Praise for *The Blue, Beautiful World*

"[An] excellent outing on a near-future Earth irrevocably altered by climate change and political turmoil . . . heartfelt . . . thoughtful . . . action-packed." —*Publishers Weekly*

"The third book set in the Cygnus Beta universe offers a unique take on the first-contact novel. . . . Fans of complex space operas will enjoy this immensely." —*Library Journal*

"*The Blue, Beautiful World* is compelling and deep with rich world building, and the characters are endearing and interesting . . . inventive and big in a way that many science-fiction readers will find satisfying and exciting." —*Booklist*

"Dr. Karen Lord is one of our greatest, and in her latest novel, *The Blue, Beautiful World,* she shows us exactly why that is. . . . In the way that all great speculative fiction is, it is a story about what makes us human, and how the connections we form with each other are vital to our survival, and it's told in the most exquisite prose." —*Tor.com*

"A gorgeously detailed story of invasion, negotiation and diplomacy." —*The Daily Mail*

"This complex, engaging novel takes an unusual approach to the classic trope of aliens in our midst, with a warmth and intelligence reminiscent of Ursula K Le Guin." —*The Guardian*

"Karen Lord weaves a complex story of first contact from a unique perspective that is warm, engaging, and wildly original. I thoroughly enjoyed this book!"   —Martha Wells, *New York Times*
                              bestselling author of *The Murderbot Diaries*

"Wherever you are, whatever your genre of choice, Dr. Karen Lord is essential reading. This is the thrilling, cerebral, empathetic, and hopeful speculative fiction the world absolutely needs—now and always."
                              —Samit Basu, author of *The City Inside*

"Brimming with sharp characters, action, espionage, and audacious ideas, *The Blue, Beautiful World* subverts the idea of first contact, and then inverts it, too—just in case. Lord delivers profound insights on charisma, identity, cooperation, and family, all wrapped up in a cracking high-stakes story of intergalactic intrigue."
                              —Malka Older, author of *Infomocracy*

"A wise, ambitious, and beautifully crafted novel of first contact, the future of Earth, and the challenges posed by survival, change, and compassionate connection."
                 —Kate Elliott, author of *Unconquerable Sun* and *The Keeper's Six*

"*The Blue, Beautiful World* is unlike any science fiction you've read. It is a treatise on global diplomacy, a first-contact adventure, and a meditation on the transformative power of pop culture. Most of all, it is a gorgeous, wise tale of our shared traumatic histories and potential futures together, on a planet whose mysteries humans have only begun to explore. Step into Karen Lord's world and be changed forever."
                 —Annalee Newitz, author of *Autonomous* and *The Terraformers*

"An exquisite novel of galactic diaspora, of long-lost humankind coming home, *The Blue, Beautiful World* is a thoughtful and dreamlike examination of the goodness and potential in humanity. It will change the way you think about family, empathy, and the mysterious ghosts born here on our own world."

—Tessa Gratton, author of *The Queens of Innis Lear*

"*The Blue, Beautiful World* launches you into an exquisite world bursting with people and ideas that reach beyond its pages. If you enjoy large-scale, big-brained fiction with a heart of gold, this is the book for you." —Suyi Davies Okungbowa, author of *Son of the Storm*

"*The Blue, Beautiful World* is science fiction at its best—unexpected, wise, and compassionate. We all need this book, more urgently than ever." —Zen Cho, author of *Black Water Sister*

THE
BLUE,
BEAUTIFUL
WORLD

THE BLUE, BEAUTIFUL WORLD

KAREN LORD

 NEW YORK

2024 Del Rey Trade Paperback Edition

LIBRARY OF CONGRESS CATALOGING-IN-PUBLICATION DATA
Names: Lord, Karen, author.
Title: The blue, beautiful world / Karen Lord.
Description: First edition. | New York: Del Rey, 2023.
Identifiers: LCCN 2023032415 (print) | LCCN 2023032416 (ebook) |
ISBN 9780593598450 (paperback) | ISBN 9780593598443 (ebook)
Subjects: LCGFT: Science fiction. | Novels.
Classification: LCC PR9230.9.L67 B58 2023 (print) | LCC PR9230.9.L67 (ebook) |
DDC 813/.6—dc23/eng/20230713
LC record available at https://lccn.loc.gov/2023032415
LC ebook record available at https://lccn.loc.gov/2023032416

Printed in the United States of America on acid-free paper

randomhousebooks.com

1st Printing

Book design by Fritz Metsch

THE
BLUE,
BEAUTIFUL
WORLD

ONE

THE EMISSARY KEPT on digging his own grave, centimeter by centimeter, word by word. He had been ill served by a poorly trained spy service, but that was no excuse. A coronation was a time for traditional platitudes and ceremonial courtesy, all the small flourishes and grace notes that such formal occasions demanded to ensure that the usual hierarchies were firmly in place and the new names alongside the ancient titles would be honored and respected.

It was certainly not a time to bring up family gossip.

The newly crowned monarch all but glowed with attentiveness, and her attendants, knowing the trap well, made no attempt to hustle the emissary away and move the next dignitary forward. They waited. One idly adjusted the fall of ice-blue fabric that poured from the monarch's left shoulder to puddle at her feet. Snow white her robe, ice blue her mantle, platinum bright the embroidery on her vestments, telling in symbol and sign all the tale of her dynasty.

The dynasty the emissary presumed to speak of.

How her mother must be proud of her . . . at last.

How their blood had returned to the purity of prior generations . . . eventually.

How reassuring it was that her brother—apologies, *adopted* brother—would no longer embarrass the chronicles of their line with his whims and oddities.

The monarch made no reply but smiled and smiled until at last the emissary, uncouth as he was, faltered in his performance, like an actor who realizes he must have missed a cue somewhere.

"Esteemed Lady, where *is* your brother?" No nonsense about his adoption then, the old fool. Simply a direct question that she could answer freely in the comfortable knowledge that the information was too late to be of any use to anyone.

She matched the now-sincere smile on her lips with a gleam of hungry humor in her eyes. "Paris, my dear ambassador. Did you not know?"

IN PARIS, THE streets were screaming.

Not literally. But nearly. The sound reverberated from every paved road and brick wall. A vibration of thudding feet strummed through lines of traffic stopped by bodies moving too thickly to be pushed aside by mere motors and machinery. Up ahead, a few cars still managed to press forward through the crush of the crowd. One car, anonymous with dark-tinted windows, made as if to break away. The crowd scented quarry and surged toward it.

Another car took advantage of the space temporarily created to nudge its way into an alley. To the uneducated eye, in the darkness of evening, this vehicle appeared to be normal in every respect. The make and age were common, and the occupants were visible behind clear glass—but then the left rear window rolled down, and the high-tech VR glass flickered, dropped its display of an upset and frustrated family of four, and showed instead the pop star, his driver, his manager, and his security.

The family had been fake, but the frustration in the car was real.

"Get that window back up," the manager snapped.

The pop star gave her an apologetic glance, quickly blew a stream of smoke outside, and obediently put the window, and their disguise, back in place.

"Can't you do something about the crowds?" the bodyguard asked him quietly, as if already knowing the answer.

The star took another drag on his cannabis cigarillo and exhaled slowly, not caring where the smoke went. His eyes were very tired. His fingers trembled slightly as he leaned forward and tapped the ash into a used mug sitting between his feet. "Well," he said simply, "it's a lot."

The driver said nothing. In a few minutes the street behind them cleared. The decoy had done its job. The driver maneuvered the car around with a precision that was entirely her own human skill and turned onto the main road.

Behind them, the streets continued screaming.

OWEN OWEN OWEN!

Only the rich could buy that special kind of identity—the fame of a single name, the hush of origins unknown. Whoever he had been in the past, he had been wealthy enough to completely bury his old self before embarking on a new career. Which, given the fawning curiosity of the world of film, virtual reality, and media, was still amazing.

People considered the manager, Noriko Fournier, to be the real brains of the operation, but to what degree was anyone's guess. Did she pluck him from obscurity and train him in the way that she wanted him to go? Was she the Higgins to his Eliza? She was legitimately, verifiably pre-moneyed when it came to the Owenmania industry, thanks to her family's banking roots. She could have done it. But what would make her *want* to do it?

She was famous for her scowl, her brusqueness, and her general air of hating her job no matter how many billions it made her. People said the only reason Owen put up with her was to get a break from the incessant adoration. If so, she delivered and then some, and not only to him.

She glared across the table. "You will entertain no other bids. Owen will pay whatever you ask."

The man in the pale linen tunic cleared his throat nervously, no doubt unaccustomed to being threatened with large sums of money. "It's not us. There's a procedure. Our laws require sealed bids and approval by a committee."

Noriko raised her eyebrows in disbelief and displeasure. "There will be no other bids," she said again with greater emphasis. "Owen's offer is to the players, not to the club."

Linen Tunic looked helplessly to his left. His colleague, a heavyset man made more imposing by a deep red jacket, spoke with all the care and caution of a man trying to defuse a bomb. "The players have contracts with the club—"

Noriko whisked away the explanation with an impatient brush of her hand and completed the gesture by slamming four well-manicured, hard-lacquered nails into the wooden surface between them. The men flinched and eyed the black tips with concern.

"You have *not* read the proposal that I sent in advance of this meeting. You are *wasting* our time. Compensation for amending the players' contracts is *included*." She breathed out and repeated softly, "There will be no other bids and this offer will expire within twenty-four hours."

Red Jacket slid a black leather folder from a space ten centimeters to his left to the exact center of the table, where it was perfectly aligned with his breastbone. He laid his fingertips on the folder with a light but firm touch. "But we *have* read the proposal. Thoroughly. And we cannot help but wonder . . . why is Owen so desperate to own a football team? And why *this* one?"

"He has his whims," Noriko stated in a tone that was too flat to even register as disapproving.

"Why this one?"

"He sees that they have potential."

"We are sixth in the league and falling. There are other, more successful teams for sale at the price you're buying. *Why this team?*"

Unexpectedly, Noriko smiled. She flexed her hand from tense claw to resting palm down, mirroring his own hand. "He sees their potential, and when your players rise to the top of the league, there will be no doubt that their success is due to him."

In the small moment when he could not think of what to reply, she touched her own fingertips to the proposal and shifted it five millimeters farther under his hand. It was the softest, most subtle movement she had made all day.

Then she stood abruptly and tossed a small black chip onto the table. "Should you or your committee manage to make a decision within that time, you can reach me via this closed network."

She stalked out without a farewell. Madame Noriko Fournier was also famous for her indifference to greetings, apologies, and small talk of any kind.

The luxury carriages of the Magistrale Privée were soundproofed. State-of-the-art shock absorbers dampened even the smallest vibrations of the train's motion. As far as overnight trains went, you couldn't ask for anything better, but Owen wasn't sleeping. For once, he wasn't even smoking, though he restlessly turned a cigarillo over and over in his right hand while staring out the window at the starlit sky and the mirroring scatter of lighted human habitation in the landscape. His bodyguard reached over and took it away. Owen didn't react.

"You should be sleeping."

It was an observation, not an order, and Owen replied to the question lurking in the shadow.

"Even the cannabis doesn't help," he explained with a brief glance at his bodyguard's expressionless face. "Anyway, Tareq is joining us in Munich."

"You don't have to be awake for that."

"Sleep through the carriage unlink from the MP Est and uplink to the MP Nord? I'll be awake and outside and recording, thank you very much. My aunt would never forgive me if I neglected my journal."

"Your aunt would never forgive *me* if I let you collapse from exhaustion."

Owen's smile was half fondness, half exasperation. "You're my bodyguard, not my nursemaid. I've done this before, you know. Declaiming and debating for nearly twenty hours at a time. Eight-hour concerts are easy after that. Yes, I'll sleep for a week when we stop, but I won't break."

The cold mask fractured and revealed a weary resignation as the old gendarme, for such the bodyguard was, rubbed a hand over graying hair. "I came out of retirement for you."

"Thank you," Owen replied softly, sincerely, completely deflecting the implied reproach and offering in turn something strangely close to affection.

Sharp black eyes pierced him, not questioning his motives but demanding a larger portion of truth. "I'm afraid for you. I'm afraid for us, our chances. Did you bring me here to share a hero's death with you?"

Owen shuddered. "Hellfire no, not in my wildest nightmares. Don't be melodramatic. And *trust* me. I wouldn't have come here if the chances weren't good . . . well, at least reasonable. I trust *you* to let me know when I'm starting to go too far. I respect you and I will listen to you."

Owen and Ahn regarded each other seriously for a long, silent moment. They both knew what was coming.

Finally, Ahn said it. "Go to bed."

Owen grinned. "Yes, General."

Suddenly, there was a loud chime. Owen frowned, glanced at his wrist, and chuckled. "Noriko closed the deal. Looks like I might get a good night's sleep after all."

*   *   *

People wondered how Owen could be everywhere at once, performing, negotiating deals, expanding his empire. The truth was simple: he had the knack of traveling light.

Concerts, for example. He had no backing band, no roadies, no equipment, no favorite accessory or costume without which he could not take the stage. He would draw from a pool of the best instrumentalists and backup singers in the area, order a bespoke outfit from a local fashion house, cover a popular song by one of the region's most famous musicians, and debut a song written by a local songwriter in the national style and rhythm.

The rehearsal phase was intense, relying on several in-the-flesh and virtual reality practice sessions, logistics planning, fittings, and more. Media speculated that Owen's residence had a military-grade VR hall that could connect to and mimic any location on Earth and a few beyond (remember the Orbital Tour, which covered all the space stations and included a thrilling piece of spacewalk choreography?). They weren't entirely wrong, but no one, not even his so-called inner circle, could confirm or deny the existence of such a thing. When Owen played host to colleagues and other celebrities, it was at rented ranches and long-leased mansions, and never, never where he slept.

The result was remarkable, unique, and very lucrative. Every country, every city claimed Owen as their hometown hero. He spoke just enough of six languages to charm his audience, and did so with a flawless accent. He could sing in any language, from the challenging clicks of Xhosa to the subtle tones of Vietnamese. He became the global Everyman, but somehow personalized, like that distant cousin on the far fringe of the family tree who is still recognized as kin. In addition, the attention of the fan bases of all the local talent he employed combined to exponentially enhance his appeal. No wonder his true nationality was a secret.

"Don't worry. I pay my taxes in full," he told the media, and it appeared to be true. One investigative journalist drew up a complicated chart of Owen's tour schedules and the laws of various tax domains to claim that he could *not* be from a country that taxed by citizenship rather than duration of domicile. But a team of independent auditors verified that taxes were indeed being paid to *some* entity, so the story fizzled out.

Of course, he had his detractors. One critic noted with great snobbishness that Owen's many awards were all secured by popular voting rather than by a jury of his peers, and the best that could be said of him was that he had redefined the genre of ethno-folk pop. Another, sounding more bewildered than bitter, said that attending an Owen concert was indeed an experience, with spectacular performances from the backing musicians and so much audience participation that it felt like the world's biggest and best karaoke party . . . but Owen had such an *ordinary* voice, just about able to stay on key and not much more. And he never wrote a lyric or a tune. So *why* was he so famous?

Dammit, he wasn't even that *cute*.

"He'll burn hot and bright and fast, and then he'll crash," Juergen, the guitarist, predicted cheerfully. "And until he does, it's an honor to ride on his generous coattails."

"That's a little disrespectful," Mariane, the bassist, murmured. She wasn't really paying attention. This was her biggest paying gig in ten years, and she would say and do absolutely nothing that could jeopardize her great good fortune, or screw up the chance of opportunities in the future. Muttering the occasional aside to chatty Juergen was a low priority. Communicating clearly with the sound engineers was key. Maintaining a good rig and learning how to sweet-talk audio engineers had carried her far in her career. "Juergen, focus. He'll be here in twenty minutes."

"He'll be late. His kind are always late."

The public address system suddenly kicked in at high volume. "I'm here. Early. Having a quick word with the mixing engineer."

Mariane tucked her chin down to stifle a giggle. Trust Juergen to forget that his mic was potentially live to all the audio engineers. And trust Owen to pull a little trick like that. They'd seen some of his personality during their VR rehearsals, and thankfully he wasn't an asshole. He would embarrass Juergen for a brief moment, then continue as if nothing had happened. Not a grudge-holder, not a bully. A rare gift among the megastars. She was inclined to like him. Nothing more—he wasn't to her taste. Too young and weedy. The mere idea made her feel like a pedophile; she shuddered and shook off a brief wave of chilly nausea.

"Let's have the intro to 'Days of Summer,' shall we?" The mixing engineer's polite, Welsh-accented voice brought her back to reality. Those butterflies in her stomach weren't for Owen's witty remarks. She was nervous, that was all. A natural physical reaction to a frighteningly huge and exciting night in her life. She pressed her fingertips hard against the bass's strings, defiantly playing a quick, complex riff to ground herself. Time to focus. Time to perform. Time to shine.

"I love you, man!"

Mariane allowed the giggle to escape this time and lifted her head from Owen's lap for just long enough to take another pull from her bottle of pilsner. They were all high for various reasons and on various intoxicants, but Juergen was reliving some old California holiday memory and had turned completely into Surfer Dude Cliché.

"Love you too," Owen replied casually. He drew hard on his cigarillo, lighting it to a sharper glow in the semidarkness, then glanced anxiously down at Mariane's face and cupped a shielding hand under his cigarillo and its few millimeters of dangling, hot ash.

"Not, like, in a sexy way, because I'm nineteen, you know? And you're at least two decades older than that, so . . . ew."

Mariane felt Juergen's shudder of disgust through her knees. They were all slumped in a pile on the floor of a glass-roofed penthouse, drinking, smoking, and watching the stars. Other humans were in similar piles around them, some within a hand's brush. Everyone waiting for the sun to come up.

"Doesn't have to be in a sexy way," Owen replied calmly. "Non-sexy is fine too."

"It's just . . . I've never felt that . . ." Juergen's arms described big

circles in passionate speechlessness, creating surging waves of movement along Mariane's legs. "It was transcendent," he said, finding the
word at last. "The musical zone. We were one. We were . . . It was like
religion. You could start a church! Church of Saint Owen—"

Owen's sigh sounded like pain rather than weariness. "No, don't
say that." His hand found Juergen's shoulder, softening the harsh words
with a brief touch. "You did great. You all did. Put your heart and soul
into your music. Couldn't have asked for more."

Mariane listened pensively. Owen sounded sincere . . . and yet sad.
Burning, then crashing. His legs shivered under her, an unconscious
tremor of remnant adrenaline. The energy of the stage, still taking its
time to leave his body and find earth. He drew deeply on the cigarillo
again, as if desperate for the cure to hurry up and take effect.

Suddenly, Mariane felt profoundly sad herself. It was such hard
work, and worse yet if you had to be a celebrity too. She wanted him to
be okay, not dead in his early forties, used up by all those coasting
along on his *generous coattails*. Saint Owen the martyr. It wasn't fair.
And now she felt both sad and angry, glaring up at the stars as if it were
their fault.

Slowly, as the edges of her vision cooled from red fury to gray resignation, Mariane realized that Owen was looking down at her with a
warm smile. She smiled reflexively in return. For a long moment they
remained like that, gazing into each other's eyes in perfect, non-sexy
understanding.

And that was fine too.

Owen crushed the last of the burning weed into the concrete floor.
"Sun's up. I'm off." He quietly shifted himself out of the weight of
limbs and warmth of skin. "Mariane, Juergen, I'll see you in Prague."

Noriko was still in Paris, but not for long. She had a few more meetings
to get Owen's new football club a fresh set of coaches and admin personnel, and that meant two stops on the road to Amsterdam. She didn't
need to be present at the Berlin concert. She had competent staff in

place to handle everything Owen would need, and they didn't need supervising. For *these* meetings, she was the only option.

Owen had told her his full plan in confidence. "Let them think I'm just having fun. You know otherwise and you know who and what are key to this project working out. Negotiate accordingly."

He hadn't needed to add that. Noriko's talent and curse was the depth of her competitive nature, and even if the football club had been, as she claimed in meetings to outsiders, the mere whim of a man with too much spare cash on hand, she would have fought to get the best deal regardless. She had her own reputation of excellence to maintain. While she respected Owen for his strong work ethic and infallible ability to organize and get results, she too felt that his life was not exactly sustainable. She would keep herself prepared to launch a post-Owen career. He would understand. They both knew no other loyalty than competence, no attachment but success, no stability but the next adventure.

Owen impressed her. His look varied from the delicate, waiflike freshness of a teen idol to the grizzled, whipcord-and-washboard toughness of a decades-seasoned rock star, but beyond all sense, he reminded her of her maternal grandfather—a broad, fat man who could be as placid as a mountain or as volatile as an active volcano . . . all dependent on which mode would get him what he wanted.

For that reason, or other reasons she had yet to identify, she wanted very much to make Owen proud of her.

In Strasbourg there was a postgraduate research associate specializing in sports science whom Owen particularly wanted. Noriko hoped the terms would be enough to entice. She also hoped she could, however briefly, tap into her grandfather's wisdom and be the mountain for this encounter instead of the volcano.

The meeting took place in a large office crammed with three desks, a treadmill and a stationary bike connected to a hanging-grid array of tablet computers, and a small kitchen table pushed under the main window. Boxes of assorted energy bars, nutritional supplements, and vividly tinted bottled liquids cluttered the table's surface, while a small dog slept peacefully in the clear space underneath.

"Sorry about the mess." Isala Kuria waved Noriko in and limped after her. "Claude is teaching all morning today. Briana is out sick. We won't be disturbed."

Noriko looked around for a place to sit. Kuria cleared a bundle of papers from a chair. "Here we go. Something to drink? There's coffee, just made."

Mountains aren't fussy. Noriko accepted a mug of strong but murky arabica and made her own important first step in the negotiations by offering a bag of palmiers and pains au chocolat that she'd bought from a neighboring bakery. Kuria smiled and found a clean plate, and for a minute or two they were content to eat and sip in comfortable silence.

The dog opened his eyes and blinked sleepily at them, but didn't budge.

"He's very well behaved," Noriko said at last in mild surprise.

"He's lazy," Kuria corrected. "But yes, Claude has trained him well about food. We don't want him poisoning himself with the free samples." She nodded at the stuff on the table.

Noriko realized that Kuria would continue the small talk for as long as it took to make it clear that she was not desperate to say yes to whatever Noriko might say. However, the atmosphere was friendly, almost relaxed. Kuria wasn't playing a game for spite.

"Our offer has intrigued you?" Noriko said at last, keeping her tone light, as if she too were merely curious.

Kuria gave her a reproachful look. "It's too much. I thought it was a joke. I didn't expect you to turn up."

"It's not a joke."

"There are far more experienced coaches available."

"My employer looks for other qualities than experience. He wanted me to tell you that he read your paper on physiological effects of VR training that enhance team performance." Noriko watched Kuria intently to detect what, if any, impact her words might have.

The young woman's face remained serenely neutral, but her eyes lit up. "That was presented at a very obscure conference and it remains unpublished. Your employer has an unusual hobby."

Noriko shrugged. "Some rich men buy yachts. Some buy knowledge. Perhaps you would like to visit our library one day."

Kuria's eyes did that expressive flash again. "A physical private library?"

"Oh yes, although its holdings are all available in VR mode. Please accept this access chip as a token of our very serious interest in your future career choices." This time when Noriko offered up the black chip, it was with a courteous, almost shy half bow.

Kuria took it and examined it with a look of part admiration, part disbelief. "How soon do you need a reply from me?"

"You graduate in five months. We hope to begin training in eight. Three months' notice will give us enough time to make arrangements. However, if you wish, you could join me earlier for the process of negotiating players' contracts. We would, of course, value your input on team selection." Noriko smoothly stood and gently raised a detaining hand to keep Kuria seated. "But do not decide now. Browse the library. Talk to your colleagues and your supervisor. Call me when you're ready to chat."

When the driver asked, almost diffidently, where the next meeting would be, Noriko nearly told her, then hesitated. "Why did I take you instead of using autopilot? I could have sent you on to Berlin to enjoy the concert."

The driver absorbed the veiled rebuke without a hint of concern. "Now then, Madame Noriko. You know why."

"Don't call me Madame Noriko." There was weariness to the request, a suggestion of words repeated several times again and again and never heeded.

"Habit of the uniform, Madame. Let's maintain our little rituals."

Noriko sighed, slumped a little lower. "It doesn't matter. The next appointment is in VR, not in-flesh. Bonn will do."

The driver keyed their destination into the car nav. She didn't turn on the sound or put the autopilot on standby; she loved driving too much for that. "You're tired?"

Noriko bristled. The driver's unique blend of courtesy and presumption was sometimes more than she wanted to deal with after a long day. "Pre-tired. Thinking about our schedule exhausts me."

"Take a nap," the driver suggested. "I'll wake you when we're a half hour out from Bonn."

"Fine." Noriko had already reclined her seat, and now she increased the angle. "Wake me early if anything exciting happens en route."

BANG!

Noriko woke up with a gasp like drowning and flailed her arms against the seat restraints until she woke up enough to realize she was being held snugly for her own good. The car was spinning a full three-sixty on the road. She swore.

"Was anyone expecting you in Bonn?" The driver spoke through clenched teeth in an almost conversational tone as she finally got the car straightened up. She took a sudden left turn.

Noriko's face slammed sideways into the window glass. The car's video system, the mirrors, and her own eyes confirmed that there was another vehicle pursuing them, an illegally modified van with a blackened windshield and a thick bar of a bumper, which hit into them again with the force of an unyielding battering ram. Unfortunately, there was not a lot of road to maneuver. They were on a narrow country lane with trees on the left side and fields on the right.

"How long—"

The car swerved into an even narrower track. "Never mind. Let's discuss this later."

Noriko shut her mouth, held on tightly, and let the driver do what she was so very good at doing. People wondered why Owen preferred small cars instead of long, luxurious limousines for his entourage; this was why. Tight city alleys, small country lanes, anything that would offer a quick getaway . . . their cars could handle it. Even the occasional off-road adventure was possible with a quick adjustment of the ride height and tire pressure.

There was a thump and a hiss as the car went through its transformation while juddering through deep ruts of dried mud and scrabbling over loose gravel. The rear cam showed the van leaning awkwardly into a curve and settling on the straight. Poor stability. Noriko knew her driver would capitalize on that.

She did. The next curve was sharp, slightly inclined, and with a helpful ditch alongside. Their car whipped around it neatly while the van slid, tilted, and went over the edge. Noriko's safety restraints finally loosened and withdrew so she could turn around and stare for a scant three seconds at the accident, until the next bend in the road took them out of view.

"Shouldn't we . . ." she began, then shut up. Stopping for potential kidnappers, injured or not, was the absolute worst thing they could do.

"Let's go straight on to Amsterdam," she decided quickly. "No stops. We can teleconference there, with our full security detail."

"Wise choice, Madame Noriko," the driver agreed. "Sorry about your nap."

A shiver of tension stopped Noriko's reply in her throat. She let the tremor pass, then spoke in a steady voice. "Let me review the footage from the car cams."

The driver slid her a questioning glance, but without hesitation she input the command to send the video to Noriko's tablet. "Time stamp around 2:29 P.M.," she said.

Twenty minutes ago. At 2:29 P.M., they had still been in heavy traffic on the highway, moving north-northwest at about eighty kph. For a while all seemed normal, then the footage showed the car stopping once at a charging station, then at a snack stop drive-through, and again at another charging station minutes later.

"You realized we were being followed," Noriko murmured, and flipped to the rear footage to search for the van. The shape gave it away, eventually, but it was blending in beautifully by changing color periodically—a common feature of advertising vans, but not often used to display solid color instead of moving images. The windshield was transparent but slightly blurry, and Noriko knew she could not trust the figures behind the glass to be real instead of a VR projection.

At 2:46, the front-facing footage lurched right as her driver made her move, crossing two lanes briskly to take a sudden exit from the highway. The rear footage showed the van veering off quickly but far less tidily, leaving behind other drivers swerving and swearing. Then came the unexpected surge of speed, the slam into the rear that had woken her up, and the spin to regain control and distance.

The final minute didn't take long to view, and it put the shiver of tension back into her belly. Turning off her tablet, Noriko sat back and made herself breathe slowly.

"Were you expecting this to happen?" she asked suddenly.

There was a reproachful pause. "Madame, you know I report only to General Ahn."

"And Ahn will report—"

"To Owen."

The brusque answer brooked no reply. Noriko was left in open-mouthed, blinking silence.

The driver relented and spoke in a gentler tone. "Don't worry, Madame. I know what to look out for now. I'll get us safely to Amsterdam by nine P.M."

TWO

TAREQ LEANED AGAINST the wall, away from the knot of tension in the center of the room.

Noriko was furious, he decided, but it was the kind of fury created by fear and uncertainty, not hatred. He wondered very briefly whether Owen would understand that, whether he should tell him, but instead he instinctively sealed his lips shut and watched the argument unfold. Noriko was furious, but Owen was aghast.

"Why do you have to go off by yourself anyway?" he said reproachfully.

Tareq sampled the nuance. Fear from Owen too, of course, but also guilt, and a slight distractedness that meant he was trying to figure out what to do next.

"She was not by herself. She had Bernice. Bernice Jones is one of my best, and she proved it again by handling the situation appropriately." Ahn spoke in a voice that sounded almost reasonable, except for the hint of a leash in the drily deliberate tone. *Listen to me. Imitate me. Be careful what you say, and how you say it.*

Owen shot a quick glare sideways. *You I will deal with later.*

Tareq tried not to giggle. The situation wasn't funny, but he was nervous. He'd watched the Berlin concert from an engineer's booth, close enough to see the stress beneath Owen's stage face but far enough to remain unseen. Owen had claimed to be happy to see him when they greeted each other in Munich, but they both knew the reason for his visit, and Owen had put off the inevitable by immersing himself in concert prep and avoiding Tareq completely. For a group of people who claimed to be close, there was too much unspoken and little actual communication going on.

Owen faced Noriko again and put on his calmest mask. "I think you should use the translator bug from now on."

Noriko all but threw her hands up, choking back strong emotion. "Look," she managed eventually, "we've talked about this. Why should I, the only member of your team who speaks five languages and understands eight, need a translator bug?"

"Because if the next creep who attacks you speaks in that ninth language you never bothered to learn, I don't want you to be at a disadvantage," Owen said.

Tareq shook his head. How could Owen not know how patronizing he sounded, with that excess of patience?

Ahn was already speaking, trying to salvage the conversation. "We have a bug that's also an emergency communicator. Sapphire and platinum, very lovely piece of equipment. Come on, Noriko, you'll put it on, won't you? Just to give me peace of mind?"

Impressive. Tareq now understood why his family said that Ahn had matured into quite the diplomat. Noriko frowned, trying to stay angry at Owen, but Ahn had made her curious.

"Only if you show me your full report on this threat and any others you're expecting," she bargained.

"Deal," Ahn said easily, and the two left Tareq and Owen alone in their little privacy cage that served as both office and shelter from everyday public surveillance.

Owen exhaled slowly. "Thank you, Ahn." He sat down and passed a hand over his face.

"You really are overextended," Tareq stated.

"If this is some kind of intervention—" Owen began.

"It's not. You're beyond your own help, and you should recognize that. What else do you think I'm here for?"

"To lecture me?" Owen said with sad humor.

"To take you home whenever you need it," Tareq replied quietly. "And you need it."

A hopeful light brightened Owen's eyes, but he caught himself and it faded. "Soon, but not yet. I'm concerned about the attack on Noriko. We have to be vigilant, at least until we're out of Europe."

"Trust Ahn to do their job. Let me do mine."

"After tomorrow's performance, then." Owen thought a moment and amended, "After we reach Prague."

"No farther than that, and no longer than that," Tareq insisted. "Constantly putting things off is how you got to this point in the first place."

Owen was visibly twitchy, but even without that sign, Tareq could feel the crackle in the atmosphere like an itch. "What is it?" he demanded.

For once, Owen didn't pretend not to understand. "I'm out of smokes," he apologized.

"Surely you don't need them that badly?" Now he was the one with the excessively patronizing tone.

Owen treated it as it deserved—he ignored it. "I'm going to take a nap. Wake me fifteen minutes before rehearsal."

"I'm not your personal assistant. Set an alarm."

Owen laughed weakly, but he took out his pocket calendar and did as he was told. Then he flopped into the reclining chair in the corner and was instantly still and silent.

Tareq turned away, giving him space and quiet, and went to find Ahn.

In Amsterdam, since the population collapse of the 2070s, it was possible to book not merely a suite of rooms but a plot of land, complete with environmentally appropriate, low-impact dwellings and offices, security points included, and bordered by a grid of canals in a moatlike manner that was both aesthetically pleasing and slightly isolating. The walk between the cabins was short, but uncomfortable. The Netherlands was suffering from a summer heat spike, and everyone was either staying in during peak sun hours or huddling near the massive misting fans installed by civic administration along the banks of the canals.

Tareq found the setup primitive, not because of its low level of technology but because of the sense of too-rapid change, evolution without consolidation. This city was no longer building on the foundations of an irretrievable past but scrambling to keep ahead of the razor-sharp blade of a future that promised death to the unprepared. The climate had shifted, the design of older buildings was obsolete, and the city was trying to adapt with the ponderous speed of a battleship trying to change course.

During his earlier travels, Tareq had seen a little of Amsterdam and a lot of the cities on other continents. Some places were more stable than others, but many of the once-prosperous states of the northern hemisphere exuded desperation of various types and flavors. There was the desperation of a rich man in a mansion trying to enjoy the last of the party before the bill collectors broke down his door. There was the frantic virtue of a criminal-turned-monk flagellating himself in vigorous but useless penance. Most of all, there was the manic optimism of incompetent politicians, assuring their public that the measures being employed were not at all too little and too late, and begging them not to erect the guillotines just yet.

He knew his history, and this present had a familiar echo. Old empires were slowly falling; new orders were struggling to become established. Here, the new factor was the reach of it—this was not a single city to be sacked, burned, and left to crumble to ruin, nor a mere country decimated and taken over by wildflowers and beasts amid the lingering threat of live minefields and unspent chemical shells. This was the whole basket overturned, all the eggs smashed, all the hopes crushed. Humankind had lived for two centuries with the ability to self-immolate utterly and a tendency to play with matches. It was only a matter of time before they followed through on that somber promise. No malice aforethought needed. Something—error, neglect, or the unpredictable and unprecedented—might easily tip the balance against them.

The entire planet was at a tipping point, ripe for salvation or destruction, angels of deliverance or barbarians. And, in the meantime, bread and circuses made life bearable and occasionally diverting.

And here comes the circus. Tareq understood what Owen was doing, though he was not sure that he fully approved of it.

He stepped into Ahn's office, another low metal building identical to the one he had just left, and paused a moment to exhale in pleasure at the cooler, richer air. Ahn, sitting on the edge of their desk, glanced across in sympathetic understanding, and returned their attention to Noriko. The new bug was already perched on her ear, and she was avidly scanning a small tablet, choosing her language settings for the onward journey.

"Owen's agreed to take a trip home after we reach Prague," Tareq told Ahn quietly.

Ahn's smile held relief and amusement. Noriko blinked, her attention caught. "What did you say?"

"Obscure dialect from the old country," Tareq said teasingly. "You've probably never heard of it."

Ahn kept smiling and took the tablet from Noriko. "He's being an ass. It's a language constructed by linguists that we use sometimes when we don't want to be overheard. Here, let me add it to your settings."

Tareq's eyes widened. "Are you sure?" he said warily.

Noriko laughed. "I understood *that*."

Ahn held Tareq's eye and gave a slow, firm nod as their fingers flew over the tablet screen. "There. That's about thirty in total, far more than you need. You can do a fresh upload when we start the Asia leg of the tour." They set the tablet down on the desk. "And the security report is waiting in your inbox. Never say I don't keep my promises."

"I will never say that," Noriko agreed, giving them a warm hug. "If anyone wants me, I'll be in my cabin doing some light reading."

She left with a happy spring in her step.

Ahn looked after her fondly. "Give her new tech and new knowledge and she's forever yours."

"Is this appropriate?" Tareq said sternly.

Ahn raised their eyebrows at the younger man's tone. "Definitely. When you have someone as intelligent as Noriko on your team, it's a huge mistake to keep them in complete ignorance."

"But putting her in danger instead?"

"Risk assessment is *my* job, Tareq. Let me do it. Now, you mentioned Owen will take a break when we get to Prague. How much time do you need for that?"

"Two days, no more," Tareq replied brusquely.

"Then we shall ensure that he has two clear, uninterrupted days after his performance. Let me know where you want us to stop, and where you want to be picked up."

Tareq nodded, eyes downcast, apparently chastened, but he was already thinking about what he was going to tell his sister on their next chat. She was always willing to listen to him rant, and vice versa. She was also an important part of the journey home.

In spite of all her concerns, Noriko had little time for reading about security. The Bonn VR appointment had been rescheduled, but she still had an afternoon appointment in Amsterdam and another in The Hague the next day. The Amsterdam meeting was a routine catchup with ParaVee, their main VR tech supplier, whose R&D team had some cutting-edge features and fancies they wanted to show off in person and ask her to persuade Owen to try out. The meeting at The Hague . . .

out of all her non-concert work on their European tour, *that* was the most important encounter on her schedule. She had no idea how to prepare for it, and it made her scared and excited in equal measure.

She forced herself to stay disciplined. She took a nap, had a light lunch, and began to read the report thoroughly. As she had expected, it was not solely a record of the attempt to run them off the road but also a description of Ahn's network. The latter was more interesting to her, and so, perversely, she dedicated time to the former, committing to memory the make and capabilities of the vehicle used by their attackers, the follow-up with the police, and the list of possible suspects in that area.

When Bernice came to tell her that it was time to go (*Bernice Jones*, she thought, *I mustn't forget her name again. I owe her that much.*), Noriko was dressed and ready and clutching her tablet close. "Tell me when we get there," she said, and sealed the partition between driver and back seat to better immerse herself in the details of Ahn's strategy.

Of course, Owen wasn't the only one to use VR. Ahn had recruited foot soldiers in every European city—recruited, vetted, and trained. Ahn had even appointed their own officers and met with them face-to-face to discuss tactics. The officers included ex-police, former military, and retired border and coast guards. They had remarkable levels of access and trust with current police organizations and military outfits.

In fact, Ahn's network was so entrenched, so well established, that Noriko could not imagine anyone would be able to penetrate their impermeable borders. She was quite certain that Ahn had come to the same conclusion and was on the lookout for an insider spy.

Noriko was a fast reader, but the drive to their destination took barely twenty minutes. An electronic pass guided them up a ramp into dimly lit multistory parking and a reserved priority spot beside an elevator.

Bernice dutifully said, "We're here," and Noriko put away her tablet and stepped out of the car. Their welcoming committee, a group of three, was already approaching.

"Noriko!" The foremost figure, bright and slender in an exquisitely tailored yellow suit, grasped her hands and pressed an exuberant kiss to each cheek, unmindful of the crush that set his tiara and translucent blue shades temporarily askew. His facial filter blurred slightly in protest but quickly adjusted. Smiling, Noriko leaned back and gazed admiringly at him—high cheekbones, smooth rich-toned skin, hooded dark and dreamy eyes, lush lips with a defined curve.

"Peter. Ageless and glamorous as ever," she pronounced. "And so subtly responsive!" Her finger rose and approached (but did not quite touch) the mask filter in a caressing gesture. The tone of awe was more than simple flattery; it was flattery of the grandest scale, complimenting both the face that had been his, and would always be his, and the mind that had designed the means to maintain the aesthetic peak of his appearance.

"Dushi, you are too sweet, and even better, you are not a liar. Come, love, I have so much to show you."

The elevator capsule was clean and minimalist, softly illuminated, and free of any buttons or indicator lights. Acceleration pressed gently on them for a half second at the start, and the end of the trip was heralded by a dizzying lightness, but Noriko could not guess how many floors they had traveled. The doors swooshed open to reveal a vast glass-paneled hall filled with sunbeams and all manner of greenery, from tiny patches of lawn to spreading, three-story trees.

"Don't even try to guess what's raw and what's enhanced, dushi," Peter said with a smug yet beautifully rendered smile as they walked the central pathway through the greenhouse, past various employees and workstations. "This is our playground, and even I can't keep track of it anymore. Now, *this* . . . is *my* playground."

He paused for a moment before a huge black door that bore his bare name, Peter Hendrix, in restrained metallic font. Then he tapped it once lightly with a finger, and it swung gracefully inward. Noriko's mouth dropped open and she drifted in as if in a dream.

"The old city! You've got a view of the old city!" She walked the semicircle of window panels and stared at the intricate detail. Pure VR, of course, but the true textures and tints, the larger crowds of decades past, the blessed untidiness and imperfections of a lived space, all were present.

Peter sat at his desk and swiveled his chair to follow her movement, savoring her reaction. "If you look closely enough," he murmured, "you'll probably see me walking broodingly along the streets of De Wallen, a memory from the good old, bad old days, when our shelf life was far too short."

"Well, you changed that. You changed everything."

He spread his hands, accepting Noriko's words with no false modesty. "If we do not control the use of our own faces and bodies, can we call ourselves free?"

Noriko turned to face him, impressed. "This is why you understand Owen so well."

"A pop star is just another kind of sex specialist, dushi. Of course I understand him. And I want to protect him." That last was spoken with just a touch of pleading.

Noriko heard it and laughed softly. "He's not ready to upload his likeness with you, not yet."

"He's not getting any younger."

"Pop stars *can* have a longer shelf life than sex workers. He has time."

"Only if he paces himself, which I do not see him doing. This is quite a punishing tour."

"And it will be followed by a long hiatus."

Peter sighed deeply in surrender. "I see you want to protect him too. I only hope you are not protecting him from the wrong things. Tell him I wish him well. Tell him I miss our Monday teas, and I look forward to resuming them after his tour."

"I will tell him," Noriko promised. She left the window, seated herself on the other side of the desk, and leaned her elbows on the surface. "Now, tell me what new delights you have for us."

For the stage, Peter offered new audio-to-video abstract holograms, designed by the VR artistic house BelNomen and actualized at high-resolution values that would make them work on a distant stage as well as onscreen. In similar vein, he suggested that since so many of their guest performers had already uploaded and licensed their likenesses to him, he could also offer cameo appearances for mass finales. Noriko was tempted but opted to leave that decision to Owen. He preferred to use VR for rehearsals but was a purist when it came to live performances.

For security, Peter's two associates had already taken Bernice to their offices for a briefing on the latest tech to acquire and to be aware of, but Peter had two things to show Noriko.

"Masks," he said, tossing one over with a flourish. "For when Owen wants to walk the streets broodingly without being torn to pieces by his adoring mob."

With a waving gesture, he called up a mirror projector from the surface of his desk. Noriko slid the soft textile over her forehead and cheeks, adjusting the two wide openings for her eyes and nose so that all sat comfortably. Then she looked to see what others would see: a face not her own, pale pink instead of light brown, thready hair in dirty blond flying away around a sharp-chinned, broad-browed shape. She smiled, frowned, narrowed her eyes, scrunched up her nose, and it was as responsive and swift as Peter's own state-of-the-art filter. The difference . . . and this, too, was art . . . was in the ordinariness. This face promised the opposite of glamour; it was forgettable, average, the face of a thousand Europeans with French, German, Spanish, and Russian ancestors tumbling around in their bloodline.

"And you will walk with him, of course," Peter said.

"Sometimes," Noriko murmured, still turning her new face this way and that in utterly absorbed curiosity. "I'm not his bodyguard, you know."

"I know. And yet . . . here is something else that might help."

A few black beads, not quite spheres, with multifaceted surfaces like cut gems, were placed on the desk before her. She took one between finger and thumb, examining it.

"Toss one into that corner," Peter suggested with a sly smile.

She did as she was told, and immediately jumped back when the bead rolled, stopped, and threw up the shadow of an armed man, threatening in a loud voice, "Police!"

"My God," she breathed.

"To be used judiciously. Better at night, with other confusing shadows about. Throw it toward a light source. No sense creating a shadow in darkness. But the audio might save you even when the shadow can't be seen."

"Thank you, Peter."

"No thanks needed. My accountants are in touch with your accountants as we speak, submitting a full invoice. It's thanks to your prompt payment and generous patronage that we are able to push the envelope in this technology."

"Quality recognizes quality," Noriko replied, pushing the mask over her head and moving to return it to Peter.

Peter stopped her with a raised hand. "No need. Yours. A little memento of our all-too-brief in-person meeting today. Along with this . . ." He handed her a silver chain bracelet with beads like charms hanging in a fringe.

She smiled, folded the mask into a neat square, and slid the bracelet onto her wrist. The beads swung and clicked in a satisfying manner when she made a fist and twisted it in sharp rotation, and, most importantly, they did not explode into sound and shadow.

"Take care, Peter. See you soon in the VR."

If Bernice had received any complimentary tokens, she did not flaunt them openly, and Noriko did not inquire. Noriko already had plans to speak to Ahn after she finished analyzing the security report, and she would discuss their VR tech additions then. For now, the weight of tonight's concert was growing, and she needed to be fully present this time. For all her certainty when speaking to Peter, she knew he was right. Owen was nearing exhaustion, and Noriko had to make sure everything was running smoothly so he would have no distractions.

Her biggest worry about the arena was that it was too accessible. This place was no Paris maze, with corners and alleys to hide in. She had seriously considered arranging for a hopper to snatch Owen up from the stage at the finale, but he hadn't liked that idea at all. In the end, a small canal berth near the back rooms under the stage was chosen as their escape route. If she could just convince him to finish on time instead of getting caught up in the multiple encores that had become typical of this tour, they might have a chance at a clean getaway.

Tareq told her to relax. She had met Tareq about a year or two ago, and she knew he was some distant relative or friend of Owen's family or some such, but she couldn't really tell what Tareq's job *was*. She didn't dislike him—Owen didn't do entourages, and anyone who was in his inner circle had earned their place—but she was puzzled by him and the vague authority he seemed to wield over Owen. Even Ahn gave him a strangely respectful space, and Ahn wasn't easily impressed by anyone.

Tareq's return now, in the middle of the European leg, might have been a mere accident of scheduling. No doubt, as she had her side trips and additional responsibilities, he had other tasks beyond hanging around Owen and making sure he ate and rested regularly. As long as he didn't interfere with *her* projects, she didn't really care.

She chose to spend the concert in the assigned back rooms, observing Ahn, who had made it their command center, as they monitored the eyes and ears of the venue with the help of an Argus AI. The setup resembled Peter's accessories: a plain headband with audio inputs and translucent shades with several visual inputs.

"I read your report," she said, approaching them with tablet in hand. "I appreciate your thoroughness on Owen's behalf."

Ahn shrugged and continued to meditate attentively under the Argus crown.

"I would like to be present at your security briefings," she said.

"There's a lot of data," Ahn said slowly, distracted by the incoming information. "Most of it meaningless to you. Why not look at occasional reports?"

"We're on the road and the situation is fluid. Isn't that worth frequent updates?"

"You don't have to worry about being attacked again. We've already isolated what went wrong and put precautions in place."

"And that's why I won't know what to expect. The next attack will be entirely different, correct?"

"This isn't your area of expertise. That's why I gave you Bernice. Listen to her and she'll keep you safe."

Noriko backed down a little. "Well then, who do I tell when I notice something? You or Bernice?"

"Both, just in case. Can we have this discussion later? Time for the finale, and the exits are going to start getting busy."

Noriko withdrew. She put her tablet away in her briefcase and went down a short flight of stairs to a small landing. A canal boat bobbed slightly in its mooring, looking very much like a vintage black stretch limousine on water. She stepped on board to find Bernice already in the cockpit and seated in the captain's chair, maintaining the engines at a soft, idling hum in preparation for a quick departure.

"How does it look?" Noriko asked, nodding at the viewscreens to the outside.

"Quiet as two A.M., for now. Few people trickling out early."

"Why couldn't we have a decoy, like last time?" Noriko muttered to herself, not really expecting an answer.

"Wouldn't matter. Only one waterway for this venue." Bernice sounded wistful, as if she too would have preferred an aerial escape.

They waited. Impossible not to feel the tension rising, impossible not to count the minutes obsessively in anticipation of that final note that meant they had to spring into action. No matter how many times they went through it, Noriko hated this last part.

"He's left the stage," Bernice whispered, touching her ear bug.

Noriko's hand drifted to her own bug, and she wondered why she had not asked Ahn to enable the communications feature.

Loud voices sounded through the open doorway and two men came down the stairs—Tareq and Owen arguing some triviality. Ahn followed behind them, almost shooing them in haste, still crowned and shaded with pale patches of light chasing over their skin as the screens in the lenses shifted. They herded the two men over the short gangway and into the innards of the canal boat.

"Go, Bernice, go!"

Canal boats in Amsterdam were speed-limited by law and by tech, but Bernice paid no attention to the former and had already bypassed the latter. After a few seconds' caution to ensure that the gangway was fully retracted and the boat clear of the mooring, she opened up the engines to full capacity, and they shot out into the main canal. The parallel road was for pedestrians and emergency services only and should have been almost clear, but the viewscreens already showed a small crowd moving alongside the canal, loudly singing Owen's last song.

"Slow down, Bernice," Ahn ordered.

"Too late," Tareq murmured. "They've seen us."

Too late to try to look like an ordinary canal boat moored for the night or casually drifting on a nighttime wander. Bernice chose a middle range, fast enough to outpace the shouts of recognition, too slow to attract the notice of those ahead. But crowds are beasts with a special kind of instinct, if not intelligence, and soon there were shouts behind and ahead and above. Windows of moored boats began to glow bright; casual cruisers paused and even veered to look more closely at the focus of the crowd's attention. Nearby houses also lit up, and a footpath bridge ahead began to fill with moving bodies. All the faces turned eagerly toward them.

"Now they're jumping into the water," Tareq said with a kind of disgusted disbelief.

"Nightmare," said Noriko very quietly. Wasn't it the greatest of ironies that the manager of the century's greatest pop star had a mild, secret phobia of crowds?

"No other route," Bernice reminded them in a tight voice, glancing at her superior as if hoping to be told a miracle to the contrary. Ahn shook their head somberly. Whatever the screens showed now on the Argus, whatever scenes were being compiled from the data of traffic cameras, personal devices, and home security systems, none of it appeared to give them any comfort.

"I have to do something," Owen said, and laughed wearily.

Tareq frowned at him. "No, let me—"

Owen cut him off. "This is my thing. Let me use it."

And then, while everyone remained in place as if frozen by indecision, he stepped out onto the open back deck of the canal boat. His voice floated back to them through the open door, one word, one command.

"Lights."

The boat's security lights turned and fastened to his image. It was not stage lighting, but it sufficed. The crowd roared their pleasure and passion at him, and the sounds of the last song started up again even louder.

That was their journey back to home base, a Stygian cruise along a waterway with the souls of the damned howling on the banks and bridges, while their guardian angel stood in a halo of light and held the crowd's attention long enough for the boat to pass unscathed.

Bernice increased speed little by little until at last they were clear of it all. Owen stumbled back inside and sat heavily in the nearest chair, his face dazed and unblinking. Suddenly, he vomited. Tareq went immediately to Owen's side with a water bottle and a towel. Noriko turned away, feeling nauseous herself.

When they docked at the base camp port, Noriko went directly to her cabin and dry-retched as quietly as she could manage over the sink. Splashing cold water onto her face helped, and in a few minutes, she stopped shaking. She methodically cleaned her teeth and took out the ear bug, then fell across her bed, fully dressed, on top of the covers. She shouldn't have been able to sleep, but she did, worn out and drained of all resources.

She shouldn't have woken up, but she did, rising uncomfortably from a dreamless sleep to the sound of voices, hushed but tense with fear and anger, speaking words she could not make out. The bug lay beside the sink, forgotten, as she opened her door to the cool, humid dawn light. It was so dim that she knew it was still far too early to get up, but it was not yet so dim that she could not see Ahn, Tareq, and Owen speaking and pointing, agitated, at something. She looked across the canal, and there they were, faint in the pale light, half-hidden in a slight fog but unmistakably present. Not a crowd to rival last night's terrors, not at all, but a sizable number nevertheless. Perhaps a hundred, perhaps more farther back in the mist, enough to set her phobia crawling cold fingers up her spine.

Their lips were moving, but there was hardly any sound beyond the occasional higher note or a chopped phrase carried on the changeable wind. They swayed with weary rhythm from side to side, as if singing, as if they had been singing all night and could not stop. Their soft chorus was an oddly surreal counterpoint to the louder argument nearby.

Owen slowly turned to face her. The other two stopped talking, followed his motion, and stared at her. Owen walked away from them, right up to her door, to where she stood just beyond the threshold. He rested his hand gently on her cheek and spoke in a whisper.

"Go back to bed, Noriko. You're dreaming. Don't worry; I'll fix this."

Noriko nodded, feeling a deep peace come over her, wiping away all fear. Of course. Nightmare, predictable as ever. She stepped back and closed her door in his face, went straight to her bed, and once more collapsed over the covers.

A diffident knocking woke her later that morning. She rose and answered the door, groggy and vexed with herself for the deep wrinkles in her clothes. Bernice Jones stood before her, holding two coffee cups. She was sober of expression, but still entirely too awake and fresh-faced for Noriko's liking.

"What," she growled.

Bernice gently transferred one of the coffee cups into Noriko's hand. "Change of plan. We're taking a city hopper to The Hague, and I've booked accommodations for us there. Leaving in an hour. Can you be ready?"

Noriko stopped mid-slurp and shook her head sharply, trying to wake up. "Sure."

It wasn't until she had showered (tepid, almost cold), dressed (jumpsuit, an uncomplicated choice), and packed (thank goodness she had barely unpacked since arriving in Amsterdam) that she began to wonder how Owen was doing. She sent a message updating him on her morning trip. There was no reply. The compound was busy with local roadies packing up the baggage for transfer to their private carriage. Prague by train, the next step on the schedule. She would travel with them that evening, after her meeting in The Hague. Except . . . why would Bernice book accommodations when they would not be staying the night?

She wanted to ask, but there was so little time, and Bernice was busy up front with the hopper pilot, and then she saw something that made her forget everything she wanted to ask Bernice.

The grass on the west canal bank was trampled and muddied in a swathe about ten feet wide. The trail of crushed grass led away toward the main highway. It looked as if someone had called a spontaneous rave at the edge of their base camp. Noriko's blood chilled as the memory of her nightmare returned.

The hopper tilted away and the bruised land disappeared in the distance. After a few minutes, Bernice returned to the passenger seat and settled in beside her.

"When do we leave for Prague?" Noriko blinked. Those were not the words she had meant to speak. She wanted to ask Bernice, *Did you see that? Did you hear anything last night? Am I delusional?*

"We fly to Prague tomorrow night," Bernice replied, not meeting her gaze.

"Where's Owen?" Noriko asked, gritting the words out with an effort.

Bernice gave her a steady look. "We'll see him in Prague on Monday morning."

Noriko sat back, frowning slightly. The world was more than surreal, it was askew. Something about last night was wrong and strange and she couldn't articulate *what*.

"He's taking a short break, that's all," Bernice added, unprompted. "Don't worry. Everything's fine."

Noriko did not reply. She stared down at the landscape below. There was one good reason to take air transport from Amsterdam to The Hague. The journey provided an excellent view of the new sea-wall rising high and dividing into two curves, one facing the sea to take the brunt of the water, the other curling protectively over the sunken civilization. Ships arriving from the North Sea stepped down from lock to lock to the lower inner waters, but they were barely visible. The broad arc of the outer face came inland at an even height, like a walled city of old, enclosing and protecting. But the inner curve continued as well, reaching higher and higher, fading into translucence as heavy materials gave way to sunlit panels, like Peter's greenhouse.

In another generation, maybe two, the Netherlands would become a country of domed cities connected by sunken canals. Noriko wondered if Peter had already designed a landscape for that future, and if he ever displayed that landscape on his office windows.

THREE

OWEN WOKE BRIEFLY to the smell of cardamom and a feeling of warmth at his back, which spread deliciously along his aching spine and unfurled gently into his brain. For a moment he simply breathed. Coffee, slightly burnt sugar, the air of the edge of desert tamed by a brief drizzle and transmuted from dust to petrichor . . . it was familiar enough that he did not need to open his eyes, nor did he want to, just in case he was dreaming.

A voice in the distance, also familiar, querying something he could not quite make out. And then the reply, spoken softly but close, above his head, coming from the mouth of the man whose hand rested so kindly against his back. "Soon. A little while longer."

Owen inhaled on a deep sigh and went back into a deep sleep.

When he woke again, his stomach was rumbling and his eyes opened immediately. He was tucked in tight under a light cloth wrap, swaddled but not overwarm. He wriggled a hand free and unwound the cloth, yawning leisurely.

"I could hear your stomach from downstairs." Smiling in welcome, a woman entered the room with a bowl in her hands, just as Owen freed himself enough to stand up.

"Siha," he said warmly, taking the bowl from her and putting it aside on a table so he could embrace her without encumbrance. "So good to see you. I'm sorry it's been so long."

She shrugged within the squeeze of his arms and patted his back before pulling away and returning the bowl to his hands. "No need for regret. It is Kirat's traveling time now, and I'm glad to rest and be anchor. But you—why did you wait so long? We all know you've already done great things, but do you really think you're invincible?"

Owen sipped the fragrant liquid. Herbs, soaked pearls of grain afloat in circles of buttery fat, the aged salt of the mountains . . . it was the taste of home . . . it *was* home. Siha watched him carefully, her eyes alert for any sign of discomfort. He drank a quarter of the bowl under her critical gaze and asked, "Can we go to the roof? I want to see the sky."

She led the way into the corridor and up a curl of stone stairs set into the thick wall. Owen trailed his hand along the rough-hewn blocks and so brought himself up to the last step, where his fingers could grasp the top of the tower's high outer wall. A flowering tree, gnarled and nearly leafless, grew from a square meter of earth in the center of the stone floor of the rooftop. It was useless for shade, but a canvas sheet sheltered a heap of cushions on a carpet and served that purpose instead. He went to sit there, and Siha joined him in silence as he finished his broth.

"You're right," he said at last, setting the bowl carefully down at the edge of the carpet. "This is different from anything I've ever done before."

"Please don't let the next words from your mouth be 'and I'm the only one who can do it,'" she said drily.

His lip quirked in a wry smile. "I'm no savior, I know that. I'm merely trying to face my fears, and maybe give something back to the ancestors."

She made a disapproving noise. "You're still trying to make it sound noble."

Owen looked at her soberly. "I have to find some good in it, or I'd stop right here, right now."

She gripped him by the wrist. "Why don't you?"

He pulled his hand away, but gently. "Guilt. Guilt if I do nothing, guilt if I go too far. It's a delicate balance."

He could feel her softening a bit, tilting more toward pity than censure, but she let nothing of it show in her face, nor her words. "Your uncle wants to speak to you."

Owen laughed softly, remembering the supporting hand on his back, the gentle voice near him, and knowing that none of it would save him from the lecture to come. "Oh dear. Is there more food below? I'll need fortifying."

Siha's expression changed to amusement, sympathy, and a little bit of gladness. "Ask your aunt. She's in the kitchen with Kirat."

As he charged recklessly down the curving staircase, bowl in hand, Owen reflected that it was not only the promise of food that gave him energy but the full treatment, quasi-parental admonishment included, that made him feel so light. At last he had reached an oasis where someone else was in charge, if only for a day or two. He jumped the last three steps with a boyish carelessness and threw himself at his aunt, crushing her small body in a hug of pure affection and enthusiasm.

"Oof," she said, but she sounded pleased. "I thought you were supposed to be fragile and exhausted."

He pulled back and showed her the empty bowl. "Your pottage restored me. Is there more?"

"Credit this one." She nodded to Tareq, who was known as Kirat when at home.

Owen raised his eyebrows in admiration at Kirat, who took the compliment and the bowl and refilled it from a pot on the stove. Owen turned back to his aunt and her bright, beautiful grin. Her face held hardly any wrinkles beyond a few deep etchings of years and character. She was retired, unstressed, well looked after, and it showed. He was so glad that *someone* got to be, but more than that, he could not do this at all if his family were not well and flourishing and strong without him.

She hit him lightly on the arm. "Now, finish your food and decide quickly. Lecture from your uncle first, or catch up with me first?"

Owen groaned and buried his face in the steamy goodness of his fresh bowl before bothering to reply. "Let me get the punishment out of the way."

"He's not going to punish you," she said, shocked, but then her eyes narrowed at him. "But he *is* going to say words that you will pay attention to. Do I make myself clear?"

Why did he always foolishly forget that his aunt was the one to be feared in his family? She could always make you feel so happy in her presence, so calm and content, and then speak a few words like a knife thrown to your heart that you'd never see coming and never be able to dodge.

"Clear as day, Aunty," he replied soberly and respectfully. "I'll go to him now."

The old watchtower had been extended years ago into a larger compound with several rooms and an interior courtyard that held an irrigated garden and a small pool of fish. Owen stepped from the kitchen into a corner of the courtyard and saw a figure seated at the opposite corner with a tablet in hand. His uncle glanced up briefly but said nothing, merely waited for him to slowly walk through the courtyard and pull up a bench to sit opposite him. Only when Owen was settled did he raise his head to speak.

"I—"

"You look tired," Owen blurted out thoughtlessly. His uncle had gained all the wrinkles, deep and light, as he grew older, but the shadowed skin was unusual.

"You came late at night, and I spent some hours with you." The words were said without reproach, but Owen cringed nevertheless.

His uncle raised a hand and Owen shut his mouth on the apology that had reflexively risen to his lips. No apologies would be expected from him, only change.

"When last did you meditate?" his uncle inquired calmly.

Owen cringed again in spite of himself and hung his head. "I . . . can't remember."

The pond's aerator gurgled quietly. Fish made the occasional surface splash. Slowly, the burden of shame eased and Owen looked directly at his uncle.

"Kirat will spend some time practicing with you so you can return to our tradition of daily meditation." A neutral statement should not sound so threatening, but it did.

"Yes, Uncle."

"I want you to understand what I found when you came to us last night. You are very good at binding people together for a cause, any cause, good or ill. You can do so swiftly, painlessly, and without permanent harm to anyone. However, you are less adept at untangling those bonds when the moment of need is over. Your state on arrival was like that of a tangled skein, frayed and knotted and ready to snap. I do not speak metaphorically. For you, a snap is a loss of control. I believe neither of us wants that to happen."

"No, Uncle," Owen whispered.

"Meditation allows you to comb the skein, to remove the ties made and restore your ability to make new connections as you please, when you please. Incidentally, it will also improve your sleep and your concentration, but these are mere side effects to the primary goal—which is not to lose control. Do you understand?"

"Yes, Uncle." Owen murmured. He felt close to tears. This was a man that he never wanted to disappoint.

"I cannot fix things for you if they go wrong, you realize."

That straightened Owen's spine. "Of course not. I'm an adult. I can handle my own business, and Aunt Grace would kill me if I allowed you to put yourself in danger."

"That is not the point. I did not say 'will not.' I said 'cannot.'" His uncle smiled sadly. "I am old, Rafi. You are far stronger than me now. Mistakes and all."

The sound of his childhood name almost undid him. He could not trust himself to speak. Instead, he laid a hand on his uncle's shoulder and sent all his love and determination in a single warm grip. His uncle answered with a mirroring gesture, hand to his shoulder, a fond grasp and hold.

"You can always come home. That's why Kirat is with you. It's not an imposition. He and Siha have been molded for this kind of travel since birth, and they both need and want the practice. Don't forget."

"I won't . . ." Owen cleared his throat. "I won't forget."

The old man sat back, his posture relaxed, a visible sign of a mind more at ease. "I think I understand a little why you decided to carry your father's name for this task, but you are not the son of Ioan Adafydd. He had no guidance, and used his gift to coerce and control. You have learned discipline and restraint from many traditions and teachers, and what you do is not for your own selfish desires, but for the benefit of all. Your aunt and I . . ." His voice suddenly faltered, as if uncertain how to proceed, but after only a small hesitation, he continued firmly, "You are *our* child, and we are proud of you."

Owen's breath stopped. In spite of his many accomplishments in his adult life, he still bore the scars of his childhood and needed certain reassurances. His heart was touched by the depth of his uncle's understanding.

A voice came from the kitchen, lilting, cautious, and still the authority over them all regardless of how soft it sounded. "There's . . . um . . . there's more food in the kitchen." She stressed the word "food" so sweetly that Owen burst out laughing, and his uncle also cracked a smile.

"Your aunt wants her time with you. Don't keep her waiting. We will meditate on the roof at sundown."

"Yes, Uncle." He scrambled up from the bench, gave his uncle a quick, firm hug (*how much harder he was, how close his bones to the skin!*) and went to eat with his aunt.

"You will not *believe* who I saw at the pilots' guesthouse in Masuf just a few weeks ago."

"Go on," Owen prompted messily around his final mouthful of food.

"Your little friend from school! The one who grew up in that religious community. I haven't seen her in ages. She looks well."

Owen blinked. "You saw Serendipity? I thought she was still off planet."

"She moves around a lot, it appears. Still with the pilots and their ships. She seems happy."

"Good, good. I was so busy, I lost touch. I should really send her a message."

"That would be nice. Now. Tell me all about your travels. Is it anything like you imagined?"

Owen took a moment to wipe his mouth, fold the napkin and set it aside, and sigh reflectively. "I braced myself for disappointment, so of course I was fine. But . . . it feels strange. The eras we idolized, they're long gone. I doubt they ever really existed. I see a lot of that now—the raw reality versus the enhanced romance. All you need is a little distance and a willingness not to look too hard."

"Paris?" she asked almost wistfully.

He laughed. "Paris is always Paris. It's been both raw and romantic for generations. No illusions there. But most of Europe is changed. It lives in virtual reality templates and canned history tours. Some cities are fighting back, trying to control their new incarnation for the next century, but some are already completely transformed. The cost of maintaining the status quo is too high, but it's hard for many to adjust to being less.

"I think people are hungry to be seen as they *are*, not as they were. I think the concerts give them a little bit of that. I don't just bring the

world to them; I show them to the world, a little shabby and dimin-
ished, but still with character."

"You're trying to make a global team," she said slowly, attempting to
understand.

"Any way I can. Music. Sports. Even a little politics in an area no
one pays attention to. I don't know how well it will work. It's too early
to tell." He frowned slightly, thinking to himself how flimsy the strategy
sounded as mere words.

"Seen any interference yet?"

Owen looked at her. He thought about Noriko and Bernice being
almost killed on the road, the things Ahn told him and the things he
knew that Ahn didn't tell him, and most of all he thought about how
much he did not wish to worry his aunt, who was also old and in many
ways powerless to help him fix things.

"Ahn is staying alert. We all are. There have been hints, but of
course it's very subtle. They'd rather keep hidden and have their pup-
pets busy ruling Earth. But no one has tried to attack me. Not even a
little."

"Attack can be subtle for people like you," she said shrewdly. "Think
of Kirat as another kind of bodyguard. Listen to his warnings."

"You thought I was being attacked when I came here?" he asked.

She nodded. "First thing we thought of. Siha even prepared restraints, just in case."

Owen's jaw dropped. "I . . . *really?*"

She nodded soberly. "Really. One would have thought we were pre-
paring for an exorcism. But honestly, we didn't know what we would
find."

He mused silently for a while. "I won't be overconfident. Uncle
Dllenahkh says I'm strong, but I know how even the strongest can be
stopped. I'll listen to Kirat. I'll be careful, I promise."

She smiled approvingly. "Kirat says you have one more day with us,
and then you go back. Are you sure you'll be ready?"

He shrugged, not wanting to lie. "I'll be better prepared," he said.

* * *

Noriko's memories of her nightmare, and of the view from the hopper that had so vividly turned the surreal into the real, were sinking.

Sinking, not fading. She could feel the knowledge of what had happened lying dormant in her brain like a layer in the fossil record. Present but not visible without focused digging. She wondered vaguely if she should be more worried. Perhaps the stress of the tour was finally getting to her.

"More?" Bernice asked, nudging the dessert basket in her direction.

"Thank you," said Noriko, and took two, pleased to be diverted by such delightful means. She bit into one and a burst of delicately flavored cream filled her mouth. No need to dwell on nightmares. The day was cool enough to sit outside at half past noon, and she could observe the bustle and gleam of a prosperous, modern city at her leisure before her meeting at three.

Without question, the dome around The Hague would be the first to be completed. What had once been the International Court of Justice, now Global Law, was housed in a larger, even grander complex as it evolved into the global legislature. The work of codifying and synchronizing the laws, practices, and customs of over two hundred states was intense and unending, but somehow it had become a desirable goal, or at least a useful one.

Certain countries had canvassed for Global Law and its auxiliary bodies to be moved out of The Hague to a safer, more protected location. Gaborone was a strong contender, and Bogotá had the support of half the Western Hemisphere, but the Netherlands clung to Global Law, and the rest of Europe helped them cling. They had already lost more than half the organizations in Geneva to Nairobi, Addis Ababa, and Putrajaya, and Global Agriculture had left Rome for Accra as soon as the planting of the Saharan Arboreal Boundary was complete (not that the two were related, but it was a dual coup for the African Union, and they made sure the entire world knew it). European investment in

The Hague was considerable at both the corporate and government level. The buildings carried well-known names and logos for the top financial and legal companies in the world.

If Noriko leaned far enough to the right, she could just make out the familiar characters of a famous corporate name—Kaneshiro—*her* surname before she married, divorced, and kept the Fournier name from her brief but enjoyable marriage. At least it helped to differentiate her successes from those of her siblings and various cousins. Speaking of which, she really should pay a courtesy call on her first cousin. A failure to do so might be seen as a snub, and she needed to maintain peace and mutual respect with her family.

"Where are you from, Bernice?" she asked casually, trying to make conversation.

Bernice spluttered and choked slightly on her tea. "Me, Madame? Mostly Southeast Asia, I guess."

Noriko grinned. "Sounds like a complicated story."

"You have *no* idea, Madame." Was that emphasis a warning to not pry further, or relief that the conversation was likely over? Probably the latter. After all, how long had it taken Noriko to even register the woman's name?

Guilt made Noriko take out her tablet to write a short message to her cousin. *So* sorry for the short notice, and *quite* understandable if things were too busy, but since unexpectedly finding herself in The Hague over the weekend (not a lie; the original plan was for only a single Saturday afternoon), perhaps they could lunch tomorrow? *Please say no,* she pleaded silently as she sent the invitation. Duty done, she set aside her tablet. Time for one more cup of tea.

Noriko had been looking forward to this meeting for a while. The World Council had invited Owen to join the ranks of their celebrity ambassadors for a special project: a VR simulation of a model of global government with the participation of a full complement of youth representatives selected from the best and brightest of each country.

A documentary was being planned and she had been advised that the meeting would be recorded for potential footage. Nice to be warned in advance, although she always dressed camera-ready.

Noriko strode confidently through the Global Law compound with Bernice at her side in assistant mode, holding her briefcase. They ran the security gauntlet (*unnecessarily obvious and intrusive, but perhaps that was the point, to deter the common or garden activist from trying anything foolish?*) and were ushered into a meeting room where glass window panels showed the raw, real landscape of The Hague in unaugmented, mild summer smog. Noriko did not spend too long examining it. Her attention was all for her hosts. Professor Dorian MacLeod was known to her and an expected presence at this meeting. The woman at his side, however . . .

"Charyssa," Noriko breathed, and immediately hated herself for sounding like a starstruck idiot. But this was only the greatest star of three decades, with a career spanning the beginnings of VR, the resurrection of film, and the rise of quantum-based hi-res VR. Ingenue, action hero, femme fatale, and ageless matriarch, she had played every part, sometimes even in the same movie.

"Madame Fournier, such a pleasure to meet you at last." The great lady inclined her body gracefully in response to Noriko's reverent bow.

"Please, call me Noriko." She cleared her throat and tried to inject a warm but brisk professionalism into a voice that was still too shyly awed in tone. "The pleasure is mine. I was looking forward to seeing Professor MacLeod again, but he gave me no warning that I would be meeting you today."

"Charm offensive," MacLeod said slyly, watching Noriko with amused eyes. "Is it working?"

"Too well, I'm afraid," Noriko said calmly, pulling herself together at last. She seated herself at the boardroom table and pulled out a file from her briefcase.

"To business. Owen loves the concept you've outlined here, but he's worried that it's just a training simulation at best, or a game at worst. Do you have any plans to develop this further?"

Professor MacLeod answered, "We have some ideas, and we'd be grateful for his input, but for now it's all about making sure the model runs successfully before considering real-world applications."

"Owen has already expressed his interest, and there will be no problem at all attaching his name and image to the project, but to be honest, I think he was looking forward to . . . well . . . not being *Owen* for a while."

"No one understands that better than us," Charyssa said with a depth of feeling that was palpable. "That's why we have the avatar in-structors, to give us anonymity when we need it. Your friends in Para-Vee have been doing some remarkable things in bringing VR into the real world. You know about the masks."

Noriko opened her mouth, about to say "yes."

"Of course you do," Charyssa continued, raising a finger to trace an expressive circle in the air around her view of Bernice's head. "So sub-tle, so well done, but I see it now." She pointed to her own chin. "There's a shadow under the chin, just a little bit of a blur, if you know what to look for. I've been using them since the earliest models, and I know all their tells."

Years of experience set Noriko on autopilot. She closed her mouth, smiled calmly, and consciously relaxed her shoulders. That was *her* tell . . . a tensing of the shoulders when thrown off guard. "Peter is in-deed marvelous. I'm sure Owen will be very much reassured to hear that ParaVee tech is being used in all areas."

Bernice sat silently, invisibly still, ever the consummate subordi-nate, but Noriko noticed when she quietly slid her hand from the table to her lap, as if hiding a flex or tremor of the fingers. Everyone had their tell, the edge where the mask was about to slip.

Fortunately for Noriko, the rest of the meeting was courtesy, small talk, and a ritual shared beverage on the balcony of the meeting room, where the breeze of ten stories' height freshened the sluggish summer air. Part of the package, no doubt, to show that Owen was so important to them that an icon like Charyssa would spend time idling with his representative. She was not so distracted as to neglect to get a photo with Charyssa. MacLeod captured them beautifully against the city-

scape, with the seawall etching a line behind them and the sky blending from faintly lavender below to brilliant blue above. The moment
was memorable for more reasons than one.

The drive back to the hotel was too quiet. Noriko said nothing. She
waited. She received a message from her cousin with apologies—said
cousin was in the country for the weekend—and a very thoughtful
prepaid reservation to one of the best restaurants in The Hague. Noriko considered inviting Bernice simply to smile knowingly at her over
the table until she broke, but decided against it. She went by herself
and savored the time alone as much as the very expensive wine and
seafood.

The following day, she ordered breakfast in her room and spent the
morning on correspondence and reports. She tried, and failed, to research Bernice. The ordinary employee record was accessible, of
course, but there was so much nothing there. Nothing of her past,
nothing about her family (*Jones? Really?*) and nothing about any prior
occupations. Her qualifications were standard global certifications
with no particular institution attached, and her identification photo
was the same as her real-life appearance.

Might as well go to the source, she thought. She fired off a message
to Ahn.

Who is Bernice Jones?

The drive to the airport was initially quiet, but at last Bernice broke the
silence.

"Ahn knows about my mask. They suggested I wear it."

"Really?" Noriko inquired with polite disinterest. That was easy to
check.

"They said it would be easier if I didn't stand out in a crowd. If I
looked a little more average."

"I am familiar with the concept," Noriko responded coolly. Perhaps
she should sound more sympathetic . . . Was the mask hiding terrible
scars? Aestheticians could do so much these days, and all with the
promise of permanence. A mask was temporary and suggested a desire

to maintain two faces to show the world, which did not signal trustworthiness.

"If you want me to take it off—"

"That won't be necessary," Noriko snapped, almost horrified. She would not be accused of harassing and intimidating a subordinate. She would harass and intimidate Ahn instead.

The accommodation in Prague was simply another generic hotel room. Their train carriage had arrived and was parked at a private station. Ahn was elsewhere, having briefly replied to her message with a noncommittal *Speak soon*. Owen and Tareq were not in the city at all but were due to arrive in the morning. Messages to Owen remained unanswered and marked unseen.

After all the years of preparation and months of intense teamwork in close proximity, Noriko felt strangely isolated, and even a little unsafe. She unrolled Peter's mask and stared at it for a long time, then put her tablet to "do not disturb," dressed in her cheapest, most casual clothes (hooded jacket included), and left her room. She entered the stall of a public bathroom in a shopping center across from the hotel and emerged as a stranger, her own personal Jane Doe, indistinguishable from the masses.

Reveling in her disguise, she walked the streets for hours, paying with paper instead of credits, lingering in art galleries, then a café, then a nightclub. She wondered how bad it could be, to simply walk away with this new face and this new lack of concern.

And then . . . then she realized that her risk-taking was meaningless. The mask was ParaVee tech. Bernice had been updated as well. She was quite sure that her bodyguard was nearby, wearing another face, discreetly monitoring her temporary rebellion.

That killed the mood. Mask off, hood up, she walked back to the hotel and back to her responsibilities.

FOUR

THE EARLY MORNING sunrise gilded the low stone and high steel towers of Prague ancient and modern. Another hot day had been predicted, but at that hour it remained a distant promise. Owen had returned, and he felt so rested and content that it seemed like a gift, a sign that all would be well for the rest of the tour and beyond. His optimism was fueled by a sense of virtue; he was watching that sunrise from the roof garden of his hotel suite, where he was sitting with Tareq, dutifully meditating according to his uncle's command.

Meditation was a challenge for him, perhaps because it felt too easy. He understood everything that his uncle said about the calming of the mind, the disengagement from past encumbrances, and the refreshing of the spirit, but for him it was still a fairly passive practice, nothing like the communal dependence his uncle's people had developed over generations of growth and adaptation.

He sometimes wondered whether his uncle put too much stock in meditation as a cure-all, like the placebo magic of a regular ritual. If that were the case, he might as well light a candle and finger some beads and lean on that instead. And then, just when he had convinced himself to drift away, to reduce the time to minutes, to skip a day here and a day there until daily became weekly and weekly became not at all, he imagined he could feel a warm buzz at the fringes of his consciousness—inexplicably but undoubtedly Tareq, nudging at his agnosticism with a mild humor mingled with exasperation.

The sunrise came like a reward for being up early, for persevering, and for deciding to keep his promises.

After meditation, they quietly returned to the suite, delaying speech to savor the stillness of their minds. The sunlight came through the glass doors of the lounge area, warmly bright on the round dining table. Owen tapped the screen in the center of the table, adjusting the door and window glass to a cooler filter, ordering a light breakfast, and sending an alert to let Ahn know that he was up. Then he poured a cup of coffee from the full, freshly brewed flask on the table, sat back, sipped with eyes half-closed against the fragrant steam, and exhaled.

Tareq joined him on the opposite side of the table, poured his own cup, and took out a small tablet, which he scanned for a few minutes. "Better?" he eventually asked Owen, half genuine query, half dry rebuke.

"Better," Owen confessed.

"Noriko will be joining us for brunch. Ahn is already up and going places with Jones. They say they'll update us later."

Owen nodded. "What should I do about Noriko?"

Tareq paused, then replied, frowning as he spoke, "Ahn turned her translator on for Standard Galactic and a few other non-Terran languages. She's not aware."

Eyes wide open and considerably less calm and content than before, Owen stared at him. "And when was Ahn going to tell me that?"

"You weren't fully available at the time. Security-wise, I can understand why, but it causes some problems. The more incidents occur during the tour, the harder it's going to be to hide who we are. You should have left her in Paris."

"But there were all those other projects to be managed, and she's the best," Owen murmured, half distracted at the various nightmare scenarios running through his head. "What should I tell her?"

"Something as close to the truth as you can manage. Don't wait for a crisis. Don't wait for someone else to feed her an alternative narrative. She'll be susceptible, and it won't be her fault if she falls for it."

Owen's cup hit the table sharply. "I *know*. Is there anything you can do?"

"Not without her consent. I don't need to tell you about that, do I?"

The only response to that was a cutting, hurt glare. "I can't tell her all the truth. I can tell her *some* of it. And I can tell her that I'm not at liberty to tell her everything. I can't do this alone. You, me, Ahn . . . we need do this together. She's worked with us for too long; she deserves that at least."

Tareq shrugged. "I'll support you in that. Can we go over which truths in advance? I'd hate to say the wrong thing."

"Call Ahn. Get them in here as soon as possible."

"Call them yourself. I'm not your employee," Tareq said tiredly.

"I *know* that. I mean *call* Ahn. They're not picking up my calls or messages, but if *you* call, they'll know."

Tareq raised his eyebrows at that—Owen's voice had grown unusually sharp for a man only minutes removed from the blissful detachment of deep meditation—but he nodded. "Very well."

Half an hour later, a hopper descended on the landing circle in the roof garden, and Ahn disembarked, stiff irritation already evident in their stride. Ahn was not in the habit of meditating, and it showed as they entered without a knock and without a greeting.

"I know this must be important," they said, moving straight past them to the glass doors for a brief glance at the hopper taking off again, "but I hope it is more important than the work I was doing just now." They paused, took a self-collecting breath, and turned to face Owen fully. "How are you feeling. Better?"

"Yes, thank you for asking," Owen replied, imitating their neutral tone. "It *is* very important. I have to tell Noriko a few things before brunch. You're going to guide me in which things are necessary."

"Ah," was Ahn's only reply. They sat heavily in a nearby chair, looked hungrily at the room service breakfast that had been delivered minutes earlier, and grabbed a croissant. "So, I authorized a range of languages on her translator. She'll hear more, but she won't understand everything she hears. What do you need her to understand?"

"A little more about who might be against us, and why," Tareq suggested.

Ahn shrugged. "I'm not even sure about that myself. For example, I thought the road incident was meant to target Noriko. Now I'm rethinking that. I believe Bernice was the aim . . . specifically to injure Bernice badly enough while she was away from us that she would have to be seen by public health authorities."

"That's a lot of tech they wouldn't be able to explain," Owen mused.

"Precisely. So I sent some messages through the network, and although nothing is certain, I'm getting the feeling that some group is gearing up to frame you as the big, bad alien."

"Me?" Owen said indignantly. "I'm more Terran than any of them."

"Of course, and that's the advantage they want to strip from you as early as possible. If I were doing it, I would select the truths like *this*: Your father was a dangerous criminal, a wild card so feared by the government that they had to make him disappear. You were under surveillance for some time as the inheritor of his unusual skills. Then you escaped, went off and studied some form of psychological control from a truly alien civilization. You rose in the ranks of their mafia and soon set your sights on exploiting Earth. They sent you to lay the groundwork for a subtle conquest by making yourself into a new messiah, someone so charismatic that the people of Earth would naturally choose you as their emperor." Ahn spread their hands out. "And here we are, with the stage set for the Galactic Judiciary, or what remains of it, to detain you, try you, and convict you."

"*I'd* believe it," Tareq said unhelpfully.

Owen groaned. "That makes me even more worried, and it doesn't help me figure out what to tell Noriko."

Ahn took time to finish their first croissant and start another while considering. "Tell her you have a cult fixated on you. The stalker problem, but several orders of magnitude larger and weirder. You don't know exactly what they want, nor whether they want to worship you, kill you, or merely control you, but you and anyone who works for you are at risk. All that is demonstrably true." They finished eating and stood up. "I need to change out of these clothes. I've been out all night. Noriko is probably going to want to talk to me anyway, so if she presses either of you for details, send her to me."

Ahn started to walk out but paused at the door and looked back. "Are you *sure* you're fine, Owen?"

Owen nodded. "I'm fine."

Ahn stared at him for a while, then gave a single brief nod of acceptance. "Please stay that way. We're doing everything we can with tech and tactics, but I'm afraid we're going to need you at some point. Work out in advance what you *can* do, and what you *should* do."

The door shut. "Well, *that* was chilling," Owen said.

Brunch was a delightful menu of fresh-pressed juices, flaky pastries both sweet and savory, cured meats, soft cheeses, and a sparkling rosé. Owen appeared to be more rested, somehow steadier, showing no sign of harm or concern about what had happened in Amsterdam—what *had* happened in Amsterdam? Noriko still wasn't sure. They chatted on a wide range of topics. She passed on Peter's message about looking forward to future Monday teatimes and told Owen all about the new ParaVee tech. Telling him about the mask caused a segue into a slightly breathless recounting of her meeting with Charyssa. She commented breezily about aging beauties like Peter and Charyssa holding on to their best years . . . but when she wanted to turn the conversation to Bernice and whatever she might be hiding behind *her* mask, she felt a resistance, like a soft touch on her mouth, like a finger on her lips, and she didn't feel like bringing it up. Not when there was still rosé in her glass and such a light, happy atmosphere in the room. Tareq dropped a fresh strawberry into her glass and smiled at her warmly, though a little sadly. *Strange*, she thought, but smiled in return and toasted him.

At last, when all the news was shared, Owen swiped his face with a napkin, glanced apologetically at Tareq, and said, "Noriko, we need to talk."

Noriko's good humor vanished. When Owen said *we need to talk* in that tone, it often meant a gentle prelude to letting go a substandard musician, changing some previously nonnegotiable contract, or explaining with firmness and kindness that someone had overstepped a boundary somewhere and consequences were about to follow. Even though she knew she had done nothing wrong, Noriko still felt her pulse pick up a little. What if, to be dramatic about it, she was about to be fired before she could discover Bernice's secret identity? Had she been framed? Outsmarted and flanked before she could fight back?

"Yes we do," she replied bravely, and set her briefcase down on the table between them like a siege wall. "I'm feeling a bit out of the loop on certain things."

What followed next was unexpected. Owen sagged and slowly put his face in his hands. "This is hard," he mumbled. He raised his head and looked at her pleadingly. "Please don't interrupt, don't laugh, and don't trivialize this."

For the next few minutes she listened to a confused ramble that consisted of irrelevant and slightly sordid information about his past (well, families could be embarrassing, she knew that personally), a conspiracy theory about some wackos following him on tour as if on a pilgrimage, and the very important, very relevant fact that she and other recognizable members of Owen's staff might be at risk of direct assassination, or might get caught in the crossfire for reasons that were not entirely clear. But reasons did not have to be clear when the enemy was operating from their own fractured logic.

"So, no more side trips. We stick together so Ahn can protect us more easily," Owen concluded.

Noriko sat in silence and digested things while Owen looked at her in concern and Tareq leaned against a wall on the far side of the room and gazed through the window, apparently disengaged.

"How long have you known about this?" she finally asked.

He shrugged. "We suspected. Stalkers are always a concern. But this isn't one person. This is more organized. Ahn only told me the scale of the problem this morning."

Relief eased the tension in her shoulders. She hadn't been purposely kept in the dark after all. The attack on the road, Bernice's mask . . . the things that had thrown her ordered world into uncertainty were once more making a kind of sense, even if it was something she would rather not have had to deal with.

"What can I do to help?" she said.

Tareq glanced across at her, briefly assessing, perhaps unsure of her intentions, but Owen immediately broke into a smile. "Let us know . . . let *Ahn* know if you hear anything strange. Don't go out alone. We have better tech on board to use if we need to, but we should still move in groups of at least two or three, with bodyguards."

Noriko sighed. "It's a pain, but I can't say I'm not used to it. Just for Europe?"

"For now." Did his expression freeze for a moment? Was that a tell or just the slight discomfort of telling a comforting half truth? Probably the latter, because he grimaced and sagged again. "I'm sorry, Noriko. This is stupid and complicated and you deserve better."

"I'll manage. *We'll* manage." Impulsively, she leaned forward, put her hand past the wall of her briefcase, and grasped his wrist bracingly. "You make sure you're okay. I haven't seen a smoke in your hand for a while now, but I notice you're not jittering today. That's good, right? No stronger drugs in play?"

He covered her hand with his. "Nothing chemical, I promise. Smokes were a bad habit for my voice anyway. I'm quitting."

"Wow, good for you!" She looked across the room. "Thanks, Tareq."

"Why are you thanking me?" he asked warily.

"Don't think I haven't noticed. Things may have got a bit weirder since you turned up, but it looks like you're a good influence on Owen. So . . . thank you."

He huffed, a mild retort to her cheekiness, but allowed a small smile of acceptance to show.

Age might slow down the body with the pain of accumulated injury and everyday wear and tear. But beyond physical age, the passing years brought experience, experience of how quickly and how badly things could go wrong. Mental wear and tear, Ahn called it. For some things, it smoothed the edges of the mind in creative ways. Youth would drive straight ahead when a dodge would do. The big swing, the dramatic leap, those were the preserve of those who had not yet learned their mortality. Age knew how to exploit a strategic weakness with a single touch, microstep sideways at the right moment, and save all that desperate energy for when it would be most needed.

For other things, mental wear and tear dulled the mind. Ahn realized they were seriously losing their appetite for adventure. Being risk averse was not always a bad thing, but when it led to a refusal to see the storm on the horizon, that was maladaptive. Or, conversely, a tendency to see trouble everywhere. That was chaos.

"Jones," they murmured, "tell me I'm being an old fool."

Bernice shook her head. "Not yet, General."

She sat relaxed in the presence of her superior, still wearing the informal uniform of Ahn's support staff: black trousers, blue long-sleeved shirt, black bomber jacket, and black cap. Ahn stared at her.

"Jones, take off your mask."

Her head tilted questioningly, but she was not offended. She took off the cap, eased a finger under an edge of fine fabric near her hairline, and drew the illusion down to her neck. Ahn took a long moment to stare at her, trying to imagine what would appear normal. The long groove along the browbone would be considered the most disturbing, not only for its depth, but for the slightly metallic sheen to the grid work that held it in a close, calibrated shape, ready to accept any standard pilot's interface. Some countries had experimented with temporary helmet interfaces, but no one on Planet Earth had managed to develop a cranial shunt of this complexity.

Ahn sighed. "Put it back on, thank you."

Bernice obeyed. Her hands were steady as she replaced the mask and cap. Her voice was steady as she said, "Are you going to reassign me, General?"

"No," Ahn said quickly. "I can't replace you. You are our last resort, our final route of escape. But you're also a huge flashing sign that we are not of this Earth, so I would like you to wear *two* masks; a partial with a visible forehead scar, and a full face one over it. Let us hope any curiosity will be only skin-deep."

"Good idea, General," Bernice approved. "And what else?"

"Prep the jump jet in freight storage. Make sure everything is ready to shift from ground to air at a moment's notice. If the four of us need to leave in a hurry, we can't depend on Tareq."

"Four of us?" Bernice asked quietly. It sounded like an accusation.

"Noriko lives here. We'll make other arrangements for her. We can't take her with us, you know that. It could kill her."

"Yes, General." Her response was a little subdued, a little chastened. Had she forgotten so easily? In a way that was good; maybe the differences were superficial, maybe there could be a great joining of hands and hearts that would take only a generation or two instead of a few millennia of upheaval, destruction, and rebuilding. Ahn wondered how much of their present security choices would influence that outcome, and how much would be down to people like Bernice Jones getting attached to Noriko and similarly self-absorbed Terrans, like a small child making a pet of an aloof cat.

"But leaving is our *last* resort," Ahn reminded her. "So stay close to Owen and Noriko. Keep them both in your sight if you can. Tareq will always find us. I'll be at the train station, using our freight car as headquarters, but you may see me at the Prague Arena as well. The station will also be our rendezvous point if anything happens that we can't control and we're forced to leave the city, the country, or the planet. I'll make the call as to which that will be. Are you clear?"

"Yes, General." Bernice was experienced enough to be very slightly worried about the options that were being presented.

"Good. Here are our numbers and locations for tomorrow night." Ahn spread their fingers and opened up a map on their tablet. "Thirty within Prague at present, covering rehearsals and all travel between locations. Sixty more will be in the city by tomorrow for arrival at concert, concert duration, and extraction from the Arena, both scheduled and emergency."

"That's the full contingent," Bernice noted neutrally.

"Precisely, Captain Jones. I'll need to see detailed plans from you within three hours. If you have no other questions, you're dismissed until then."

"I have one question. Do we know yet . . . *who?*"

"Could be any of three groups, Jones. When I know, you'll know. I'll say this much, you should be able to handle anything that comes your way. Arrange your sections accordingly, with a mix of physical and mental skills. No one should stand out. We have the extra ParaVee tech if there's a danger of discovery. Use it as much as you like. For the rest, be careful. Earth is going to find out sometime, but not because of us. Understood?"

"Understood, General." Bernice looked gray at the mere thought of kicking off a galactic-level diplomatic incident.

"Don't worry. We're stocked, we're staffed, and we're prepared. They have no idea *how* prepared. This show of force should make them think twice. Nobody wants a war right now. Later maybe, but not now."

Bernice smiled weakly. "Much later, General. Let's hope for that."

Noriko was extremely annoyed to hear that she would have to endure the concert from the backstage greenroom, in the very thick of things. "Why? Why not at least in a quiet room where I can enjoy it on my personal screen at the volume of my choice? Do you know how crowded it gets when the supporting acts are going on? What happens if—"

"Noriko." Bernice's voice shocked her silent. There was no *Madame* in that, no hint of deference at all. "I have my orders from General Ahn. Do you need me to provide you with a sedative?"

Noriko flushed, angry that she had been so transparent. "I'll be fine. I'll have something to drink, I'll sit well out of the way, and I'll be fine."

She was not fine. She could feel the tension, see the slight difference in movement. There were a lot of security people on the ground for this concert. None carried arms openly, yet all looked alert. She imagined that that was only half of them; more would come in with the audience, dressed casually, pretending to dance and sing while listening to the bug nestled in one ear, safe within their noise filters.

"Let Ahn do their job," Tareq told her when she fretted. Easy to say, when security was the one part of Owen's empire over which she had zero control.

She grabbed a bottle from the catering table and went to sit grumpily in a corner. Why couldn't Owen at least insist on his own room for concerts? He welcomed the mayhem of common rooms, only allowing himself a small, sectioned-off area for his costume changes. Something about "bonding in the flesh after being merely acquainted in VR." It was all part of the Owen mythos. The idea of a cult following gone wrong wasn't such a stretch when you thought about it. He should have been one of those drugged and difficult stars, trashing hotel rooms, crashing cars, and pissing off journalists. But he was intensely reserved offstage, and stupidly generous backstage and onstage. The crowds fed him and drained him and she could never understand how he kept coming back, because the only thing that made her more nervous than crowds was the naked vulnerability of being in the spotlight.

Noriko poured out a large glass and put on her noise-silencing headphones. If there was nothing she could do, she'd do nothing but drink.

Twenty minutes into the concert, Ahn heard a humming and realized the sound was coming from their own lips. This was an old staple on a varied set list, a song Ahn had heard so often that they often failed to notice when it was playing. When they paused to listen, listen properly, the cadences of the popular music of their home planet were obvious . . . but the music Ahn had grown up with was itself so influenced by the musical traditions of Earth's cultures that it was impossible to find anything alien about the song.

The Argus played audio of Bernice's lieutenants coordinating their observations and movements. Bernice occasionally chimed in to override or clarify a command. Ahn watched several screens at once with different filters, looking for patterns, strange data, sudden changes.

A screen shimmered with a moiré gloss over one small section of the crowd. Hardly noticeable, until you also noticed how the crowd parted around the slowly advancing disturbance, stepping aside in unconscious synchronicity.

"Jones, there is a ghost in the crowd. I say again, you have a ghost in the crowd, floor seating, northeast side, near the second exit corridor, north of the stage. Confirm when you see it." Even as Ahn spoke, their fingers traced out commands on their tablet, activating tech both at the Prague Arena and in the sealed bunker of a carriage that was their headquarters.

"Seen. Closing in now," Bernice replied within seconds.

"Joining you as avatar," Ahn continued, and pressed the final switch.

They saw and felt a portion of their consciousness materialize beside Bernice as she huddled behind a stage backdrop, using her own venue-limited Argus to probe the area in front of the stage. "I can get Owen offstage whenever you give the command, General."

"Stand by," was all Ahn said as they scanned more deeply. No weapons. No large tech of any kind beyond the shielding. "Jones, take off the Argus and look with your own eyes!"

Bernice swore softly and obeyed, pushing aside the lenses with a smack of her palm. The blurred space showed itself to be a pair of humanoid figures, just a little above Earth average height, wearing full-face mask tech. They could still pass, if you didn't really know what you were looking at. But if you did, you would quickly realize that there was no reason to cover every inch of exposed skin during one of the greatest European heat waves, in a crammed auditorium with heat radiating off so many bodies that the environmental controls had failed to keep up . . . no reason unless you had something to hide.

"Grab them now, Jones!"

"Section will get them when they're at the stage, General! I won't reach in time. Too many in the way."

"Too late," Ahn snarled. "They've got range."

The two strangers had plenty of range and focus, and they were using it to target the bassist and the second guitarist. The music thinned as their parts dropped out. They stopped playing, stared into the crowd, moved toward the stage edge, and began to scramble down. The guitarist moved faster and jumped past Jones's own troops, who were caught unawares. The audience surged happily toward him; he swung the instrument viciously around, and then the screaming began.

"Too late," Ahn repeated. "Get your psy-troops up, quickly. Cut off those two. Knock out our people if you have to. Get a grip of the panic before we have a stampede on our hands."

"Yes, General," Bernice replied, a little breathless as she relayed commands. She began to move out.

"Stay where you are!" Ahn barked. "Watch Owen."

At first, Owen was bewildered. He quickly signed to the rest of the band to keep playing and tried to reason with the crowd. More than reason. In spite of not being physically present to feel the effect, Ahn recognized Owen's stance, the change in timbre of his voice, the way the people around him turned to him as if he had become the only sun in their universe.

But it was too much. Too many varying demands, too many different emotions. Encourage the band. Calm the crowd. Seek out the enemy. Protect himself from influence. Owen swayed even as he spoke, slowly, persuasively.

"Get ready to grab Owen," Ahn warned Bernice. "He's going to fall."

FIVE

HE'S GOING TO FALL.

Owen was aware that several things were happening at once and he was powerless to stop any of them.

Juergen Stein and Mariane Vanzetti were rampaging, out of their minds as if drugged or hypnotized. The crowd was turning, roiling, crushing in on itself, hysteria spreading from the margin to the center. The other band members were perplexed, uncertain. There was a fight for control, and he was at the very edge of it, trying to do too much with too many.

And he was falling.

He hit the stage hard, knees first, and vomited. Out of nowhere, stage fog puffed around him, cool and insidious. Bernice was at his side, and then, with a huge rush of relief, he felt the physical and mental touch of Tareq steadying him and pushing away his nausea.

"Hold on," Tareq said, and then . . .

. . . silence.

*   *   *

A hot, dry wind on skin; white-bright sun squeezing eyes tight shut; hard, uneven ground pressing against feet; the deep, delicate quietness of a wide, empty landscape.

Bernice blinked and looked up. She had curved her body around Owen by reflex, head down, shoulders braced. In a lightning-lit instant she saw a blooming tree, a velvet cloth, and, in the mid ground between the two, a pair of dark, angry eyes framed with shining hair. The instant faded to nothingness, and then she was head down once more, staring at a familiar floor, dark gray steel stamped with a nonslip texture.

"Blast and hellfire!" That was Ahn. They ripped off the Argus and lunged toward the huddled group with Owen at the center, Bernice on the left, and Tareq on the right. Tareq and Owen gripped each other in mutual support. Bernice was shaking, wide-eyed, looking around to orient herself.

"You're at headquarters, in the train station," Ahn confirmed. "Don't ask. Get on the Argus quickly and contact your troops. I'll speak to Noriko myself."

Bernice followed orders automatically, scrambling to switch her tech to the longer-range Argus Ahn had been using. Frantic reports came to her, and she fielded them with a necessary calm. The stampede had been averted. Minor injuries only, perhaps ten to twelve people in all. The stage had been cleared and the PA system was informing the audience, in formal, sober tones, that there had been a small incident that was now under control, and there would be a short fifteen-minute break in the program.

"And the two ghosts?" Bernice demanded.

"Detained and removed from public view," her lieutenant said. "What next, ma'am?"

She looked to Ahn, who was still following her audio via their bug. Ahn was kneeling beside Owen, holding up his drooping head in both hands. "He can't go back. Tell them to make an announcement that Owen was taken ill and can't perform. Let them bring on the supporting local bands."

She relayed the message as Ahn got Owen to his feet and moved him and Tareq to a nearby couch. The small space rang with their overlapping conversations.

"Lieutenant Jelínková, secure the prisoners and bring them to headquarters for questioning."

"Hey, Noriko! Ahn here. Yes, we had some excitement. Nothing to worry about, it's all taken care of. Can you pack up for us? We'll meet you at headquarters. Corporal Musilová and her section will help you with the baggage. Bernice is with me for the moment. Oh yes, Owen's here too, everyone's fine. Don't worry. Can you pack up in two hours?"

"Lieutenant Marek, detach Corporal Musilová and her section to report to Noriko Fournier. Packing up and moving out immediately. Maintain security around the hotel."

"Yes, it wasn't exactly what I was expecting, but you'll be safe with Corporal Musilová. See you soon!" Ahn ended on a ridiculously sunny note.

"Lieutenant Svoboda, how did those ghosts get in? Any backup with them?"

Ahn returned to their desk and sat beside Bernice. "Right, that's taken care of. Now, let's go over our positions. We're going to have to adjust."

Across the room, Owen roused himself, sat a little straighter, and muttered to Tareq, "That was a rough transition."

"Sorry," Tareq said, and he looked like he truly meant it. "I had to decide quickly. Siha's very angry with me, trust me."

Owen passed his hands roughly over his face and stretched his hands out, clinically assessing the shaking of his fingers. "How are you?"

"A little unsettled. It'll pass. How are *you*?"

"Embarrassed. Uncle Dllenahkh keeps telling me to remember I'm not omnipotent."

"He says you care too much." Tareq paused for a moment, then continued in a rush, "That's why you make yourself sick afterward. You hate doing this, and you make sure that it costs you. Isn't there another way?"

"I'm trying to make another way, but when they bring this kind of war to me, I don't have a lot of choice."

They fell silent for a while, listening to Bernice and Ahn directing the aftermath.

"The psy-troops are doing a good job with the crowd," Tareq noted.

"They are," Owen agreed grudgingly, "but we don't want to make a habit of that. We have to keep within the law, no matter what our intentions are. This is all going to come out into the open, and our reputations will be on the line."

"Yours, not mine—" Tareq began teasingly.

"Ours," Owen repeated, an edge to his voice. "Ours because you're my family now. You agreed to that, don't forget it. You don't work for me, but I *am* responsible for you."

Tareq sighed and said, "This is going to be a very long night."

After a few more minutes, Bernice stood and came over to them. "We're wrapping up soon. I'm going to speak to the stationmaster, get our carriages linked up and ready to go. Do you need anything?"

"I'll get us some food," Tareq said. He glared at Owen. "*You* should get some rest."

Owen was about to retort when Bernice unexpectedly agreed, "You should. We have two prisoners coming here in a few hours and I want you to be present when we interrogate them."

Her calm request disarmed him in a way that Tareq's quasi-sibling needling would never be able to accomplish. "Of course. But promise you'll wake me if anything happens."

She nodded. "Of course," she said in turn.

Owen found his sleeping compartment dark and lonely, and blissfully so after the crush of minds and bodies he had recently endured. He fell asleep instantly, as if knocked out by a drug, and immediately passed into surreal dreams that tired him as much as wakefulness. "You need to make a new way," a many-masked Noriko told him, flash-

ing her features from age to age and person to person. "But you're trying so many at once! Pick one! You're overextending yourself."

"Who are you?" he asked her, but he really meant *Stop doing that!*
The changes were dizzying and he hated them.

"I'm necessary," she replied. "But you'll need more of me in the
end. You're not omnipotent. Even an Argus uses avatars. Even a kitchen
uses soup spoons. Even a gargoyle uses downspouts."

"Oh hellfire," Owen grumbled, dragging himself into half wakefulness and out of the weird loop. He seriously considered drinking to
shut up his conscience, but lost the train of his thought midway and
fell into another dream.

His sister, the one he had chosen and who had chosen him, stood
before him. "Congratulations, Brother. They underestimated you and
you used that brilliantly. You have served our House well."

The warmth that he felt upon seeing her was a memory and a
reality. He touched the hem of her ice-blue mantle fondly, respectfully.
"I serve you and our Mother, and will keep doing so for as long as you
both continue to do good."

"We serve you as well, Little Brother. Do not forget. We are responsible for you; you agreed to that."

Memory and present met with a resonant poignance. His own
words to Tareq, nothing but a repeat of what had been told to him,
years ago and less than a year ago.

"We shelter under the same roof." He gave the ritual response with
his heart. Then, perhaps due to some tension loosed in his subcon-
scious, his dream collapsed into a meaningless jumble of sound and
image.

He woke at last to someone gently shaking his shoulder. "Prisoners
have arrived," Tareq murmured. "Ahn wants us to watch and listen
from a screen at first. We'll decide when we need to come in and question them."

Owen swung himself up, adrenaline speeding up his body to a false
alertness that his thoughts did not yet have. "Noriko?"

"With Bernice. Getting us ready for a quick departure." Tareq stopped short of the door that would have taken them into the windowless carriage Ahn used as their headquarters. A table had already been set up with an audiovisual system, and the screen showed Ahn wearing the Argus, leaning against their desk, facing two figures in wrist and ankle restraints. The prisoners had been stripped of their masks and their faces were in full view—symmetrically, classically beautiful, with a soft glow like a faint sprinkling of some mineral. Fairy dust, glamour, or simply some alien tech . . . they were not of Earth and it showed.

Owen and Tareq, who were also not of Earth, were unfazed. They settled in, facing the screen, and connected their bugs to the audio.

Ahn exhaled and looked up in mute recognition of their presence, then fixed the prisoners with a stern glare. "State your identities," they began.

"You're assuming we recognize any tradition or convention that requires us to give you our names and titles." The prisoner's voice was a smooth, amused alto . . . They reminded Owen of Charyssa's famous persona from the Spyminder franchise. Ahn seemed to have the same reaction because they smiled and bowed their head, as if conceding the point.

The moment passed, and Ahn looked up again. "I've trained long enough and hard enough for that little display to have no effect on me whatsoever. In addition, a number of my best psy-troops are within range and ensuring that no undue interference or influence happens within this room. Please don't waste what little time I have to give you. Who are you, and what do you want?"

"We represent the combined corporations of Alpha Lyrae, and we want you to respect the extension of the Terran Embargo," the second prisoner said in a harsh tenor.

"Respect it? Like you are respecting it now? You are the only reason we are here at all." Ahn pushed away from the desk and took a few meditative steps across the narrow space from wall to wall. "You were found with ferotropin, a synthetic compound known to cause euphoria with an unfortunate side-effect of occasional psychosis and violent behavior. But you didn't use it. You turned your considerably powerful minds directly on Mr. Stein and Mx. Vanzetti as they performed on-stage. I'm not sure why. Perhaps they were the most susceptible. Perhaps they simply had the capacity to cause the most damage with their instruments."

Ahn paused, leaned on the desk again, and pointed a finger at the prisoners. "I think you never intended for it to be used. After you un-leashed the riot, you were going to plant this substance on Owen or some member of his team. Reveal to the world that his popularity had a bit of chemical help and suggest that perhaps he's a lot less benign than people imagine. That would turn opinion against him overnight. Have I guessed right?"

They didn't wait for an answer. Owen could not tell, but Tareq gave a nod and he assumed some sign, some hint of confession had escaped the prisoners and been detected by Ahn's psy-troops and relayed via the Argus.

"That's the opposite of what I expected, but it makes sense if you don't want Earth to know about aliens too soon. Discredit us, but use a sensible, Earth-normal narrative to do so, ignoring all existence of psionics. I approve. It could have worked."

Ahn took their seat and hovered their hand over a tablet, poised to take notes. "Now, the attempt on my captain's life in France—was that you?"

The second prisoner laughed. "Not us. It appears your enemies are many."

Ahn calmly made a note. "The failed infiltration of my Berlin re-cruitment program. You?"

Silence, but again Tareq nodded next to Owen, and Ahn checked the item off their list.

"Sabotaged equipment just prior to the Madrid concert? Theft of VR shielding in Paris? Successful infiltration of Paris hotel staff?"

Ahn reeled off a number of middling to minor incidents that were news to Owen. He didn't know whether to be worried or impressed by his security chief's reticence, but he was definitely comforted by their competence.

At the end of the recital, Ahn tapped their tablet off and stared at them coldly. "You two are not as important as you think you are."

Even Owen couldn't miss the prisoners' flinches of chagrin. Tareq chuckled outright. Owen had a sudden idea. "I want to go in," he said.

"Definitely," Tareq agreed gleefully, quickly bouncing up to open the door.

The reaction from the prisoners was gratifying, and familiar. The moment Owen stepped into the room, Tareq one protective step ahead of him, the two shuffled back in their shackles and tugged futilely at their wrist restraints, flight and fight reflexes combined.

"What do *you* want from Earth?" Owen snapped without preamble.

"We already have what we want—Earth itself. Your silly musical empire won't change that," said the first prisoner dismissively.

"You think you rule here?" Owen asked, pushing back just a little. He made them focus on him completely. He knew how to turn attraction to hatred, and hatred to loss of control.

"Yes, we do!" she spat back at him. "Our leaders are already in place in several countries, and we will hold influence over several more. We have been here for centuries, and no one will usurp us. When the embargo is finally lifted in twenty years, we will be the de facto government."

"Twenty years," Owen repeated softly. "You think we have that long? I thought you were better informed."

He glanced at Ahn, signaling with a nod that he was finished.

"And now what will you do? Hand us over to the authorities in Prague?" the second prisoner said mockingly.

Ahn sighed. "Yes, that would be awkward, wouldn't it? Fortunately, *we* have already successfully infiltrated the Prague gendarmerie . . . so we are free to take you, and you will not be missed."

Two guards entered the room in swift response to Ahn's silent command and removed the prisoners via the far door of the carriage.

"They underestimated me," Owen said. "They underestimated everything we're doing. That's comforting. They see what I can do, and they hate that anything from Earth could be stronger than they will ever be, and yet they underestimate me and what I would do with that power."

"We can't take them with us, but we can't let them go. What do you mean, they won't be missed?" Tareq asked worriedly.

"No need to contemplate execution, tempting though it is," Ahn answered placidly. "I've assigned Bernice to fly them out. And, on another note, we either bring Noriko fully on board, or you must find her some other work to do. Your inner circle must be just that—people who know you and understand exactly who you are and what you are doing."

"Ahn's right," Tareq agreed. "The situation has me on edge." He tilted his hand in distraction, held up a hand as if listening to something. "Wait . . ."

"Can we decide this after Byzantium?" Owen hedged.

The door beside them opened, and Ahn and Owen jumped. Tareq sighed—embarrassed to be caught before he could give warning and embarrassed that he had forgotten to switch off the screen outside when they left to join the interrogation.

"No," said Noriko.

Her face was drawn, her posture spoke of exhaustion, and there might have been a suggestion of alcohol and stimulants in the twitch of her hands, but her voice was steady and implacable as she faced her colleagues.

"Not Byzantium. We need to talk . . . *now*."

Bernice rolled her shoulders, flexed her fingers, flapped the ailerons, and revved the engine. Putting on the pilot's helmet was like being wrapped in the skin and skeleton of a large, powerful beast—exactly like. Nothing on Earth could compare. Even VR designed to create a cyborg state, pairing human minds with huge industrial robot avatars or anthropomorphized vehicles, could not compare to galactic standard mechanical pilot interfaces.

She could even sense the two prisoners sealed in life support capsules, knocked out to ensure no shenanigans en route. Their full names and corporate affiliation had been discovered; that information plus all the data concerning their crime and the consequences had been temporarily banded to their wrist restraints, like a gift tag on a festively wrapped box.

She had traveled this route many times before. She had all the necessary clearance codes and access to appear as a regular addition to Earth's air traffic. Even with a destination so rare and remote, her presence would raise no questions.

The roof of the freight carriage opened slowly to a dark sky growing pale gold in the east. Treetops fringed the horizon as the train whipped through the forest. Bernice waited.

"Captain Jones, you are cleared for takeoff."

"Jones, cleared for takeoff," she acknowledged, and eased the jump jet into a stable hover above the train. Slowing slightly, she let them pull away for a few seconds before turning southward and engaging the main thrusters.

Antarctica, still ice-shrouded at its core, still terra incognita to most people on Earth, awaited her and her cargo, with its gateway to galactic civilization. As always, General Ahn was staying strictly within the rule of law, and the two prisoners would be facing galactic justice in less than forty-eight hours.

Peter showed his teeth in an approximation of a cheerful grin. He had always been good at faking expressions, but working on the masks had taken mere artistic talent to a precise and scientific practice.

Monday tea appointments were for friends, valued colleagues, and anyone who could be counted on to provide that small boost of positive energy that was needed for the first workday of the week. On Monday afternoons, he could be a little vulnerable, slip a sedative or a stimulant into his cup, and let the hour of fellowship extend into the evening.

On Tuesday, when he had hit his stride and full strength for the week's activities, lunch appointments were saved for rivals, enemies, and fools who had to be suffered gladly for the sake of the business. Sometimes, an appointment held all three in one person, and Peter found himself working hard with every ounce of his experience and skill to control his face and his mask.

"Molyneaux, my *dear* sir," Peter exclaimed with enthusiasm. "You are too, too much! You must think I am naïve, to let you into the secrets of my research division."

His guest looked downcast, almost apologetic, but Peter was as good at recognizing posturing as committing it. "Hendrix, I left UniVis almost a year ago. I've been a private consultant and contractor since then. You *know* this. Why continue the corporate competitiveness? I'm small beans next to ParaVee. I want to collaborate with you on a tiny, niche project. How can that hurt your sales?"

They were in an upper lounge—not Peter's office, he truly didn't trust the man—but it had a similar wide-paneled window, which was presently showing the rather dull cityscape on a drizzly day. Peter slouched in a deep, velvety wing chair, fully at home, comfortably but fashionably dressed in shades of bright blue: tailored trousers, a close-fitting tunic, and a light kimono over all. Contrasting silver embroidery marked his collar and the cuffs at wrist and ankle, but the rest was a rich, subtle damask. Mr. Molyneaux wore a common gray business suit to match the weather. Blending in, as usual. Peter wondered what that was like, and if people honestly enjoyed doing it.

"It will not hurt my sales," Peter replied, "but it may hurt my future. How do I know that you will not grow tired of ParaVee and return to UniVis, or even LeviaThon? I've seen your résumé. You are a man constantly on the move."

"I learn wherever I am. Advancing the technology is my sole aim. Wouldn't you agree that is more important than who wins and who loses?"

Peter rested his teacup on its saucer, extended it lazily to the server for a refill, and poised the freshly steaming cup under his lips as he spoke smilingly. "Oh, I already know who wins. Graves International, who owns UniVis, LeviaThon, DANN Inc., and a few other places you

have worked at or consulted with. You are quite predictable, Molyneaux, if one has the resources to get the information."

The man stiffened, about to protest, but Peter held up his hand to
forestall him. "And now you are about to tell me that this is not news,
because ParaVee is the last unaffiliated independent in the VR industry. Very well, let us go with that for now. Do have another sandwich.
The salmon comes from our very own in-house pisciculture farm, and
the arugula from our hydroponic gardens."

The server offered a tray to Molyneaux, who hesitated, frowned,
and then shrugged and accepted. "I wish I could persuade you, Hendrix," he said in a voice that was full of regret, warmth, and just a touch
of hope.

Peter's head went back against the velvet and he sighed, savoring
the glow. "Ah yes, I am quite certain that you wish you could. But no
hard feelings, Molyneaux. Let me show you something new I am working on. Look at the window."

Munching appreciatively on his sandwich, Molyneaux obediently
peered around the edge of his chair's right wing. His chewing slowed
and he settled himself slightly back in the chair.

Peter stood up and approached the now-mirrored surface, smiling.
At arm's length he paused and fondly touched the reflection of his
face. "Old age comes to us all. I have always been at peace with that.
Look how well it becomes me." He examined the creases, the slight
mottling of the skin, the soft sag and wrinkle of the neck, thinned lips,
and drooping eyelids. "A regal elder. This is the face I show my family
and my closest friends, Molyneaux. My colleagues call this window
setting 'Truth.' I wanted to call it 'Intimacy.' Who do you think was
right?"

Molyneaux remained seated and still, showing a mere crescent of
his features, a partial eclipse shining at the edge of the chair. "Both
terms are suitable."

Peter spun away from the mirror and turned his beautiful, smooth-
skinned, bright-eyed mask to his guest. "But you must not be shy.
Come closer and see the difference. I do not mind. Unless . . ." He

paused, allowing a little touch of drama. "Of course. I am too shame-less. You, too, have a facelift mask, and you do not want to feel old today. My apologies." He gestured, and the window switched to the gray outdoors once more. "Better?"

Molyneaux did not reply. He stood, shyly keeping his head lowered. "When you refused my offer, I wondered why you had agreed to meet with me at all. Now I think I understand a little."

"I am not a cruel man," Peter said sweetly. "At times it is simply pleasant to have company. At other times, I enjoy company and the chance to send a message. Please, let ParaVee flourish. There is room for all of us in this rich and varied market. Let us be, if not friendly, at least neutral. And let us not hide our true faces from each other. The time is soon coming, and indeed may already be here, that what is done in secret will be made manifest."

"Thank you for your hospitality. I bid you farewell." Molyneaux ex-ited swiftly, leaving a half-eaten sandwich on his plate.

The server—actually Peter's personal assistant—came to stand be-side him. "Was that wise?"

Peter shrugged elegantly. "Probably not, but it amused me."

"You're getting very good at spotting them," his assistant said admir-ingly. "I had no idea."

"They're getting very bold," Peter snapped. "I hate colonizers. They always slip and show their contempt."

"I want the Truth filter as a portable lens option."

"In development," Peter assured him. "Still a few more tweaks. I'll put you down for the third prototype."

The assistant opened his mouth, clearly on the verge of asking who had the first two, and closed it again. Peter observed his restraint and smiled in approval.

"Do you think a portable lens would sell well? Something a little retro with a vintage sunglasses look?"

"*Very* well," his assistant replied without hesitation.

Peter chuckled. "Excellent. Make a note of it."

* * *

The immaculately dressed businesswoman stood to welcome Noriko, taking her hands with unfeigned enthusiasm. "Noriko! So good to see you! I expected you would be in Zagreb by now."

Noriko gave a faint smile and greeted her cousin warmly. "Thanks for making time for me, Hana."

Hana sat down again, but Noriko remained standing, looking around the restaurant. Such a small thing to notice, infinitesimal in difference, easily second-guessed, and yet as she turned her gaze quickly from face to face, every third or fourth person seemed to have a little fuzz, a little shimmer, in the shadow of their chin. Her eyes saw the mask, or was it her imagination? Were there demons leaping unsummoned from her newly forged paranoia?

"Can we go somewhere a little quieter?" she asked.

Hana's eyebrows went up. The restaurant was elegant, tasteful, and filled only with the hum of soft conversation between executives and diplomats in very expensive suits. "If you like. Or . . ." Her eyes narrowed as she tried to parse the deeper meaning behind Noriko's request. ". . . would you prefer to go back to my office? We can order in a meal."

"Please. That would be lovely," Noriko murmured. "Sorry to be a bother. My nerves are a little shot."

Hana glanced at her, but said nothing. They walked the short distance to the Kaneshiro building and went up the elevator capsule in relative silence broken only by Hana's cautious attempts at conversation and Noriko's monosyllabic replies. Even after the office door was firmly closed and Hana coaxed a meal preference out of Noriko, the silence continued as Noriko stood staring out the window, wondering how the hell to begin the conversation without sounding completely insane.

She sighed and showed Hana a rueful smile. "I'm sorry. It's been a difficult few days."

There was a quiet knock on the door, and then one of the company

ancillary staff came in, dressed in the familiar long-sleeved teal tunic
and black trousers with the company crest on the breast pocket. Thin,
translucent gloves covered his hands completely and disappeared
under his sleeves. He pushed a trolley before him bearing cutlery,
plates, glasses, a carafe of cold water, and the sealed containers of the
food they had ordered.

"We had a terrible crowd incident in Prague," Noriko heard herself
say distantly.

Hana made a noise of shock and sympathy. "Are you all right? Is
everyone all right?"

Noriko nodded, watching as the man set the coffee table in front of
Hana's desk with all care and precision. "Quickly controlled, thank
goodness. Minor injuries, barely a note in the news. Bigger news was
that Owen left the stage early, so tickets were partially refunded." She
managed a weak smile. "Crowds stress me out. It could have been
worse, but that's my personal nightmare come true."

"You need a vacation," Hana declared.

"Are the gloves necessary?" Noriko said suddenly. The man straightened and slowly rested his hands on the rail of the trolley, duties finished, his eyes toward his boss, the shimmer under his chin
unmistakable as he moved under the bright office lights. Too easy, Noriko thought, remembering Bernice with some shame, to move among
those long socialized not to look at who was driving their cars, pouring
their drinks, silently present and observing.

"Standard food handling regulations . . . I think." Hana frowned,
sounding slightly confused at the digression.

Noriko smiled brightly at her. "I'm being silly. You're right. I need a
vacation. What are you doing this weekend? Let's go to a spa."

Later that night, Noriko adjusted her bug and opened a call to Owen.

"They're everywhere, aren't they?" she said quietly.

Owen hesitated only slightly before replying, "Yes."

She said nothing more. Owen waited patiently. The silence was almost companionable. He could have tried to use that voice on her, a tone she had heard a woman describe as the experience of happily drowning in warm honey. But he didn't, and as far as she knew, when it came to her, he never had.

Noriko examined her options and her feelings and came to a decision that scared and reassured her all at once.

"See you in Byzantium," she said.

The knock on the door was diffident, quiet. If Peter had not been expecting it, he might have thought he had imagined the sound.

He opened the door to his private lounge. Tea was already laid out on the table behind him. No server today; there would be things spoken that had to remain private. His guest stood propped against the doorjamb, as rumpled and sweat-stained as if he had just come from a long, hard rehearsal.

"Peter, I'm sorry. I can't stay long."

"Dushi!" Peter grasped his hand and gently drew him in. "I was afraid you wouldn't come at all; you've been so busy. But look at you. You're exhausted." He rested his hand briefly against Owen's cheek, pushed him to sit down, and poured out a cup of Ceylon.

Owen took the offered cup and drank obediently. "It'll be worth it in the end. Right?"

Peter didn't speak but busied himself pouring out his own tea. It wasn't the kind of question that wanted words, so he put salmon sandwiches on a small plate instead and handed that over in answer.

Owen smiled and accepted it. "Noriko knows. For better or for worse, she knows. She'll have questions, especially after the tour is over—"

"Leave her to me," Peter said firmly. "I've already traced that learning curve. I can break it down for her."

"She thought I was investing in a post-music career era. Now you get to tell her—"

"That you're taking over the world?" Peter concluded sweetly.

"Something like that," Owen said with a pained laugh. He bit into a sandwich and hummed lightly in appreciation, but the moment of bliss was all too brief.

"Ahn has briefed us on the Prague incident. We will, all of us, be better prepared." Peter leaned forward and held Owen's attention with a steady, intent gaze. "What I want to know is . . . what happened here, in Amsterdam?"

Owen regretfully finished his sandwich, hoping it would fortify him. "You were at the concert."

"I was. I left quickly, by hopper. I expected you would do the same."

"Canal boat," Owen confirmed. "An error, in hindsight. We had nowhere to turn when the crowds came."

"So, you did . . . what you had to do," Peter said gently. "How did it feel?"

"Afterward? I was sick. Out of control. Had to get away, take a couple days to rest, recalibrate." He spoke in choppy spurts, unable to meet Peter's eyes.

"And during?" Peter inquired, again with that painfully gentle tone, promising an impossibly infinite understanding.

"Afire. Immense. As if the universe belonged to me and me alone." Owen meant to say it meekly, but his voice grew slightly louder with each word and ended in defiance.

Peter looked away, a thoughtful frown creasing his forehead. He leaned back, picked up his cup of jasmine tea, and drank, silently musing.

"It *is* going to work, isn't it?"

This time, the demand for verbal reassurance was clear, and Peter rose to the occasion.

"Of course it is, dushi. You have me, after all, and I have ParaVee. How can we possibly fail?"

SIX

TODAY'S PREP ROOM attendant was Telarialhaneki, one of House Haneki's fearless, bright young things. There were many: all talented, all eager, and from all corners of the galaxy. Hanekis did not discriminate when it came to genius.

"Apology?" the Patrona inquired over her shoulder, swiping her finger quickly through the wardrobe catalogue screen hovering before her.

Telarialhaneki grimaced as she balanced inputs and outputs from two mobile screens and an audioplug. "Explanation," she replied. "It's all we'll get, though they *have* recalled their emissary."

The Patrona frowned. "Not good enough." That was an understatement. No one had *died*, but what audacity, to target a former Patron's people! "Submit an objection. That emissary may not have been acting on a direct order, but his government is responsible for his actions. Otherwise they're no better than the cartels."

Telarialhaneki leaned in, pointing at an image in suggestion. The Patrona shook her head and continued to browse. Telarialhaneki stepped back a little and made a whispered verbal memo to her audio-plug. Multitasking was the norm.

"Speaking of objections," Telarialhaneki began cautiously, "rumor has it—"

The Patrona made a scoffing noise. "Rafihaneki has ties of blood, occupation, and kin-contract on three different planets. He's well con-nected everywhere, Earth included. How dare they accuse us of being behind this operation?"

"Aren't we?" came the amused, impertinent query.

"We're not the *only* ones, is my point. And thanks to him, we now have conclusive proof that the interference by cartels and others has gone too far. I predict the process of lifting the embargo will go much more swiftly and smoothly after this scare."

Telarialhaneki pointed again, and this time the Patrona nodded in approval, but then she made a change—a single, simple tap that made Telarialhaneki's eyes widen. "I didn't mean to imply—"

The Patrona's fingers slowly curled into a fist. "Oh, but *I* do."

The wardrobe fabricator hummed in acceptance, hissed in a final phase of steaming, and discharged the garments the Patrona had se-lected for the Galactic Council meeting. The suit was in a classic, utilitarian style similar to the uniform of the Galactic Gendarmerie. However, with a different color, the message shifted from solidarity to challenge, from support to declaration. Robes of state would still be worn over the suit, but with their dark hue, their open flow and fall, the message would only be bolder.

Their world's mighty glaciers and icebergs might now be in rapid melt phase, with green once more visible at the equatorial belts, but several past centuries of snowy battlefields had firmly established white and gray as the colors of war.

"Really, Patrona?" the bright young attendant murmured in dismay. "Has it come to this?"

The Patrona stroked the still-warm fabric. "Not yet, Telarial, not yet, but the fight is coming soon, and we *will* be ready."

Eleven years later

THE MEMORY DREAM began as it always did, with a sweetness, a heaviness, as if the universe itself were sorry and trying its best to be kind. But it also felt like the kindness of a vaccination needle to a small child. *You will not understand why I'm doing this. You cannot. This is going to hurt. This is also for your own good.*

Kanoa found that his main emotional response to the kind cruelty of the universe was resentment and a strong desire to be left alone.

For now, he would enjoy the good bits. He would appreciate that glimpse of the best of home. the gritty, pale sand under his feet, gleaming with sea-foam and darker gray streaks of volcanic mineral. The green land behind him, playful yet majestic, with high hills, deep-cut streams rushing into small waterfalls, and the heady scent of the night's light rains on wind-bruised greenery and rich, dark earth. The salt breeze in intermittent puffs like shy kisses, telling a lie of warmth that the sea would soon dispel. And his father, standing with feet wide and arms akimbo, grinning at the ocean as cheerfully as if he were personally responsible for the glorious start of the day and the beauty of all nature.

"Come, boy. You'll age like a raisin if you don't do this. Locked in your VR gear half the day. You'll shrivel up."

"We're moving about all the time," Kanoa protested tiredly.

He yawned. Not only was it still too early in the morning, but the argument was old and repetitive. His father was convinced that something about the use of virtual reality made both brain and body atrophy, like a caged animal in a zoo habitat designed to be adequately stimulating but nevertheless finite. The remedy was the wide world, the real world, the "raw" as designers called it, and his father applied that remedy diligently. Every morning, their ritual was the same: walk to the beach, give and take a little teasing about the limitations of technology, then swim past the breakers and out into the merciless ocean for a four- or five-kilometer stretch to the other side of the curving bay.

At twenty-two years old, Kanoa was just able to keep up with his sixty-seven-year-old father, who had been a competitive swimmer in his youth and a part-time lifeguard into his middle-to-late years. Now he swam merely for recreation, and his present fame was all about his work as one of the councilors for Samoa in the Federated States of Polynesia. Kanoa was slightly relieved that he had at least managed to surpass his father in that area, with his qualifications in international relations and his work in the governor's office. His father was very strict about his children achieving more than he and his generation could ever have managed.

"Progress!" he insisted. "We are building a dynasty, and there is no room for slackers. I would rather have an adopted son with ambition than a lazy child of my blood."

In another family, those words would have been all cruelty and no kindness, but for Kanoa, growing up with two adopted siblings and a keen sense of his father's slightly twisted sense of humor, this was more than normal; it was fine. He was used to his father laughing at how he cringed from the cold water or when he failed to avoid being smacked in the face by a sudden rush of foam from a breaking wave. Kanoa was just a little grumpy because it was early and he didn't like talking this early in the morning. He would have preferred a peaceful, gentle awakening, not this rude shock, but he understood that his father meant well and was genuinely trying to make sure he was at his best.

He would soon be representing not just a city, nor even a district, but the entire Federated States of Polynesia, comprising several natural islands and an ever-increasing number of artificial islands. Of course he wanted to be at his best. He knew that, and he hoped that his father knew that, even as he struggled to be more than half-asleep and grumpy at five A.M.

In spite of the breeze, the waters beyond were calm, and Kanoa soon found himself in that smooth, steady swimming action his father called "strolling." Even breathing, long stretch, relax into each surge and rise with every swell. So hypnotic . . . he almost found himself drifting off again into a kind of moving meditation. He almost forgot to listen for the parallel splash of his father's progress beside him, but it registered nonetheless as a strangeness, a distressing absence that shook him to full awareness. He stopped . . . alone; looked around . . . alone; looked back . . .

His father was floating some twenty meters away, mercifully faceup, with his lips pouting in labored breathing. Kanoa sprinted to close the distance and immediately positioned himself behind his father's head, one arm across his chest, supporting him and cradling him close.

His father laughed weakly. "A little discomfort. It'll pass."

Then he turned his head to the side, convulsed, and retched a little into the water. Kanoa gripped him more tightly as a swell washed over them.

"I've got you," Kanoa said, forcing all hint of fear from his voice as he raised his wrist to activate his emergency beacon. "They'll come for us soon. Hang on."

"No, wait." His father's voice was soft and sleepy, his eyes half-closed, but he smiled. "Don't stress. It's a good death. Can't complain."

In that moment, Kanoa knew that he had fallen asleep again, or had never woken up, and was dreaming about swimming at dawn with his father, because at no time in the real world would his father be dying while the ocean surged around them. And only in a dream would the horizon grow higher like a rogue wave while the water around them turned gray and dark yet mildly turbulent like waves over shoals. Only in a dream would the ocean stop behaving naturally and turn into a badly rendered VR mockup, something too bad to be even a place-holder mid-design.

He did not panic. The brush of water against his skin, familiar as breathing, became a tickle of seaweed, then a numbing tingle that took away all chance of panic. His arms slackened, and his father's body slipped away from him. The gently churning waters parted them, and then he could not think or feel anything.

That morning, when he came to his senses again, he had found himself in the shallows of the bay with many hands around him and under him—brothers, sisters, friends bearing up his slack body. His mother's face hovered over him, and her hands cradled his head.

"Where is your father?" It had not been a question, but a wail. She already knew.

"Gone," he murmured as he rose from slumber into the bright sunrise, the chilly water, the urgent hold of his family. "He's gone."

Then the dream deviated from memory, as it always did. Unseen by anyone but him, his father appeared on the beach, looked down at him, poker-faced, and said laconically, "Get up, Kanoa. You're going to be late."

Everyone else vanished. The beach was deserted except for the two of them, standing facing each other, heavy silence between them.

"Goodbye," his father said at last, before turning away and walking into the sea.

This morning, when he rose out of the hold of the dream memory, he was as alone as when he had first missed the sound of his father swimming beside him. There was no one to pick him up, to ground him, to get him out of bed, to force him to be at his best. So he did it himself, swinging his unwilling body heavily out of bed and to a fully upright position. He dressed, took up the towel that he had laid out on a chair near the door the night before, and walked into the darkness to the usual place. The Governor's House maintained an indoor saltwater lap pool. Finite, walled-in, and horribly absent of breezes, sun, and sky, it was hardly up to his father's prescription, but it would have to do, and he had been making do with it for the four weeks since his father's memorial and his move to the capital.

Four lengths into his half-hour swim, he heard a ringing chime, like an old-fashioned doorbell. With a smooth half twist, he flipped to a backstroke and spoke his access password to the room. The drab, half-lit walls pulsed once, then flashed back to become a far larger and brighter space, with several marked lanes, pale blue water, a young woman swimming on his left, and a man of similar age to his right.

The Governor's House had excellent VR facilities in several rooms, including this one. The woman, Bay Kaneshiro, was in Morocco; the man, Faisal Al Hajri, in New Kuwait. Both liked a daily swim, though it was definitely not morning for either of them. Both had VR facilities in their own homes, a luxury and level of wealth that Kanoa could barely grasp and doubted he would ever attain.

Faisal splashed him with a whooping cheer, an invitation to race. Kanoa's heart skipped almost painfully, caught between excitement and complete disgust at the idea of moving this quickly just minutes after rising, but he took only a moment to decide and then he was racing after the competitive one. Fast enough to seem serious, but not fast enough to beat him. Kanoa had already discovered that Faisal tended to sulk when he was beaten, and he was far better company when people allowed him to win at small things.

Faisal reached the other end first, as intended. Kanoa pulled in a second later, breathing only a little harder than usual, and when he glanced back, Bay was taking her time, bobbing along in a leisurely breaststroke, her head sleek and gleaming as she dipped along in her lane. Kanoa kept his eyes on her even though he knew Faisal was staring at him, waiting for him to start a conversation. *Too early for that,* Kanoa thought.

"We get our assignments today," Faisal said at last, sounding a little annoyed that he had to be the one to speak first.

"I heard," Kanoa replied, glancing his way. No more than two words, no more than a glance. He didn't want to do what so many other people did around Faisal . . . stammer, talk too much, stare too hard, hang on every word the young prince uttered.

Bay reached them at last and pulled herself out of the water to sit on the side. One hand twisted the excess water out of her hair, the other hand delicately swiped water from her eyelashes. "It's been today for hours, Kanoa. You're the last time zone. Check your status and tell us what group you're in."

Kanoa gave a guilty flinch. Although not a compulsory requirement, most of his peers had chosen to adjust their sleep cycles to a midpoint time zone, or near enough, so as to be able to interact with as many people in their cohort as possible. He had meant to do so, but he was still so tired from everything—the grief, the moving, the extra testing during orientation—that he simply hadn't bothered.

He pulled himself up to sit beside Bay and asked the VR room for his status. The three listened silently. Then, without warning or farewell, Faisal's avatar blinked out of sight. Bay gave the vacated space a frown and shifted the background to a more pleasing view of a spa pool shaded with green bamboo.

"What's his problem?" Kanoa asked, surprised at the abrupt departure.

"You're not in his group. He doesn't care anymore. We're expected to socialize, and he would rather not waste time doing that with someone he won't be working with," Bay explained.

"That's rude," Kanoa grumbled, feeling a pang of betrayal. He'd thought, in spite of all the evidence that Faisal was a typical self-serving son of the elite, that perhaps Faisal liked him enough to pretend to act like an ordinary human being.

"Practical. He's here for a reason, and he's sticking to his plan."

Kanoa heard her, but was distracted. "Diplomatic Group. What does that mean? The entire class is international. How does a model global government do diplomacy?"

Suddenly, his stomach growled and a tiny echo followed. Bay clutched her stomach and broke into laughter. "Lunchtime for me. Join me in the dining hall?"

"Half an hour to shower and change. See you then?"

She nodded, and her image winked out, taking the spa background with it. Kanoa sat on the narrow edge of the pool, almost taken aback at the room's transformation, snapped back to a small, drab box with no subtlety or flair. He sat for a moment with his discomfort, then slowly walked back to his quarters, thinking.

Governor Crawford had been welcoming, but filled with warnings about the project. "Some of the young people in this class were accepted mainly because they have money, or connections, or both. Others have lots of ambition and talent, but no focus yet. They chose the project for the prestige; they know what will look good on their resume. The rest are like you—outstanding in all the tests regardless of their level of education, wealth, or connections. *You* are the backbone of the Global Government Project, and you must never forget that."

Kanoa appreciated that, he really did. Remembering that made his choice to leave his family less selfish, and he could consider his new life at Governor's House a necessity rather than an unearned luxury. Most of all, it helped him to navigate the strangeness of his new classmates, too many of whom appeared normal at first but then later showed they were from what one of his sisters called "Rich People Planet." Neither in his world nor of his world, regardless of the temporary overlap. Perhaps that was the conclusion Faisal had reached.

Now, Bay was definitely on Rich People Planet, but according to Governor Crawford's taxonomy, she *might* also be one of those who had aced the tests. Otherwise, why would she still hang out with him?

When he went to the dining hall, a little rushed, a little late, Bay was waiting for him impatiently at a table for two.

"You never told me," he said quickly. "What group are you in?"

A light frown teased a line between her brows. "Trade, but I'm asking for a transfer to Diplomatic."

"But why? Trade is excellent!" Bay's family was famous, but nontraditional in how it chose its successors to the family business. She would definitely need experience in international trade to compete with all the other high-achieving cousins lined up for executive boardroom positions, which were only awarded by merit and cutthroat campaigning.

She glanced away, and he recognized himself in that moment. That was how he looked to his own hypercritical eyes when trying to appear casual in front of Faisal. "Owen designed the Diplomatic module." And she blushed.

Kanoa gave her a teasing grin. "You're a fan?"

She flashed him a dirty look. "Owen isn't just a pop star. He worked privately with Peter Hendrix of ParaVee industries to develop some of our most cutting-edge VR technologies. I'm curious to see what he's produced. Like you said, what does a Diplomatic Group do for a global government? Diplomacy is the conversation between sovereign states. If we're all equal under one law, with every aspect of our civilization negotiated under global ministries, what's left for us to negotiate in our group?"

"We'll find out next week."

"Yes." She spoke easily now, the blush gone, the awkwardness covered up and brushed away. "And they'll tell us our headquarters. No more VR. We meet in the flesh, so to speak."

"Looking forward to that," Kanoa said easily, but his mind was racing ahead. He'd been barely present for the orientation month. Slacking, his father would have called it and accepted no excuse, least of all his own death. That was going to change, starting today. There were documents to read, VR scenarios to run and study. He had to prepare himself to hit the ground running and impress his group with his competence. *You're the backbone,* Governor Crawford had said. Time to act like it.

Then a thought struck him. "Bay, which group was Faisal assigned to?"

She eyed him curiously. "You didn't look that up? I thought you had a crush on him. He's in Culture, Sports, and Entertainment. Right where he wants to be, with all the glamorous celebrities."

"That was his plan?" Kanoa said, disappointed.

"He likes a pretty face, or a challenge . . . which is why he liked you, I think. More challenge than pretty, though. His future marriages will be arranged by his father. He's looking for lovers for now, and for later."

"Rich People Planet," Kanoa scoffed lightly, forgetting who was next to him.

"Aristocracy Island, you mean. Don't lump us all together. Some of us actually enjoy working for our shit."

"Fair enough." Part of him was still cynical enough to question what benefit Bay got out of talking to him. He'd seen what she looked like when she had a crush on someone, and that definitely wasn't the reason. But most of him was glad he'd managed to make one friend in the terrible, sleepwalking month that had just passed. And yet . . . when he thought about it, he still wondered.

"Bay, have you been . . . looking out for me? Did you know my father died the week before we met?" It was a strange question to ask, and he would not have blamed her if she had given him an odd look, but she only pursed her lips thoughtfully and took a little time to reply.

"I'm sorry about your father. I didn't know." She paused, considered a while, and continued, "At our first meeting, before I even noticed you, I was standing next to Faisal and he said, 'Look at that boy with the beautiful, sad eyes. He's my next.'"

Kanoa winced. Bay cleared her throat apologetically. "Sorry. I've known Faisal for a while. He doesn't self-censor around me. Anyway, I looked at you, and he was right. Your expression was calm and controlled, but your eyes were . . . vulnerable. Faisal likes to find things that are hurting and pretend to mend them so they'll get attached to him. I've seen his process. I thought this time I should block it, for the sake of the project if nothing else."

"Thanks, Grandma," Kanoa said with a smirk. Bay was not at Faisal's level of asshole-ishness, for certain, but *that* was a motivation with just enough arrogance and competitiveness for him to believe her.

She showed a rare smile. "I enjoyed it. And you're interesting, so all in all, a win for me."

Arrogance again. Time to throw her off-balance. "Tell me, have you ever met Owen in person?"

Success! The blush was back. "Once. Eight years ago, at a family gathering. I was fourteen and it was pretty horrible. I couldn't talk. I think I screamed. He looked uncomfortable. And . . . uh . . . tired. Tired of being screamed at." She tucked her hair back, dipping her head lower in embarrassment. "My cousin was furious. My sister laughed at me. For *weeks*." She looked up defiantly and challenged his amused gaze. "I locked myself in my room and destroyed a shrine's worth of Owen material. Pictures, articles. Even removed his songs from my music list for about a day. But I put them back eventually, and I decided it was time to grow up. I don't know which was worse: Noriko yelling at me or Hana laughing at me, but for ages after that, whenever I did something stupid, I would hear one or the other in my head."

The confession was an awkward but sincere gift. Kanoa decided to honor it as such. "My father always said shame is a rough but effective teacher. He told me to embrace it. I have both the yelling and the laughing in my head too."

Much to his delight, that got a full laugh, but the light moment was far too brief. Bay grew serious again, looked at him intently, and asked, "Where do you see yourself in the future?"

"And where do you see yourself in the future?" The examiner's voice was so mellow, so studiously neutral that not for the first time Kanoa suspected he was a VR construct, an amalgam of various instructors and mentors blended and fine-tuned for optimal effect. The VR background was a studio setup, a mockup of a media interview that invited students to play the part of an established expert speaking with authority to the world.

Hesitating for too long would be seen as indecisive. Kanoa licked his dry lips and made a start.

"I want to continue to serve the public, like my father. I think he has been a good example of what can be accomplished with dedicated, conscientious leadership."

He paused, but the examiner remained silent. Too short an answer? He jumped in again, quickly. "However, I believe I should remain open to opportunities that may arise. I can only imagine what I have known, and there may be other futures more appropriate to my talents." He swallowed nervously, sounding pompous to his own ears. "After all, that's the point of a project like this: to learn what is useful, to unlearn what is outdated, and to develop to one's full potential.

"That is my hope, anyway," he ended in a rush of sudden shyness. From overly pompous to overly earnest. How he hated that question! How was anyone to foresee the future, when so much had changed so radically over the past century? "We have to be adaptable, not prophetic," he complained, and almost startled himself. He had not meant to speak out loud.

"Thank you, Kanoa Havili. The interview is now over."

His mind returned to the dining hall, the scattered remnants of rice and fish on his plate, and Bay still examining him as if his answer would matter, as if it would endure longer than the last version of himself that had dared imagine a future, only one month ago.

"I see myself successfully completing this project. Beyond that, who knows? Who cares?"

Bay gave him a knowing half smile. "We're being observed. Many people care. People will have plans for your future even if you don't, so remember to keep answering that question every day. *I* do. When I was eleven, I wanted to marry Owen, and when I was eighteen, I wanted an executive position on our company's board."

She paused. He prompted, "And now?"

"Now I'm wondering if my scope was too small. If I lacked both imagination and information. Now I'm arming myself with every weapon I can lay my hands on. Knowledge is a weapon. Networks can be a weapon."

"Am I in your network? Am I a part of your arsenal?" he wondered.

"Could be," she shot back. "Are you ready?"

"Getting there," he answered, and for the first time in a month, he smiled as if he meant it.

*   *   *

In a tidy little coincidence, he saw the interviewer in the afternoon, that same man whose appearance in the VR environment had been so bland as to make him appear particularly artificial in a place where artificiality was expected but not flaunted. However, much to his surprise, it was a meeting in the raw, with no VR whatsoever, only the governor calling him into his office and introducing him to that familiar yet ordinary face.

"Kanoa, I'd like you to meet Jon Newhaven. Jon is an instructor for your project and he'll be traveling with you to your group headquarters in a few days."

Kanoa blinked and tentatively accepted the offered handshake. A respectful nod would have been well within etiquette, but handshakes and other forms of ritual contact had become a way of verifying an in-flesh encounter. Jon's hand was very warm but surprisingly dry given the day's high humidity. The clasp was a little too firm, just shy of causing pain, something a VR program would never do. When he sat down, Kanoa sat in a chair opposite and watched him in fascination, almost anticipating some glitch or filter-slip. The man dressed well but neutrally, in the boring, unisex international style that had become established several decades ago: tailored slacks cut neither too wide nor too narrow; a matching long, fitted tunic with a single bisecting placket from mid-thigh to throat; and a high-standing collar with the round emblem of the World Council pinned on the right, occasionally throwing muted sparkles under his clean-shaven chin.

Admittedly, Kanoa was similarly outfitted, but his suit's color was a refreshing teal instead of a somber dove gray, his collar was embroidered in a geometric pattern that had been made in his mother's family for generations, and he wore three wristbands, a necklace, and a communicator bug that sat neatly over and around his ear. The bands had some other function—data storage, access, or VR enhancement. The sole function of the necklace was artistic—craft, beauty, and another reminder of his family and his heritage.

Jon looked like a man who came from nowhere and had no one, and for a moment Kanoa felt an odd sympathy for him.

"Thank you for selecting me," Kanoa said, giving the pronoun the plural, formal stress.

"You selected yourself," Jon replied with an easy smile. "We only administered the tests and observed the results you gave us. You are well suited to this work."

Kanoa struggled to keep his features under control, but knew from experience that his expression was that callow, half-shy, half-pleased, all-childish look of someone surprised by a compliment from one accustomed to excellence.

"We were sorry to learn that you lost your father so close to this time of change and adjustment." To the untutored ear, that might sound like an apology for giving him no extra time or space for his grief, but Kanoa was old enough to know better. *We regret the circumstances; we do not regret making no effort to mitigate their effect on your performance.* Fair. Public service was a priesthood: personal problems must not be prioritized. So said his father many a time during Kanoa's childhood, when he justified his fractional parental engagement as a natural consequence of his career success.

I am following in my father's footsteps, Kanoa thought a little wryly. "It is kind of you to mention it. I hope that I have not allowed my standards to slip too far. I know I have a lot of catching up to do."

"Of course. That is part of the reason I am here. My main goal is to meet you in the flesh, as I have already done with almost all the members of the group. However, I am also here to walk you and your group through the scenario for your group's first assignment, before we move to Havana and begin our work in earnest."

Excitement flooded Kanoa's entire body, and he did not bother to hide his glee. Sometimes it paid to be in the last time zone. He was the last to be visited but probably the first to learn where they would be headquartered.

"Why Havana?" he asked casually, more to make conversation than anything else. If Jon had announced they were going to set up in one of the moon colonies, Kanoa would have been just as satisfied.

"Well-connected for VR and communications, but also somewhat physically isolated. You'll understand later why that's important. We do spend a lot of time in VR, and although you'll need recreation, you do *not* need distractions."

Kanoa wasn't sure about that. He had a cousin who had studied at an institution near Havana, and culturally the old city was far from dead, with all manner of music, theater, and art on offer. However, if the aim was to put them somewhere they couldn't leave easily, or get lost, then Havana definitely fit the bill. That was intriguing, the idea that the project's administration wanted to control dropouts and leaks. Suddenly, the featureless smoothness of Jon's suit took on a more sinister aspect. *Conform! Conform!*

"We selected you for good reasons, but building a team takes work and time. We're putting you into an artificial environment under artificial stresses to achieve that quickly. It's only for a while."

Impressive statement. Had Jon guessed all that unspoken rebellion from Kanoa's slightly doubtful look? Once more, Kanoa felt moved to make a conscious effort to control his face.

The governor cleared his throat, clasped his hands, and leaned forward slightly over his desk—a pose that was both powerful and earnest. "It is, of course, a very great honor that Kanoa is representing the Federated States of Polynesia on such a prestigious project. We are all very proud of him."

Kanoa shot the governor a scared smile. He could recognize a warning wrapped in congratulations when he heard it. "I will do my best, Governor Crawford," he promised sincerely.

"I'm sure that you will. After all, you are your father's son." Meant kindly, said kindly, the words gave Kanoa a surge of warm reassurance, but Jon, no doubt operating from other cultural expectations, was visibly uncomfortable, squirming slightly and dipping his head to hide his expression for a moment before regaining his professional mask.

That moment of weakness in his instructor sustained Kanoa later when they went to the largest VR hall in the Governor's House to meet his teammates and formally start his second orientation phase. Jon did not notice; he too appeared to have an extra shot of energy, even confidence, as he spoke his access to the room and set the parameters.

"As you were," he admonished when Kanoa attempted to configure a new suit and slightly better-lit appearance for himself. "We should meet each other as raw as we can, especially when our worlds are unreal."

An interesting philosophy. Kanoa gave a slight shrug and obeyed, unbothered. He had already made himself fully presentable to meet his instructor, and his self-esteem was high. The walls faded out in a mirage of infinite darkness, then solidified and drew close again, settling into the shape of a standard World Council meeting room, with wide windows showing a slowly changing range of landscapes outside, an ancient wooden table on a carpeted floor, and six heavy chairs, also in old, thickly varnished wood. Kanoa found the small icon of his state's flag and sat down. Jon sat at the head behind the World Council flag. Four others appeared, fading in and solidifying as they sat by their respective flags. Bay caught his eye from the foot of the table and gave a triumphant little smile and nod. Not in Trade. Transfer request accepted. Kanoa fought not to grin in response, but the more cynical part of him hoped she would not regret it.

At last he was ahead of the game. He knew the three other representatives at the table as intimately as five hours' intense study of portfolios and dossiers would permit. Yrsa Helgadóttir, a young VR specialist with a talent for creating real-world applications, was from Iceland, and she looked a lot smaller and shorter in the raw. She was square-bodied in her thinness, with dark, flyaway hair that would not be contained by her ears. She looked a little sleepy, but fighting it, as if awake out of sheer interest and nothing else. Thiago Mendes from Brazil was a complete unknown, with no famous family connections, freshly obtained qualifications, and a naïve, open face that told Kanoa nothing. Dylan Cardinal was the oldest of them all at twenty-six, married with a young daughter, an early-career diplomat. Surprising that

Quebec would put forward someone already entrenched in public service, but at least he was a worker, not a representative chosen for money and connections.

In fact, when Kanoa considered it, from a technical viewpoint, the membership of this group was very satisfying. No deadweight whatsoever. The corporate heirs and heiresses, the celebrities, and the aristocrats had all made their way into more exciting divisions. Except Bay.

Genuine warmth filled Jon's voice and eyes as he looked around the table and said, "Welcome, everyone. This is the first time the Global Government Project has hosted a Diplomatic Group, and we're excited to see what you'll make of your assignment."

His hand swept over the surface of the table, and maps of familiar regions lit up and arranged themselves. Their own countries—large, small, and dust-mote micro—were highlighted against the Earth, soft focus and slowly receding, as if a camera's eye were leaving orbit and taking a last longing look behind.

"Here you are, a hand's count of individuals from a fraction of Earth's land and an even smaller percentage of Earth's surface. You will speak not only for your own people but for other countries, for all of Earth, for each orbital station, lunar colony, and Martian outpost."

Thiago interrupted with an apologetic hum. "Ahmm, Professor, how do we do that? Aren't we still dependent on the decisions of the other groups? You make us sound like the final arbiters, but surely that's the Executive Council?"

Dylan stared at him, holding his breath, frozen at the boldness. Kanoa glanced around, but Bay and Yrsa only looked mildly curious, as if they had been wondering the same.

"Good question," Jon replied quietly. "We once gave diplomatic assignments throughout all the groups, in order to teach our representatives how to achieve consensus between countries. But then we realized this thinking was flawed. Why should a global government be based on a multistate model? Consensus-building within an entity is a form of diplomacy, but it is not global diplomacy. And so . . . we designed this assignment."

His hand swept the table's screen clear again, and the image that remained was a dark, distant glimpse of the solar system from somewhere around Neptune's orbit. "You will encounter intelligent civilizations beyond Earth. You will communicate with those civilizations and learn their laws and cultures with a view to establishing formal relationships with them. You will learn how to negotiate with them."

As he spoke, the camera kept pulling farther and farther out. The message was clear. Perspective. Whatever was out there, they, as representatives of Earth, would be facing something much, much bigger than they were.

Yrsa looked unimpressed. "I've played games like this. I've *designed* games like this—"

"This isn't a game," Kanoa heard himself say. "This is a proper challenge. Earth is all connected now. We think we have differences; we don't. We're a bunch of villages in the same country with access to the same technology and media. With our translators, we pretty much use the same language. We've been having family squabbles for decades. This sounds different. This is a First Contact scenario."

SEVEN

EVERY PERSON IN the room went through a visible shift in attitude. Bay looked delighted, like someone who had gambled on a prize behind a curtain and won something far better than a pocket 3D printer and a case of wine. Dylan and Thiago both leaned forward as if pulled into a secret that they couldn't wait to start dissecting. Jon kept his face blank but Kanoa imagined that there was something significant in how he breathed—slightly slower, somewhat deliberate, perhaps calming and hiding an inner rush of excitement?

Yrsa was the only one who still looked dubious. She began to speak, but Kanoa cut her off impatiently and continued, "This is *not* a game, with cute aliens you'll want to fuck and ugly aliens you'll want to kill. This assignment probably has diseases and exploitation and aliens with bigger guns than you."

Jon's lips folded in, suppressing a smile as he listened to Kanoa speak. "Thank you, Kanoa. Eloquently put. To be fair, some of the aliens will be cute, and some may even want to fuck. However, that will not be the point of your assignment. Your goal, as always, is to secure *Earth's* best interests, not fulfill your personal desires."

"So, which civilization has the greater power in this First Contact scenario? Us, or them?" Dylan asked somberly.

Jon looked down at the table, now a deep darkness sprinkled with stars. "Another good question . . . although the 'us or them' framing is neither accurate nor useful. You will have to do a lot of research to find out the answer." That plural, formal stress on the pronoun silenced all five representatives with the weight of responsibility. Jon let them marinate for a while in that silence.

"I'll leave you now so you can discuss this as a group. Don't speculate too much. Your briefs will be made available in Havana. I'm very much looking forward to seeing you all in the flesh again."

"Except me," Bay said suddenly in a small voice. Everyone looked at her, confused. "I haven't met you outside of VR yet," she clarified in a louder voice.

"Yes. Last-minute changes to the team selection process disrupted my schedule," Jon said drily. *No more special treatment for you.* A bit harsh, the delivery. Kanoa wasn't sure Bay deserved that kind of public put-down. His eyes widened in sympathy as he watched Bay absorb the rebuke with a startled blink followed by an expression of cold resolve.

"But I will see you all in Havana very soon," Jon concluded in a gentler tone. He rose, nodded to the group, and walked out of the VR hall.

The silence that followed was more than awkward; it was painful.

"Well, who's going to speak up first?" Yrsa said finally. "We're meant to use this as a 'getting to know you' session. We shouldn't waste it. There will be plenty of work waiting for us in Havana."

Bay recovered first. "In that case, wrong background. May I suggest something less corporate?" She pushed away from the table and stood up, and their chairs morphed into a jazzier design. The table's dimensions shifted, rising, elongating, and settled with her standing behind a

bar and the rest of the team lined up before her as if about to order
their usuals.

"I don't drink," Dylan said severely.

"Everyone drinks," Yrsa snapped in reply. "If you don't drink mood-
altering substances, just choose something else."

"This is not *just* a wet bar," Bay told him, now in her element.
"Oxygen jet is at your left elbow. What would you like? Something familiar, like snowy pine with a touch of smoke? Traditional jasmine? Or
this limited-edition blend called Nineties Nightclub?"

Intrigued, Dylan leaned over the outlet and gingerly sniffed the
samples, finally selecting jasmine with a hint of petrichor. Yrsa quickly
ordered up something that might have been a gin and tonic, or simply
a tonic with a twist of lime. Thiago took ginger ale, and Kanoa chose
the same. *We're all being so careful,* he mused.

"Will they let us do this in Havana?" Yrsa wondered, speaking his
next thought aloud.

Bay made a very loud scoffing sound. "Are they going to put us in
surveillance shackles, like delinquents?"

"Sounds like someone didn't read the fine print," Thiago murmured
into his ginger ale.

Bay reacted instantly, sharply. "I always read the fine print. An
agreement to keep to 'designated areas' is just that, an agreement. Not
a shackle."

"You think our professor is going to let you roam about?" Kanoa
warned her.

"You think he's going to find out?" she countered.

They all laughed, but then Yrsa said softly, "Don't mess things up
for our group, okay, golden girl?"

They shared a long look, but Bay nodded and looked away first.

Perhaps the oxygen went to Dylan's head, because he bravely
pointed a finger at Bay and stated, "Fine. *I'll* say it. One of these things
is not like the other. Career. Career." His finger moved to Kanoa,
Thiago, Yrsa. "Career." He pointed at himself. "Most definitely career.
And then there's you. I know the rep you bounced from this group.

Fortunately for all concerned, she's delighted to expand her Trade qualifications, but your background isn't like hers. You were most qualified for Trade, if you cared about your career. And if you didn't, this is the last group someone like you should choose."

Kanoa held his breath and watched their faces, wondering if Bay would share the same story she had told him. Bay calmly poured herself a shot of vodka, downed it with a swift gulp and grimace, then said in a husky voice:

"That's a very good question. You'll have to do a lot of research to find the answer."

Kanoa joined in the laughter as Bay grinned triumphantly and Dylan acknowledged defeat with a raised hand and a smiling shake of his head. He caught the quick wink Bay tossed in his direction. *We'll keep each other's secrets,* it seemed to say, and for a moment, as proud as he was to be a member of the Diplomatic Group, he imagined that it would be a lot of fun to sneak around the nondesignated areas of Havana with Bay, in the raw, far from any glimmer of VR.

Packing and farewells kept Kanoa busy, and he did not see Jon again beyond a brief glimpse from a distance in the seaport hall, then again in the processing line at Havana. Neither did he visit his colleagues via VR. All would be making their own preparations and taking various forms of transport to reach their new headquarters. Bay had confessed to him (in a slightly ashamed tone that flagged the information as another secret between them) that she would not be traveling for very long but would take a supersonic jet from Barcelona to Havana. Kanoa was shocked, not at the expense, but the port of departure. "You're in *Catalonia?*" he asked incredulously without pausing to think. "I thought you were in Morocco."

"That was *last* week," she said, with such offhand boredom that he glared at her. He was used to representatives, especially the wealthy ones, having multiple residences. Bay was the representative for Upper Pacifica, with her primary residence based in Vancouver. But he could still be taken off guard by the gulf between their different concepts of normal. His idea of privileged travel did not include supersonic jets but VR rooms in government buildings, where civil servants and officials from Fiji, Yap, and Aotearoa could walk in off their respective streets and have a meeting in real time, if not in the raw.

He was therefore not surprised when he arrived in Havana and Bay was already there to greet him at the entrance.

"Welcome to headquarters," she said with a mocking flourish of her right hand.

"Thank you," he said sincerely. A pause. "Lovely grounds," he commented with great restraint. "Took us three minutes to clear security, five minutes to drive from the main gate. I had a lot of time to look around."

"Indeed!" she responded with fierce brightness. "Why don't you put away your things, and then we can have a nice walk before dinner?"

Some people argued that top-of-the-line VR had become so detailed, so granular, that people could now be fooled even in large-scale outdoor settings. Kanoa seriously doubted it. There was a good reason why landscapes were limited to windows and distant views, and his own deep sense of the vastness of nature rebelled against the idea that any human-crafted facsimile could compete.

And yet, when the five members of the Diplomatic Group walked the extensive grounds that evening, admiring the topiary and the hanging garden and the koi pond and the small neoclassical folly, Kanoa looked back at the quasi-fortress that was to be their residence and workplace over the next year or two and was troubled.

"It *is* real. Raw, I mean. Isn't it?" Yrsa's wistful voice pleaded to be convinced.

"Yes?" Thiago replied uncertainly.

"Yes," Kanoa declared, unaccountably angry.

"So . . . more like 'near Havana' than 'in Havana,'" Dylan said with philosophical calm. "Near . . . ish."

"It's a fucking prison!" Kanoa yelled, gesturing angrily at the brutalist architecture of the central building and the wide-open acreage all around them.

"Don't exaggerate," Bay murmured.

"No, no, give him some space," Dylan said. "I'd be mad too if I left the freedom of the Pacific for a fenced-in enclave."

"Bet you wish you were in Trade now," Yrsa said snidely to Bay, who declined to respond or react in any way.

"It's not so bad," Thiago said reassuringly. "Everything is an adjustment. We get a few nights' sleep, sync to the time zone, have a few VR runs, and start delving into the material . . . We'll see things differently in a few days."

"You're right," Kanoa said, ashamed of his outburst. "We're here to work, after all."

"The food's really good," Bay volunteered.

"We're saved!" Yrsa proclaimed sarcastically, and then they both laughed, much to Kanoa's surprise.

The afternoon walks became another way to discuss the day's work. Of course they used their scheduled sessions at the start and end of every week, but both within and without the walls of their fortress was the unspoken expectation that everything done in the VR would be a matter of record. Surveillance was illegal in private spaces like sleeping quarters and bathrooms, but they were banned from congregating there "for their own protection."

"Is this about sex?" Thiago asked uncertainly a few days later, after they had had a chance to thoroughly read the terms, conditions, rules, and regulations of their residency at Havana Headquarters.

"It's so we can't record each other," Dylan said in a gentle reminder that diplomacy and spying had never been mutually exclusive. "I'm beginning to think that a lot of the restrictions are meant to protect us, not control us."

"Still think this is just a game?" Kanoa asked Yrsa.

She gave him a tired look. "If it's not a game, what is it?"

"A metaphor."

They stopped walking to look at Bay.

"Have you noticed that all of us in this group, even me, come from the same hemisphere?"

Yrsa shifted, on the verge of dissenting, but Bay forestalled her. "You too. You're Icelandic Scandinavian and Greenlandic Inuit. In fact, through blood and beyond blood, we're connected to places where Old World met New for the first time. Like Kanoa said from the beginning, we know about the genocide by disease and battle, and the colonization and exploitation after."

"About that," Thiago said. "I was wondering why our professor made a point of mentioning our responsibility for *all* Earth. I thought he wanted us to remember all our resources, land and ocean. But then I began to read some recent research, and I began to wonder . . . are there already alien civilizations on Earth? We've taken over all the land, but so much of Earth remains impenetrable to us, like the depths of the ocean. Imagine a civilization that we can't even recognize as such, because it's so different to what we know. We could have a real-life First Contact scenario about to unfold, and this project is just a test run of how we would react." He grew more and more excited with each word, gesturing animatedly and appearing much younger than his twenty years.

Yrsa laughed. "Whoa . . . now we're really speculating. Giant sentient squid in the deep? What's next, a hollow Earth? Parallel dimensions and portals?"

The tension broke. Thiago's intensity fizzled and he chuckled in sheepish agreement, and Dylan also joined in with the laughter. Kanoa, however, froze, chilled by the memory of a gray sea, a looming horizon, and an experience of altered consciousness and sensation. He could not explain that last moment with his father, no matter how many times he relived it, both in dream and in memory.

A stillness caught his attention, and there was Bay, also not laughing, her face drained of emotion and blood. She met his gaze briefly and looked away.

"Our presentations are next week. Is everyone ready?" Dylan asked. He was the group leader for the first week, probably due to his greater experience.

"Definitely," Bay said with determination. Kanoa heard the edge—

was she already overcompensating, desperate to prove she deserved to be in Havana?

They all nodded or murmured some form of assent. Dylan looked relieved. "If you're falling behind, or can't figure something out, let's talk about it? Either one-on-one or as a group. I know we all want to impress, but let's impress *collectively*."

When Kanoa returned to his room, he immediately pulled up his dossier for some extended study. His "yes" to Dylan had been tentative, and he knew exactly why. He had kept his own promise to focus, to settle into a routine and slowly put behind him the distractions of grief. But the material was . . . challenging. He could already imagine Yrsa laughing as he made his presentation.

Was Bay right? Had this part of the project been designed by a pop star? He could believe it, because it was pure entertainment, exactly the kind of content that would make Yrsa turn up her nose and say she could have written something far better, or more original, at the very least.

The model civilizations of the scenario had been given the names of systems known to have planetary discs or planets, but apart from that, there was no real-universe rationale to their locations. They were too distant from each other to suggest even a modest faster-than-light interstellar trade, unless the fiction of wormholes or portals was lurking in the background material, awaiting discovery. But there they were, five civilizations for five presentations, four interconnected and one—Earth itself, of course—quarantined from the rest of the galaxy. An extended political and sociological metaphor, perhaps, but it made zero technological or astronomical sense.

His civilization was based on 16 Cygni B, or some alternate version of it with an Earth-like, habitable planet. Cygnian civilization was the youngest of the five, with heavy cultural and technological influences from their four galactic siblings. (*How?!* his marginal notes queried angrily. *Modes of transportation? Colonization or a sprinkling of explorers turned settlers?*) He'd read further and seen the Cygnian founding myth, and had to restrain himself from throwing his tablet at the wall.

Fucking portals! And not just from anywhere, oh no. From Earth. A population scavenged from every genocide, plague, and natural disaster and tossed through space and time to 16 Cygni B via some form of portal technology that even the other four civilizations knew nothing about.

For a moment he'd been so enraged that he put away the dossier. That old racist nonsense crediting aliens for the technology of non-Eurasian ancient civilizations was apparently alive and well in other forms. If aliens could be bothered to set up superior tech to save a handful, surely they had the tech to stop the genocide in the first place? And now even the triumph of their survival in the real world, in actual history, was being trivialized with this fairy tale.

Kanoa badly wanted to rant to Bay, but she was clearly very busy with her own work, and he was not yet prepared to bare his soul in front of the entire group in a manner that might be considered *unprofessional*.

After he'd taken a while to calm down, he returned to the material with grim resolve to look at it through fresh eyes. Metaphor. The entire shambolic scenario was an unsubtle metaphor. What, then, was the point of having a civilization like 16 Cygni B at all?

Of course, his cooled head responded. This is the same reason this group has been selected. You have one alien civilization that not only is as culturally close to Earth as you can get but is also fundamentally anticolonial and pro-heterogeneity. They may or may not be independent enough to be functional allies, but they will definitely be the bridge between Earth and the true difference of other alien civilizations.

Clumsy and hurtful in execution, but helpful in context. Now all he had to do was sell that to his colleagues during his presentation.

He delved further and at one point did indeed fling his tablet, not at the wall, but at his bed, where it bounced without harm. "Seriously?" he yelled.

Cygnians and, apparently, humans of Earth, as well, could produce hybrid offspring with the other alien civilizations of the galaxy, while the aliens, alas, had evolved too far from the common origin for successful interbreeding. "Interbreeding." He muttered it like a dirty word. A cute alien who will fuck you and leave you with more than memories. Yrsa was going to be *livid*.

Think. Rape, marriage, and hybrid populations are all present in the First Contact problem. It's a cliché, but that doesn't make it less real or true.

Kanoa sighed and went to pick up his tablet again. Fine. Sexual exploitation was on the table for this scenario. So, too, were marriages of political convenience—a concept he would have called outdated on Earth if Bay hadn't reminded him of the corporate and traditional aristocracies and their informal bloodline books.

In one aspect, the Cygnians were to be envied. They had already achieved a global government, and he was keen to see what it looked like. Which norms and cultures had proved more dominant in a world built from scattered remnants? Had they simply followed the older systems already present in the galactic order, or did they maintain their own flavor of morality, their unique quirks and practices?

Sighing again, Kanoa rubbed his eyes tiredly. There was so much more to cover before he could even begin to reframe it and deliver it to his colleagues. He tapped some settings on the tablet, reclined comfortably in bed, and watched the ceiling and walls transform and expand, taking him to the VR training facility—which, fortunately, did not require him to be sitting formally upright as he listened to the lecture.

"My name is Captain Lian, and I am your instructor for the module on Cygnian law and order."

The instructor looked a little Korean, a touch Nepalese, and entirely, humanly attractive in voice, face, and bearing. Kanoa wouldn't mind at least a flirtation with an alien looking like this one.

"Cygnian paramilitary and police forces have long operated as a section of the Galactic Patrol and the Galactic Gendarmerie."

Kanoa felt himself drifting off to sleep but let it happen. He could always rerun the lecture when he woke up. He wouldn't mind seeing Captain Lian again.

"Thiago. Are you . . . *bleeding?*" Yrsa tentatively reached out a finger to prod Thiago's sleeve.

Mouth filled with food, both hands around a large, overstuffed wrap, Thiago first tried to flinch away, but then he caught sight of the small spot of red spreading through the light blue material of his shirt. He gulped his mouthful and swore.

"The bastards actually stuck me, can you believe it? It's the twenty-second century, but they choose to break the skin. What's the point of it? They've already screened us for every disease and mutation known to humanity. Does anyone recognize any of this shit?"

No one did. They had all encountered a variety of psychosocial testing to assess how well they would fit into a team, what strengths and weaknesses they possessed, and how teachable and adaptable they were likely to be, particularly under stress. Selection should have been the end of it, but now, in addition to the research and Jon's tutorial sessions, the group found itself subject to an intermittent schedule of psychological and physical tests. The new psych tests were both strangely specific and yet random in a way that suggested there was real science behind what they were going through, but no explanation was forthcoming that would prime them to fake an emotion or suppress a reaction.

"They're testing to see if we're aliens."

"VR bots."

"Androids."

They all laughed a little uneasily as Thiago dipped his napkin into his drinking water and blotted the stain on his sleeve.

"Presentations in a couple of days. Everyone ready?" Dylan asked.

Murmurs and noncommittal grunts.

"Excellent!" Dylan said as cheerfully as if they had all given full-throated assent. "Here's the running order. Thiago, you're first with

Earth. Kanoa, you follow with 16 Cygni B, and then Bay with Epsilon Eridani and its colonies. Yrsa, you're next with Alpha Piscis Austrini and Beta Geminorum. I'll conclude with Alpha Lyrae. Kanoa, you've got a little overlap with Bay; can you both work it out?"

Kanoa glanced at Bay first to confirm mutual agreement, and nodded. "I'm covering the Eridanian colony in the Cygnian system. Bay is handling the rest."

At first they'd all agreed to rehearse the presentations together and get feedback from each other for changes and improvements. Then, as the material unfolded into greater and greater complexity and time leaked away, the agreement shifted from full rehearsal to access to drafts and permission to annotate. Kanoa meant to comply, he really did, but he also didn't want to be the first to submit his work, work that he confessed felt thin and weak, like he was still missing too many essential points. He quickly realized that he wasn't the only one holding back.

"About that," Bay said apologetically. "The Epsilon Eridani situation is *complicated*. I'm still scrambling to put together a sensible structure, but I'll at least fling up a summary so the rest of the group can get an idea of what I'm working with."

Groans of sympathy followed that admission and, with great relief, everyone agreed to put up summaries of their material rather than their full presentations.

"We're each trying to learn about a century's worth of history and politics for an entire stellar system in one week," Yrsa said morosely. "If this is the beginning, I can't imagine what else is coming our way."

"As long as it's not more stupid medieval blood tests, I'll adjust," Thiago said.

"Mistakes were made. Fine print was not read. All tests approved by the Global Government Project administration are required for admission *to* and continued enrollment *in* the project," Bay intoned.

"Who has time to read any fine print these days? I barely have time to shit, shower, and eat," Kanoa grumbled.

"Boot camp treatment. It'll get better," Dylan said confidently, and since he had more experience in the field than all of them, it sounded reassuring. "Next week's schedule moves from research to more classes. We're going to have some instructors in the VR and some in the raw. And . . . I *think* we're getting Charyssa as an instructor."

The mood around the table brightened significantly. Yrsa in particular looked dazzled, and Kanoa understood why. The Global Government Project had been supported and promoted by a lot of celebrity big names, including Owen the pop star and Charyssa the legendary actor. But Charyssa was also known as one of the pioneers of VR in both entertainment and governance. She had won top awards in both careers.

"I assumed she'd already taught us at some point. Doesn't she often wear masks?" Bay asked.

Yrsa shook her head. "To age her appearance up or down, definitely. She already does that onscreen and in VR theater. But wearing a different face entirely? I don't think that's her style."

Dylan stood. "Before I get back to work, can I get everyone's summaries up and available before midnight tonight? Let's have at least a day to take everything in."

"Mine won't look pretty," Yrsa warned.

"Don't care," Dylan replied brusquely. "Get it in, and good luck, everyone."

Kanoa appreciated Dylan's firmness when he went into the VR to check out the summaries. There was so much to absorb. Every civilization had one or two avatars speaking the history, like his Captain Lian.

He watched and learned from an Eridanian pilot of a huge spacefaring creature adapted to carry human passengers through dimensions to achieve faster-than-light transport from planet to planet. The biggest discovery from that was the near-destruction of the Epsilon Eridani civilization in an act of war instigated by one of their own colonies.

The Alpha Piscis Austrini civilization wasn't much better off. A long-established former colony in the Beta Geminorum system was thriving, and the cultural connections remained strong in spite of their independence from the Alpha Piscis Austrini government. But the home planet for the Austrinians was at the peak of a severe glaciation, resulting in a slushball situation, with a just-habitable band around the equator; highly engineered, enclosed environments at the surface; and above the planet's surface, a well-populated orbital ring and linked suborbital cities.

Alpha Lyrae was a mess, but an understandable mess. As the only system to have more than one sizable habitable planet, it was also the only system to have a fragmented government. Two ruling powers rather than one shaped the identity of the Lyrans. They, too, had an interstellar, faster-than-light fleet, not of living beings but machine intelligences interfacing with human brains.

Something prodded Kanoa's memory. Living beings. Thiago's flight of fancy about undersea intelligences—and then Bay, not laughing, struck by something in Thiago's words.

He followed the thread from Bay's brief mention of the Eridanian fleet to the full dossier she had been given to do her research. An older avatar appeared, his long, dark, shining hair streaked with gray, wearing a jumpsuit that covered his body from his fingertips to his feet.

"I am Naraldi, independent pilot, retired from the Eridanian fleet, and associate of the Cygnian fleet. I will be your instructor on the history and culture of Epsilon Eridani."

Then, unexpectedly, he leaned a little forward and looked sternly at Kanoa. "But don't you have enough research of your own to do without dipping into other dossiers? Come back next week."

For a moment Kanoa was too shocked to speak, but he quickly recovered. "I'm looking for information on your ships. There is an overlap with my assignment."

The avatar Naraldi was unconvinced. "Then why did you not research the Cygnian fleet?"

"I skimmed that bit," Kanoa admitted sheepishly. "Besides, I'm interested in the origins of the ships, which means I have to look at Epsilon Eridani."

The avatar appeared to ponder. Kanoa wondered what the pause covered. Scanning through his access permissions? Informing human instructors of his extracurricular curiosity? He began to regret his impulse.

"Very well," Naraldi said at last. "The mindships evolved as a collective intelligence from various autonomous and semiautonomous flora and fauna in the oceans of Epsilon Eridani. Over time, they formed a symbiotic relationship with coast-dwelling, seafaring humans and added them to their collective consciousness. These humans were the first proto-pilots. Interdimensional travel of the ships guided by pilots was the next phase, and finally, technology was developed to enable the transport of nonpilot passengers with a pilot and ship."

The warm timbre of Naraldi's voice washed over Kanoa in a manner that should have been soothing, but the words were accompanied by video and images that quickened his heartbeat. The modern Eridanian ships were jeweled behemoths, with prosthetic modules attached to facilitate docking, passenger transport, and shielding. Their early counterparts were nakedly svelte and infinitely mobile, like a murmuration at sea or a shoal of fish, with the constituent entities so close and mutually responsive that particles became waves.

Most images showed the proto-ships moving far below the surface of the ocean, an environment that echoed their future domain in space. However, one image spiked his heart rate to panic levels: a proto-ship rising smoothly from the water, looming like a new horizon, turning all above and all below a muted gray as it surrounded a slowly swimming human body, ready to consume . . .

He fumbled for his tablet and turned off the VR. The perfect silence of the room was marred by his harsh breathing. He waited, listening to himself as his heart and breath and blood slowed and quieted to peace once more.

He spoke his defiance aloud to the empty room. "I will *not* let the stress get to me. I will get this presentation done, and I will complete this project. I will show nothing but excellence, for my father's memory, for my country, for Earth."

By the last phrase, he was smiling at himself. So stupidly earnest, so ridiculously patriotic, like a hero in an old movie. "For my father's memory," he repeated softly. "Let's leave it at that."

The islands of the Pacific had never been closer, not even through centuries and generations of ocean crossings, than when VR became a standard element of public and private life, expanding scant, scattered miles of fields and mountains into a virtual continent. This did not mean that the oceans were neglected, far from it. The more people turned inward to small rooms and virtual vastness, the more they sought balance in raw vastness and limitless horizons. Artificial islands proliferated to join the natural rock, and both seasoned and amateur seafarers had an increased choice of transports and waystations along safer routes.

For the hardcore VR-averse, the Pacific was one of the top ten places to retreat, as long as one still permitted older forms of connection, such as the text message and the two-dimensional screen call.

Beyond the common retreats, far from the usual routes, there floated a sealed dome tethered to the deep ocean floor. Severely minimalist and starkly ascetic, it appeared to be stripped of even the most basic of communication technologies. This was a hermitage, built for those who shunned the hubbub of civilization in all raw and virtual forms—but the sole resident was not seeking silence for its own sake.

She was listening. She had been listening for years.

Today, she heard the breaking of the silence, but there was no cause for alarm. The visitor was expected, and welcome. He took his time walking through the outer shallows of the dome's stabilizer, almost showing off his skill at moving with the slight dip and surge of the surface. By the time he reached the entrance, she was there, waiting, leaning over the rail of the surrounding deck with a warm smile and a lightness in her heart.

"So good to see you," she said, and they embraced for a little longer than necessary according to most social conventions, but absolutely as long as needed for them both to reconnect and push back the silence.

He drew back a little and extended a closed fist. "I bring news," he said, turning his wrist and unfolding his fingers with a flourish like a magic trick.

She smiled at the sweetness of the gesture and delicately plucked the datacharm from his palm. It was clear that they were very old friends. "I wish I had news to give in return, but there has been no sign of them. Perhaps they have left Earth after all."

A slow, disappointed exhalation was his initial response, but then he shrugged and followed her as she led him into the dome. "How much longer should we search?"

"That's for you to say," she answered. "Something to drink?"

"Please."

They sat facing each other on a carpet, a low table with prepared refreshments before them. Her fare was simple but varied, and the carafe was filled near to the brim with cold water. She poured out a cup, and he drank first, conscious of the salt spray on his face, and then he wiped his hands on the cool, damp towel she had thoughtfully provided.

"If they are not here, then where have they gone?" he mused. "The oceans are so vast. We must be certain."

It might have been due to the age and depth of their friendship, or even something more, but he tilted his head and examined her curiously when she hesitated very slightly before raising her own cup to her lips.

"No sign of them, you said. But what else have you heard in the silence?"

A smile was the reward for his perceptiveness, but she still took time to finish half her cup and taste a strip of smoked fish before starting her reply.

"These oceans are vast, it is true. For this reason, I cannot be certain of what I hear. But I do hear something, and although it is not speaking to me, it is speaking."

His back straightened, eyes brightened, all attention to her words. "And have you tried speaking to them?"

"I am considering it. It is not a question of finding the right language but more the right . . . disposition. It's a shift of understanding, a different sense of being. *You* know."

He did know. His attentive posture relaxed a little as his thoughts turned inward. "I have not had the time or resources to search myself, but I wonder whether I should help you a little."

"You? I thought neutrality was your official stance. Famous for never meddling, never divulging a secret. What's changed?"

He pulled a long lock from his bound-back hair and showed her his new strands of gray with a rueful yet relieved smile. "At last I begin to see the end of my journey. It's liberating. And for once I know the difference between choosing to meddle and choosing to live. Let me take you closer to the conversation. Let us descend to the greater depths and see who these speakers are, and discover if they wish to speak to us."

Her eyelids fluttered and she lowered her head modestly. "Tempter."

He turned his head, a nonchalant gesture, suggesting that his conscience was clear, his hands were clean, he would never dream of pressuring her in any way. "Ask permission from whomever you feel has the right to tell you no and the power to make you obey."

Had he gone too far? An edge of anger showed in her hard stare and suddenly rigid hands. "You think you know me well, and maybe you do, but you do not need to be discourteous about it."

He refilled her cup and passed it to her, concern and apology in the simple act. "Let me know in due course what you decide."

EIGHT

PRESENTATION DAY MEANT a full day in VR. Every person in the group dressed well, but avoided both virtual and raw artifice. Only their clothes told both story and history in the weave of the fabric, the style of the garment, the national colors, and the shape of the accessories. The rest was the true raw of ordinary human bodies and unmasked faces. This was pure twenty-second-century diplomacy in full formality, where any hint of disguise was frowned upon.

Unfortunately, Kanoa found himself sweating with nervousness. He wished he could at least have a mask in the range of his own features, something to make him look a little more mature, more seasoned and experienced, and, above all, something that would not sweat.

In contrast, or for compensation, the VR tools provided for their presentations were exceptional. Kanoa expected Yrsa to excel but still pushed himself to approach the quality of what he had been able to find of her previous work. Bay would definitely want to prove herself and remove the "golden girl" marker for good. Thiago probably had the least to worry about, as the youngest and most inexperienced member of the group and the person with the most familiar and factual dossier of Earth. Dylan, in contrast, was their first assigned leader and the oldest, and already a career civil servant. He knew he was meant to set an example.

Unfortunately for Dylan's ambitions, the administration had not informed them that a second assessor was being added to the presentation audience—the iconic Charyssa herself. Bay wasn't the only one with a celebrity crush, and Dylan was red and stammering as he made the introductions for his team. To be fair, Charyssa tried to mute her effect with the same style of standard suit that Jon always wore and a mask that softened her face with the wrinkles and gravitas of an elder. It didn't really work. The mere suggestion of her presence brought to mind memories of several beloved characters in the films and VR series they had known from their parents' era to the present.

Kanoa blinked and looked again at the shadowy area where the pair of instructors sat quietly, unobtrusively. Maybe that *was* her face, completely in the raw, not only as a diplomatic courtesy but also in accordance with Jon's established tradition of walking in one's own naked truth amid the fantasy of VR.

Thiago's presentation was meant to be the easy snoozer, but he added a little zest with some innovative approaches, including a portion where he briefly interviewed the avatar of his dossier. Kanoa had not bothered to glance at the Earth presentation summary in advance, nor had he accessed any Earth content from the Havana HQ library, but he was somehow unsurprised to find that the avatar for Earth civilization was Owen himself.

Kanoa felt very proud of the restraint he showed by not turning to smirk meaningfully at Bay. Owen didn't have a fraction of the high-wattage star power that Charyssa possessed. He was said to be much better in live concert than he was in recorded audio, and as an avatar he was merely charming, not at all outstanding. Kanoa wondered if he would ever meet Owen in the flesh to compare.

Thiago ended with a small, self-indulgent segment on the possibility of discovering and communicating with civilizations based on non-human intelligence, on Earth and beyond, and ended with a relieved flourish. A good beginning, from what Kanoa could divine from their instructors' expressions.

And he was up next. He presented the Cygnian civilization straight-faced and sober, with no mockery or sarcasm, while carefully avoiding looking at Yrsa. His theme was bridging, and he made the most of it, showing the importance of the Cygnians as facilitators and translators in understanding galactic culture. He described the Lyran, Austrinian, Eridanian, and Geminoran settlements and their intertwining history with the main Earth-based culture. Naturally, he emphasized the Cygnians' semi-mythical origins as indicative of their potential openness to multicultural cooperation. Of course he hinted further that they were not likely to be positively disposed toward an imperial, conquering ethos. He managed all this with such gravity that when he finally cracked and sneaked a peek at Yrsa's reaction, he was glad to see her pensively nodding along to his framing.

Kanoa sat down feeling fairly proud of himself.

Bay was next. He should have known more about her presentation, but because of his sharp exit from her dossier after the Eridanian ship scare, he didn't. He listened carefully, resolving to close his eyes and duck his head if she began to show any images of the proto-ships in the oceans. But the ships were secondary to her theme of the fragmentation of the Epsilon Eridani civilization, crumbling from powerful and admired galactic arbiters and enforcers to scattered refugees. Beside the new Eridanian-Cygnian settlement, there was a roving fleet and community of pilots, a prison colony that appeared to have become cut off from all galactic transport, and finally, the core remnant of their population was trying to establish a permanent settlement in the Alpha Centauri system.

Oh. That's . . . close.

An attack from the prison colony in the Epsilon Tauri system had temporarily wiped out the biosphere of the Eridanian home planet. No return would be possible for centuries. The disaster led to a tumble in their power, resources, and naturally in the level of fear and admiration they commanded from the rest of the galaxy.

Kanoa felt very uneasy. He distrusted fallen empires. They tended to kick and lash out in their dying throes, and former paragons soon transformed into fallen angels. Apart from that, what did it mean for the project? Would there be a single galactic delegation sent to Earth, united in their purpose and steadfast in their goals? Or would it be several factions, the scramble of would-be empires seeking power over each other and hoping to gain Earth's resources and location as a strategic advantage?

The latter situation would be chaotic. It would definitely be that one.

In his opinion, Bay did well with a complex dossier. Yrsa's presentation, however, was oddly unbalanced. When he'd skimmed her summary, he thought there were interesting things to be said about the challenges and restrictions of climate on what had once been a proud and powerful empire, or the competitive yet warm relationship with their largest and most successful colony. After the Cygnians, he would rank the Austrinians next as most likely to tolerate difference and self-determination. But Yrsa got fixated on one aspect and completely geeked out. Kanoa had thought she would laugh at the idea of portals—well, he was wrong.

She was obsessed. The technology of Austrinian portals was somehow connected to a kind of game, which, as far as he could figure out, appeared to be some kind of three-dimensional, gravity-variable form of American football with no ball and a field that kept tilting depending on the mass and location of the players. Some of the images looked more like the players were cliff diving or rock climbing. Yrsa spent quite a few of her allotted minutes explaining the historical and cultural significance of the game to the Geminorans and the Austrinians, and Kanoa, already tired from late nights and longing for the end of class, started to drift off.

". . . collective intelligence to retain the integrity of each traveler's consciousness during transit . . ."

He jerked awake with Bay's elbow in his ribs and a phrase ringing in his head—*collective intelligence*. Where had he heard that before? The Eridanian ships! They were a collective intelligence. He straightened and paid closer attention. Yrsa was saying that the Austrinians had found a way to create a system of solely human minds that could travel from planet to planet like the Eridanian ships. And then the presentation went off the rails as the reason for Yrsa's obsession was revealed. She was now trying to connect it to her own work in VR research. Something about using an AI framework that would allow people to communicate not by words, but directly from mind to mind within a VR scenario—

"Yrsa, thank you for that information, but could you kindly limit yourself to the material provided in your dossier?" Jon interjected.

Yrsa stopped, mouth open midsentence, and the entire group froze in sympathetic embarrassment. "Of course," she said finally in a tiny voice.

She looked deflated. Dylan's expression was pure panic. *We should have rehearsed together,* Kanoa thought despondently.

Yrsa gamely, though disjointedly, ad-libbed a more relevant summary of the Austrinian and Geminoran ruling classes in the little time she had left and sat down, head bowed and face flushed. Dylan bounded up with great energy, clearly anxious to make amends and end on a positive note.

—Don't worry, Bay signed to Yrsa . . . and the rest of the sentence was lost to Kanoa's field of view as she turned her back to him.

—I screwed up, Yrsa signed back. —I was trying to show off. I really screwed up.

Kanoa raised a hand, about to attempt some short but soothing phrase in elementary-level sign language, but he was interrupted by

Charyssa herself, rising to her full height and slashing a single command in their direction.

—STOP IT!

Bay, Yrsa, and Kanoa melted back in their seats, mortified. Dylan faltered. Charyssa smiled warmly at him. "I'm *so* sorry, Dylan. Could you please go back a sentence or two?"

Dylan tried, but his concentration was shattered. He tried to compensate with humor, which fell flat. He stopped again for an awkward twenty seconds that felt like five minutes, breathed deeply, and doggedly continued. For a moment, Kanoa thought he had pulled it off, but then he looked over at Jon and saw their instructor had his knuckles resting against his lips as if to forcibly silence himself, eyes narrowed as if in pain, and his head was moving very slightly in an unconscious, silent repetition of *oh no oh no oh no*.

"Let's have a quick review of the presentations."

Jon had returned the VR hall to a neutral setting: boardroom table, seven chairs, and softly filtered light that fell mostly on him. It might have simply been a feature to highlight the speaker, or a kindness to allow the concealment of a blush or a tear among the listeners.

"Thiago and Kanoa, you two had the most straightforward and familiar civilizations, but that's not to take away from the fact that your presentations were solid. Bay, you did a comprehensive overview of a fragmented and fallen empire. Above average work, presented with nuance and clarity. Well done. Yrsa, you highlighted a fascinating common data point in your focus on collective intelligence, but in doing so you neglected the overview, the background, the context—which is the entire point of this week's assignment. And Dylan, both you and Yrsa missed an important overlap between the Lyrans and the Geminorans.

"You correctly noted that Alpha Lyrae does not have a single coherent government to represent the system. The planet which we have designated Lyra A is more compliant with galactic law and custom. Lyra B, a smaller planet with several colonies on asteroids and moons, is known for their cartels, which operate throughout the galaxy. They are much more of a wild card. You touched on that as well, and you did notice that they were implicated in isolated attacks on Geminoran cities.

"However, I have heard no mention of the fact that Lyra B now effectively controls the official capital of the Geminoran civilization, and that the Austrinians are supporting a rival city that is striving to win back full autonomy for the Geminoran people. Yrsa, you simply said that Beta Geminorum and Alpha Piscis Austrini are allied. Dylan, you spoke of Lyran-Geminoran cooperation without specifying which of the two Lyran blocs is represented in that alleged cooperation.

"The reality is far more complicated, and it has serious ramifications for Earth. At first I thought your group presentation was focused on identifying which civilizations would be supportive in a framework of mutual respect and which would impose a hierarchical relationship."

He gave a very slight nod to Kanoa, Bay, and Thiago, and Kanoa felt the heaviness in his chest ease a little.

"But that theme was lost in later presentations, which was unfortunate. I do not mean to suggest that it was the only valid approach to the material, but it would have been a very valuable one."

He sighed and spoke a little more gently. "It's been a very long day. Full feedback will be available to you in a couple of days. Tomorrow afternoon, Charyssa will hold an orientation session for the next phase. The morning is free."

"No advance preparation will be needed for the orientation session," Charyssa added kindly.

As was now custom, the two instructors got up and left the group alone so they could have their own discussions.

"I apologize," Dylan said formally, stiffly. "To everyone."

Yrsa made a noise that was half chuckle, half choking sob.

"Let's not do this," Bay said hurriedly, heading off the drama. "So, we know we've got some gaps in our coverage. We'll come together again after we get our feedback and do all our additions and corrections as a group."

"Sounds fair," Thiago said.

"Makes sense," Kanoa added quickly to show his support, both for the lack of drama and for the concrete plan. "We need a good foundation to build on. Mistakes are just that—mistakes, which can be corrected. No one died. That's the point, to work out these problems in a low-stakes environment."

"Fine," Dylan rallied. "And my advice to the leader for the next phase is this—we need to work together more. I admit it, I really didn't want people to see my messy drafts, but if the end result reflects on all of us, we're going to have to get used to being bare-assed and unpretty in front of each other."

"Yes," said Bay. "That's what Jon's getting at when he makes us enter the VR in the raw. Just ourselves and nothing else."

Was that a hint of admiration in her voice, an echo of that half-ashamed, half defiant intensity when she told him about her crush on Owen? Kanoa sincerely hoped not. But Bay caught his dubious expression and merely gave him a cheekily unrepentant wink.

Students of various countries and cultures told a generations-old joke about their teachers, claiming that during the holidays they disappeared back into their crypts and sealed themselves up in their coffins until the start of the next term.

Where had that originated, Jon mused. An old summer teen movie? A comic strip? No matter. He was the teacher now, and he felt quite the opposite, that three weeks of escape from the Havana Headquarters was a release from a crypt, and the putting off of his formal suit an unsealing of a coffin.

In unconscious agreement with Kanoa's father about the importance of raw nature as antidote to the uncanniness of VR, Jon was going to pay a visit to a friend far, far away in a place where the horizons were broad and the oceans deep.

He took a private jet directly there, because when he wasn't on official business for the Global Government Project, he liked to spend his money as he pleased—and he had always preferred to waste money rather than time. The nearest airport was still an hour away from his destination, but that was an hour well spent on the open deck of a fast-moving ferry, feeling the salt water sting his eyes and prick at his wind-chapped lips.

He had to remind himself to live in the moment more. Life had been too busy this past fifteen years, but he expected that to change soon—though he could not promise that the change would mean improvement.

The ferry slowed and carefully navigated a small path in the stabilization shield of a dome habitat, leaving him a mere two strides of gangway to cross into his friend's home. He heard the ferry depart but did not watch it. He was looking for his friend and wondering why she had not been waiting to welcome him.

Laughter sounded from an open door. He stepped through, slid the glass half-shut against the unrelenting sea spray, and turned to pause in wonder at the scene before him. Not one friend, but two, standing together so deep in conversation that they startled at the sound of his entrance.

"Look who's here!" the woman said, extending her arms as if to show off a prize.

An old family friend, close enough to be called "uncle" but revered enough to be always "sir," came forward and grasped Jon's hands warmly. "At last you're here! You look well!"

"You too," Jon replied, feeling his years fall away. There was something about this much-traveled elder that would make any ordinary man feel like a child. He turned to the woman. "Serendipity? Is this on purpose?"

"Yes, I told him when you were coming, but I thought I'd let it be a surprise for you."

Serendipity came up to him, touched his cheek fondly with the palm of her hand, and held it there for a moment. He could not read her thoughts and emotions, and she would not read his, but a remnant, resilient spark of their long-ago mutual crush glowed in the air. He kept still under her warmth with an old, odd reserve that did not entirely hide his own fondness for her.

"How is the Diplomatic Group?" the old man continued, returning to settle himself in the recliner at the center of the room. "How are your students handling the material?"

"Poorly. At best, they see it as an academic exercise; at worst, a joke. I wish I could get them to take it more seriously, but . . . well . . ." Jon trailed off, shrugged, and made himself comfortable in a chair opposite.

"We were all young once," said the old man, eyes twinkling teasingly.

Jon gave the sly remark the response it deserved—a slanted look and a curled lip—then returned quickly to good behavior. The habit of giving courtesy and respect to this man was too strong.

"You haven't asked if I've heard anything," Serendipity said sternly.

"Because you would have told me immediately if you had. And yet . . . there's a hint of intrigue about both of you. You have a new plan of some kind?"

Serendipity pointed to her coconspirator. "He thinks that since we aren't getting results at the surface, it might be worth the effort to go deeper."

"And we would like you to come with us," the old man added smoothly.

Jon had started nodding to Serendipity's words, but when he heard the rest, he immediately began to shake his head. "No offense to your lovely ship, but I don't do well with that form of transportation. You know that."

"Yes, but . . . you can't deny that you make marvelous bait."

"Your own ship is marvelous bait. Why don't you just dive down and call?"

Serendipity shot her mentor a quick glance, confirming that she had his permission to speak further. "I think we have given up on find-ing other ships in Earth's oceans."

"We haven't seen or heard of any for more than ten years. I believe it's true: the withdrawal is complete," Jon agreed.

"Being a rogue myself, I was prepared to find other rogue pilots," the old man explained. "But I'm ready to admit defeat now—at least in that area."

"Oh yes. What, exactly, am I meant to be bait *for*?"

The two looked blankly at each other, and then at Jon. He groaned.

"This is how we find out," Serendipity said, with a hint of a plea in her voice.

He surrendered. "Tomorrow, then. No, give me a few more days. I'd prefer to do this when I'm rested."

They meant him no harm, and he knew it would probably be fine, but old memories of bad experiences set a puddle of nausea roiling in the pit of his stomach. Still, he'd do it. If they were right and there *was* something to be found, wouldn't that help to galvanize his students to approach their work at a different level, less war game, more war room?

"Promise me something," Serendipity said suddenly. "When the order comes, when everything starts happening, I want to know you're safe. Promise me you'll go back to Havana and stay there."

The request surprised him. "I'll be there for the duration of the project, but why incarcerate myself otherwise? Do you think I need so much protection?"

"I think we can't be sure about what the threats will be and where they will come from. You taught me to play chess; you know that there comes a point where the safest move is to castle the king. Stay in your castle, my king. Let us be sure of your well-being at least."

He lowered his head and fixed her with an intent gaze. "Extend the metaphor. I won't be used to attack anyone, not even a pawn."

She laughed at him. "Relax. Trust in your own pawns to defend you *and* win the game for you."

Jon shook his head. "No, no promises. Not even for you."

*   *   *

"Your classes begin this week. You were not given a curriculum beforehand, and there were good reasons for that. Even now, you may question why we have decided to train you in certain subjects." Charyssa smiled that disarming smile at her riveted audience. "I ask you to be patient. All will become clear in time."

Dylan raised a polite hand. "I have a question. Why are we learning a constructed language?"

Charyssa frowned slightly as she replied, not vexed but perplexed. "I would have thought that would be obvious. Everyone here speaks at least three languages, and you all wear a bug for live translation. Learning a language that is entirely new to you, and has no relationship with any language you presently speak, is the only way to return you to the same baseline."

"Thank you, ma'am. Um . . . I do have another question?" Dylan ventured tentatively.

"Yes, Dylan," she encouraged.

"The schedule says we're learning football? As in . . . soccer? Is that a history of soccer or—"

"You're going to learn to play," she interrupted with a brusqueness that would have been unkind from anyone else, but from her it caused a sheepish smile from Dylan and a suppressed titter from the rest of the group. Except Bay.

"Isala Kuria is our instructor? *Isala Kuria?*" She turned excitedly to Yrsa but quickly crumpled in frustration at Yrsa's confused expression. She rushed to explain. "She's the head of the Kuria Institute, which specializes in motivation and teamwork. They train all kinds of coaches and leaders, not only in football. CEOs and military types love her. Come on, you should know this! She's written papers on the emotional intelligence of teams. Collective intelligence! Isn't that your thing?"

"Actually, that's another one of our classes," Thiago chimed in. "Networked AIs and human intelligence in VR frameworks. You should ace that one, Yrsa."

"But why do we have to learn to actually, physically play football?" Kanoa wondered, cutting through all the rising enthusiasm.

Charyssa leaned toward him and repeated slowly, "All. Will become clear. In time."

With anyone else, it would have been condescending. With Charyssa, it led to a blush from Kanoa and a ripple of laughter from the rest of the class.

Their first football session was ridiculously fun. Kanoa had been expecting some kind of stadium setup in the VR, but he was terribly, terribly wrong. A field had been neatly marked out, goalposts had been erected, all in the humid tropical air and raw outdoors of the extensive grounds. No VR mud could compare to the real thing, Isala explained cheerfully. She took them through some simple drills with the help of a cadre of assistants and quickly flung them into a five-a-side game with a very patient group of women who had obviously once been professional players.

"Bay, I really don't know about this," Kanoa muttered to his friend during a brief water break. "Owen designed this module—is he really this eccentric?"

Thiago overheard and nudged him, discreetly pointing with his chin. "Do you see that?"

Kanoa tried to glance casually in the indicated direction. Isala was sitting on a side bench, surrounded by three of her assistants, all of them talking with great intensity over a large tablet and moving in to occasionally point or swipe at something with a finger.

"I don't know what they're analyzing at this stage, but I'm pretty sure it's nothing we've seen before."

"Biometrics," Yrsa guessed. "Physiology. Motion efficiency. Something."

"Yrsa, I think they're using some of our selection data and the tests we've taken since we got here. We're not athletes. They're looking for something else."

"Nobody *listens* to me," Bay complained. "Collective intelligence? Remember? How the members of a team communicate without speaking and feel the same thing and move to the same goal? That's what she's assessing in us."

"How do you even do that?" Dylan wondered.

"If people would listen to *me* for a change, I could tell you about similar work being done in VR development. Multiplayer games, an option for nonverbal team coordination—" Yrsa began.

"Yrsa," Kanoa said patiently, "when your brain is plugged into a VR scenario, it's *plugged in*. We're running around on a field. The only connection we're sharing is flesh and sweat."

Thiago took a large swig of water and capped his bottle, intoning, "All. Will become clear. In time."

They were still laughing when the whistle went off to call them back to the game.

Jon looked out at the sea, suppressing a queasy feeling. He could feel Serendipity's concerned look as they walked through the inch-deep water on the stabilizing shield. At least she was concerned; the old pilot strode along without a care. Probably thinking Jon was making a fuss for no good reason. Perhaps he was. It was so disorienting and draining that he'd be no use to himself for hours, but he couldn't claim that it was painful or harmful.

The black-and-silver of the shield ended. Beyond a sliver of blue, a muted gray mass, like a vast shoal, hung below the water. The edge rose up slightly and curled invitingly closer, like a sentient, friendly wave.

"The last time I did this, I was naked," Jon said, teeth clenched. "Will this suit help at all?" His finger tugged nervously at the high collar of the silvery jumpsuit they had given him to wear.

The old man looked him over and smoothed the collar more snugly to his neck. "Wait . . . what's this? Take it off."

Jon reluctantly peeled a thin membrane from his face. The features that emerged were a little more weathered and irregular but not significantly changed. Overall, however, the effect was of greater personality and character. Serendipity's eyes sparkled in appreciation.

"Put it away," the old man ordered Jon. "You know we travel light."

"But we're staying here, in the water, aren't we?" Jon protested.

"I like to be prepared for anything."

The three figures, clad entirely in silver-sheened diving skins, plunged into the deep water. The colors shifted, the sea beyond the shield went from calm gray shallows to roiling white froth, then to random ripples that soon gave way to the regular surge of the ocean swells.

Hours later, two figures broke the surface of the water, carrying a third between them. As they scrambled up onto the stabilizing shield, their face masks unsealed and hoods fell back. Serendipity and the old pilot moved forward, breathing deeply for a while in forced, intentional rhythm. Jon, supported between them, breathed shallowly and stumbled as his feet churned sluggishly through the thin layer of water.

"Is it always this bad?" Serendipity said. Surprisingly, she sounded curious rather than worried.

"From what I witnessed of his first time, yes. Perhaps I shouldn't have asked him to come."

They pushed and carried him into the dome, laid him out on the floor, and stepped back. Jon's eyes remained closed and he stirred slightly, but neither of the two seemed distressed. Serendipity watched him in fascination, and the old pilot went to the nearest chair and perched on the edge, waiting quietly.

"Hnnnngh!" Jon turned over and spasmed into a curl, then got up on hands and knees, coughing. Serendipity quickly fetched a cup of water and passed it to him just as he got to his feet. "What was that?" he asked.

"No, no," she said brightly. "We each have a story to tell, and we'll tell it separately. No cross-contamination of the witness report."

Jon stared at her, his eyes watering from the cough and the sea salt. "Did you know . . . ?"

She nodded to the old pilot. "*He* guessed. Don't say any more. We

make a record of our experiences alone, and we view the results together. Yes?"

"Yes," Jon breathed. "That makes sense. If we're wrong . . ."

She laughed. "Go change. We have work to do."

At the end of the week's classes, Charyssa gathered them into the VR
hall and reminded them of their presentations. "We will return to your
original dossiers, but this time we're going to start adding complica-
tions. New information. Challenges, compromises, problems to solve,
issues to address, obstacles to overcome."

Thiago leaned into Kanoa and murmured, "This sounds like fun.
And here I was hoping it would be all football, VR, and learning obscure new languages for the rest of the year."

Charyssa, who never seemed to miss anything, gave Thiago a Look
and smoothly continued, "For your first complication, we have an audiovisual message sent directly to every receiving communications device on Earth. Public, delivered in every language on every country,
and therefore impossible to cover up."

Charyssa gestured to the velvet darkness of a blank VR wall, and
they all turned to look. The brightness of the image made them jump
when it appeared, and it gave off a glow like a holy apparition. This was
no gentle Mary but an imperatrix robed in white with a blue mantle.
Her hair was her crown, a profusion of short brown curls, with lighter
touches speckled throughout and shining with what might have been
purely decorative gems or an array with some as-yet-unknown function.

"Citizens of Earth, greetings. I am the Patrona of House Haneki,
ruler of Alpha Piscis Austrini and elected head of the Galactic Council. I bring a message and a warning. Your governments and commer-
cial institutions have been infiltrated by rogue actors from Alpha Lyrae.
The Galactic Council has voted to bring these criminals to justice.
This will take place over the next five weeks. Do not be alarmed. Do
not attempt to interfere with the Galactic Gendarmerie as they en-

force the laws of our galaxy. After the infiltrators have been removed, you are welcome to open talks with the governments and peoples represented by the Galactic Council."

There was a nervous giggle, quickly smothered, then silence as five carefully composed faces turned to their instructor.

"This is cheating," Kanoa spoke first.

"Oh?" Charyssa replied with genuine surprise, as if she had been expecting some reaction, but not that one. "How so?"

Kanoa swallowed but pushed on bravely. "This isn't a proper First Contact scenario. You've eliminated years, decades even, of small-scale interactions between groups. The aliens are already here and know all about us, but we know little or nothing about them. The information imbalance is huge."

"Yes. That is quite a complication, wouldn't you say?" Charyssa said coolly, and of course the rest of the group laughed *with* her and *at* him.

"We've been told not to interfere, so that defines the problem somewhat," Bay noted seriously. "Perhaps we're meant to look strategically at which governments and institutions aliens would be most likely to infiltrate?"

Charyssa smiled and pointed the remote at Bay. "That is correct. Where are Earth's weaknesses? How could we tell if someone, or something, was using our own systems against us?"

A kind of relief settled over the group. This made sense. This was well within their capabilities and, even if it was couched in a scenario ripped from an anime opera, it had real-world applications.

"And our deadline is five weeks?" Dylan asked.

"No, *their* schedule is five weeks," Bay corrected him. "I suspect we'll soon be receiving 'news' in the VR about strange coups and companies folding suddenly, and it will be our job to connect the dots for the first few cases to anticipate the final victims and the overall result."

Charyssa was nodding happily. "Excellent, Bay. That is indeed what will happen. I will only add one other thing. Do not assume that only Alpha Lyrae has a presence on Earth. Who are the Galactic Gendarmerie? How are they getting here, or are they already in place? How would we recognize them, and what kind of weapons do they bring?"

She stood up. "I'll leave you to discuss your strategy. Don't forget, you must keep up with your classes as well. We will continue to assess you in all areas."

She left the room. Thiago waited a second, then sang out "FUN!" with great sarcasm, and everyone broke down laughing.

NINE

"AT FIRST, I thought I was imagining things."

Serendipity's face hovered in the dimly lit corner of the room, fill-ing the frame. She was sitting forward eagerly, hands clasped together by her knees. She looked as excited as a child describing an adventure.

"I've been in so many different ships before, so many different modes. With and without a passenger module. With and without a suit. Piloted and unpiloted. I've heard the ships speaking in my head within themselves, among themselves, to their pilots. I've even heard them speaking to their passengers in phrases they know will never be answered.

"I've never understood them fully, but I've never heard them baf-fled. I've never heard them . . . awed.

"And I have never, *never* before today heard someone, who was neither ship nor pilot, answer them back."

* * *

"I have traveled many oceans on many worlds and in many times. No matter how much I think I have learned, there is always some new discovery to humble me, to make me consider that an eternal lifespan across all time and space might not be such a terrible thing."

The old man leaned back in the recliner. His face was peaceful, but his eyes were half-closed as he mused over the puzzle he had to describe.

"When they told me the Eridanian ships had disappeared, I was curious, but not concerned. I believed that the Alpha Centauri settlement had withdrawn their scouts on Earth. There was no political benefit to remaining here, especially after the Galactic Council agreed on a process to end the Earth embargo. I further learned that internal upheavals, kept quiet but impossible to silence, had also distracted the Alpha Centauri ruling class from any further extraplanetary activity. That did not surprise me, but it did move my curiosity to concern, because it was known that the settlement did not have oceans capable of supporting a breeding population of ships. If the ships were no longer in Earth's oceans, and the Cygnian and independent pilots had no word of their brethren, where were they hiding?

"Serendipity offered to listen for me. She has been very patient during this arduous task. My ship and I, we are creatures of the surface and the skies. I had no concept of ships visiting the crushing depths of the darkest waters. I should have remembered their origins. It was only when Serendipity told me of the whisper she heard that I began to suspect.

"Like her, I heard the bafflement, the awe. Unlike her, I was in the middle of it, wrestling with a conversation that was so far removed from my experience that I could not participate, only observe. I caught a glimpse of a man, of Earth by his appearance and of an age to be wise but not withered. He spoke to me, but I could not understand him. He knew I was trying.

"I took us back then. I could feel my ship straining, untested at those depths though desperate to stay. I promised a return and we left for a slow journey to the surface.

"I have no more to say, except that if *this* is what the pilots of Alpha Centauri found in Earth's oceans, I understand why they would withdraw.

"And yet . . . I do not believe that they wish us any harm."

"This is . . . hard."

Jon sat slumped in the middle of the carpet and rubbed his hands over his face as he searched for the right words.

"I travel like most do, in a module, in a long sleep. I might hear the murmur of ship and pilot in my dreams, but if I do, I have never remembered it. I wake at the appointed time in a new place. I go about my business.

"Once, I went into a ship without a suit, no farther than the waters of Grand Bay, just a few steps from my aunt and uncle's home. Once, I took an emergency journey between planets with no module, no suit, nothing but my bare skin and one other passenger with a pilot.

"The effects were the same then as now. I was dazed, barely able to function. My mind cannot remain fully conscious while in contact with the mind of a ship. I think, although I cannot be sure, that they also prefer it when I am asleep. I hear no communication; I can barely coexist with them.

"So, perhaps you will understand when I tell you that I saw nothing but blurred colors. I heard nothing but echoes—words that were not spoken to me, not directly, but aside, like background noise, like a recorded memory.

"I heard one thing clearly: 'It's a good death.'

"I said one thing in return: '*Who are you?*'

"What I heard . . . I have no idea what it meant. And I have no idea what we should do next."

Jon returned to Havana with his mask in place, dressed in his unremarkable uniform, and carrying a datachip of the three recordings made in the dome after the descent to the depths.

His own task was, unfortunately, quite clear—to continue his work with the Project. Serendipity and the old pilot planned to bring in more qualified reserves to probe the ocean depths and discover its secrets. For that, they could either get official permission or rope in a few more rogue pilots to help them do the work.

Unusually, he hoped they would choose the former, the formal route. Absence of harmful intent did not always equate to absence of danger, and if there was something in the deep that could make a difference to Earth's future, they needed to know both what it wanted and what it could do.

For now, it was out of his hands, and he was on a deadline.

"Welcome back, Professor," Dylan said as Jon entered the VR hall.

"Professor? They never call *me* that," Charyssa teased.

"We call you 'ma'am,' which is worse, believe me," Bay said easily.

The five representatives laughed, and Jon looked around at every face with a smile. Three weeks could make such a difference. He'd left them barely acquaintances and come back to find them friends. So much the better. He joined them at the table, sitting beside Charyssa near the head.

"Good to see you all again. I've been following your progress," he told them. "Dylan, good work on the amended first-week presentations. It's a far more coherent and comprehensive document now. Bay and Yrsa, thank you for your second- and third-week reports."

Dylan mumbled his thanks, embarrassed and pleased. Yrsa looked proud and relieved, and Bay grinned triumphantly.

Still young, he reminded himself.

We were all young once, an older voice in his head chided gently.

"The work is getting harder, but you knew that was going to happen. Charyssa will remain your coordinator for the rest of the session. My work will be a little different. I'm afraid I'm going to be taking up your football slot and replacing it with something a little different, in the VR."

"Nooooo!" Kanoa wailed. "I was getting so good!"

"You didn't even get the point of it!"

"Isala is leaving us? Already?"

"In the VR? Are we doing a multiplayer game?"

"I bet it's the Wall."

Jon turned to Dylan with such swift attention that the banter immediately hushed and everyone leaned in. "Yes. Good guess. Do you want to guess why?"

Yrsa raised a hand slowly. "I'd say we're still looking at the collective intelligence question. Organic and AI together. Something that would give us a real-world advantage if there *were* aliens?"

Bay spoke up hastily, eager to correct her. "Something that would give us a real-world advantage in creating a global civilization. That's the point, isn't it? We're the Diplomatic Group. We have to create the global culture if all the rest of it is going to work."

"Yes," Kanoa agreed. "The alien scenario is just a metaphor for our own destructive tendencies. There's no First Contact, no 'us' and 'them.' We have to find a way to become only *us*. All of us."

Jon realized that they had gone silent, watching him expectantly for approval. He blinked. "Yes. Indeed. All very good ideas and definitely something to consider."

Out of the corner of his eye, he saw Charyssa put her hand to her mouth to discreetly bite a knuckle.

During their post-class discussion on their alien infiltration assignment, the group identified three areas with the right combination of strategic importance and internal instability: the Chilean-Argentine Confederation, the Republic of South China, and ParaVee. The first two regions were no surprise. Both had experienced some form of upheaval or reconstruction since their shaky beginnings. Furthermore, they were the countries best known for their casual oversight when it came to matters like corporate taxes and labor laws.

The last choice was hotly debated, but Yrsa prevailed.

"You have no idea how much virtual reality is embedded in entertainment, governance, communications . . . everything. It's so much a part of our life that we don't even see it anymore."

"Wouldn't that be a bit too obvious—targeting the biggest virtual reality company on Earth?" Thiago hinted.

"Yes, it would, but ParaVee is exactly how you described it. Huge. How can they be sure of everyone who works for them? They have subcontracted several companies to deliver their products and services. They have excellent industrial counterespionage—by Earth standards. What if superior technology existed to tweak a design, or introduce a trojan or parasite?"

Everyone shuddered slightly, except for Bay, who stared stonily at her tablet, arms folded stiffly. She looked upset, but Kanoa had no idea why.

"Okay, you've convinced me," Thiago agreed. "But it's one thing to argue the political consequences of a weakened or compromised RSC or CAC, and quite another to talk about imaginary technology that may or may not exist."

"Then leave that to me. We're always speculating about the hacker who's ten steps ahead. I'll just stretch my guessing to ten kilometers ahead."

Dylan volunteered to work with Thiago on the CAC, and that left Kanoa and Bay with the RSC.

"It's Antarctica, of course. Lots of resources there, and very, very dubious, old land claims. The CAC is perfectly placed to take control of the area," Thiago said with enthusiasm.

Dylan was less convinced. "Didn't the World Council designate it as a global area of scientific interest back in 2090?"

"Of course, but we're not talking about people who plan to play by our rules. We're talking about *aliens*," Thiago pointed out.

Kanoa couldn't stop himself. "Hey . . . I know this isn't my area, but what's the real-world application?"

They all turned to look at him. He waved his hands self-consciously. "Sure, if there were aliens they could help the CAC take over Antarctica, but in real life, the CAC would never be able to do that alone. I'm just suggesting, you might want to lead with another motive."

Yrsa groaned. "We hate players like you. Never immersing, always trying to second-guess the designer. Kanoa, just play the game as it is, hmm?"

All that from the woman who was the first to sneer at the First Contact scenario? He blinked and drew back, offended. "I'm just saying, let's not lose perspective here. We could come up with papers that are actually useful, not far-fetched what-ifs."

Thiago looked at him sadly. "Trust the process, man. We're not in the real world yet. Enjoy testing your creativity in a VR lab, because when life happens, it'll throw things at you that you never imagined were possible."

Kanoa raised his hands in defeat. "Fine, I'll play along. Forget I said anything."

As soon as the discussions were over, Kanoa escaped to the garden. The group's tradition of daily walks had tailed off somewhat after the start of the football sessions, but Kanoa, in stubborn homage to his father, still kept a few minutes each day to stroll in the grounds and stand unsheltered under the sky. He wondered what would happen if he raced toward the horizon, let himself be late for the next session on the schedule, wandered into an area that was not designated. A month was more than enough time to develop cabin fever, even if your cabin was a massive fortress of a mansion on several beautifully landscaped acres. He started to run.

"Hey, Kanoa! Wait!"

For a moment he was tempted to pretend he couldn't hear, but what was the point of that? Some people would take a hint, but not Bay. She would just shout louder, or speak directly to the bug in his ear. He resentfully slowed his strides and let her catch up with him.

"Kanoa, don't stress. I think you're right."

"What?" In spite of his bad humor, he turned to look at her, still walking quickly away from the house.

"You're right. And so is Charyssa. We shouldn't be taking anyone's messages at face value. Have you asked yourself . . . why us? Why this group? Why are they doing things this way?"

"Bay." He stopped, sighed, and faced her fully. "I understand. You're invested in this being important, especially because you turned down an assignment in Trade to come here. But what if *you're* wrong? What if it *is* a waste of time?"

Bay's chin tilted aggressively to one side. "A waste of time? It's a year with the World Council's Global Government Project. They could have us weaving baskets for the next eleven months and we'd still be able to walk into any interview for any job and have an advantage."

"I thought you were impressed by substance, not just names." He gave the rebuke more of a sting with a slight emphasis on *you*. You, child of privilege, growing up on Rich People Planet, never expected to care about real work. And yet she *had* worked hard and proved herself to the group, to their instructors, and to herself. Only to stand before him and say it didn't matter.

Anger and hurt radiated from her. Kanoa was certain she was going to throw some insult at him and leave. But instead she bit her lip, took a breath, and said, "Listen to me. What if we did the research around that? The motives of the people organizing the Diplomatic Group?"

His shoulders slumped. He didn't *want* to be mean to her. "You want to research Charyssa? Owen? Some of the most famous people in the world. What can they hide?"

Bay's eyes narrowed, but with amusement, not spite. "I know what they can hide. I have a cousin who used to work for Owen. And . . . well, Peter Hendrix, the founder of ParaVee? I've known him forever. He's like family. I know plenty of things that I've never spoken of, like why Owen designing this module is amazing and not stupid, and why ParaVee will never be infiltrated by *anyone*, human or alien. But there's a lot I haven't been told, a lot that I suspect, and you're the only one of the group who's stayed skeptical enough to be useful to me."

Kanoa grimaced, unsure how to take that. "Flatterer."

Bay gave a long, low chuckle. "I mean it. Everyone has fallen under Charyssa's spell. Even Jon, for all that he's so bland . . ." She trailed off, frowning.

Kanoa eyed the horizon. It still seemed very far away, but the itch of imprisonment was easing a little. Was that all he had needed, some small rebellion, some diversion from the assigned material, the designated areas, and the fixed schedule? If so, he'd take it.

He put on a stern expression. "So, you want me to do twice as much work for no good reason."

Bay began to protest but quickly saw the humor leaking through Kanoa's pretense. She slapped his shoulder instead. "The job comes with benefits. I'll show you a little trick from Rich People Planet, courtesy of Uncle Peter from ParaVee. A completely secure communications channel, one-to-one, between you and anyone else who has *this*."

She dipped her hand into a pocket, came up with a dangling pendant, like a charm for a chain, or the cuff-style of ear bug. "You'll have to trust me, of course."

Kanoa took the small gem from her hand and fastened it to his bug. "I *don't* trust you. But I also don't have anything you want, so . . . I'll assume you're giving until proven greedy."

Bay managed to look both impressed and annoyed. "Fair enough. Let's go forward with that."

Kanoa kept his expectations low. Their schedule had quashed so many good intentions, so many beautiful beginnings. Like their plans to go drinking and dancing in the nightclubs of Havana every Friday (they went once), the proposed day trip to the beach (postponed by rain and never mentioned again), and even Yrsa's ongoing attempt to get them all involved in a multiplayer game that she was designing (Thiago and Dylan seemed more into that, but Kanoa was still trying to tweak his character settings).

But Bay proved steady and persistent. She used their private channel to share with him her own initial work, and what he learned made him wonder if she might not have a point. Owen was heavily involved in the development of virtual reality technologies, a side effect of his famous global collaborations, which required a fine detail of audio and video transmission for 3D stage rehearsals with artistes based in two or three different countries.

Owen was also a benefactor of the Kuria Institute. Money from his music royalties and ParaVee work was being funneled into teamwork research, both in raw games like football and in VR gaming. But it had been Charyssa, a savvy media mogul and entertainment icon in her own right, who had noticed Owen's interests and decided to recruit him to her dream of a unified Earth.

"That's perfect, that is," Kanoa muttered to himself. "A former beauty queen who really wants world peace."

The Diplomatic Group no longer looked like a frivolous add-on to the more serious work of the Global Government Project, but he was no closer to guessing what Charyssa and Owen hoped to achieve with their alien First Contact scenario.

He told Bay as much. Her reply was cryptic. "We need to go further back."

So he did. Charyssa was well documented, a teenage Miss Universe who had demonstrated massive talent behind her uniquely multiethnic aesthetic appeal. She had gone on to dominate in acting, producing, and humanitarian work for four or five decades after her debut. As a Sino African, she first ruled the box offices of two continents and two heavyweight entertainment industries, then easily crossed over to Indian and Pacific-American projects.

Reading her history made him feel more enamored of her, not less, and he didn't want to turn into another Dylan, starstruck and stammering, so he took a break and started to look at Owen's story.

Within ten minutes of research, he was angrily calling Bay.

"What Rich People Planet nonsense is this?"

She laughed at him, hard. "It's perfectly legal."

"For a given value of 'legal,' sure," he scoffed.

"Don't be so provincial. Getting a new identity doesn't make you disappear. It makes you one of the most trackable people on the planet. Taxes, security, they all keep a close eye on you. It's only your past that's erased, not your future."

"You say erased, but surely someone must know?

"It's a very long-established procedure, Kanoa. They've perfected their confidentiality and they've had very few leaks in decades of operation."

"What kind of person does something this drastic?"

"Sports and entertainment celebrities. Retired porn stars and redundant princes. Children of dictators and mobsters." Bay spoke musingly, sounding like she had too often wondered this herself.

"Criminals?" He had to ask.

"Never, not even if they give evidence. You have to have a clean record and a lot of money to do this."

"So, you're saying Owen could be anyone, even an alien, for all we know."

She sighed. "Don't be silly. The process includes thorough medical scanning and some surgery. New faces aren't only made by masks. Owen is completely, entirely human."

"Just testing you," Kanoa teased. "I bet you think he's a prince."

To his surprise, Bay answered mildly, "And if he is? What advantage would a spare prince gain by creating the Diplomatic Group and pushing for global government? What kind of aristocracy will be recognized as the focus of our collective rituals and ceremonies?"

Kanoa thought for a bit. "That's . . . a lot of effort to become King of the World."

"Just a suggestion on the table," she replied casually. "You haven't even heard my ParaVee suspicions yet."

"And what do *you* get out of this if you guess right? A seat at the table? Or a seat behind the throne?" Kanoa asked shrewdly.

"Be honest, Kanoa, wouldn't you like that, for yourself? Do you really want to go back home and be governor of a microstate in a mini federation?"

"My father always said the best rulers must be a servant to all, and master of one." The words could have been preachy, but instead they were spoken with sadness as Kanoa's grief resurfaced. At times it felt as if his father's memory were the only raw reality in a virtual world filled with people who lived and thought in ways he could barely comprehend.

Bay replied with somber respect, "Then look at it this way. Who reminds the rulers to serve? Who helps the rulers master themselves? The seat behind the throne can be an important one, Kanoa."

Three days later, the group received the news of a coup in the Chilean-Argentine Confederation—not class assignment news. Real news. At first they were confused.

"The simulation is bleeding over into reality," Thiago said half-jokingly.

"Are you *sure* this is real? Could they be fooling us into taking the assignment more seriously?" Dylan wondered.

"Why would we do that?" Charyssa entered the VR hall with a grim face and a stern look at Dylan. "Your wife is a media specialist, is she not? Why not ask *her* whether the news sources can be trusted?"

Kanoa made himself small and quiet in his chair and fervently wished for others to do the same. Charyssa was *furious*. Not at them, it seemed . . . but surely not at the situation? Shouldn't their instructors feel happy that the Diplomatic Group had made an accurate prediction, albeit from an alternative-world context?

No way to find out what Jon thought about the situation. He was nowhere to be found, and they all received a message that their scheduled VR game session would have to be postponed this week, with apologies, until further notice.

"Why is Charyssa so angry?" Kanoa murmured to Bay as they left the VR hall for lunch.

"That's not anger; that's fear," she replied, just as quietly. "Something's going on. I'm going to call my sister."

Events moved faster than they expected. Before lunch was over, news flashed over the dining hall VR panels. The Chilean-Argentine Confederation was being officially warned by the International Law Enforcement Agency. Missiles had been tracked from an Argentine base en route to Antarctica, target unknown.

"A launch error? Showing off?" Thiago guessed, as baffled as the international experts reporting on the situation.

The bafflement only increased when the ILEA reported that someone . . . *something* had turned the incoming missiles around, diverting
them neatly to their point of origin and forcing the CAC to send out a
swarm of laser drones to deactivate their own missiles prior to shooting
them down mid-ocean.

"Whose polar base has *that* kind of technology?" Dylan shouted at
the talking heads on the news panels, as if hoping they could hear his
question and answer it sensibly.

"What base on *Earth* has that kind of technology?" Yrsa corrected
him.

Bay and Kanoa exchanged horrified looks. "Let's find Charyssa,"
Bay said immediately, and they left their half-eaten meal. "We're going
to find Charyssa," she shouted back over her shoulder as Yrsa and
Thiago gave them surprised looks.

"No, stay," Dylan said, laughing sarcastically. "Any minute now, the
Republic of South China will jump into the fray."

Kanoa fled, almost afraid he might be right.

The door to Charyssa's office was ajar. Someone's hand rested on
the interior handle, holding it half-open, and that someone stood
slightly turned, speaking over his shoulder to Charyssa. The sound of
Jon's voice made Kanoa and Bay slow their brisk pace. They paused a
few feet down the corridor as Jon closed the office door. He turned,
saw them, and blinked with the usual amount of surprise, but to
Kanoa's bewilderment, he also looked a little sad.

"I thought you weren't supposed to be here," Bay accused.

"I'm not," he said sharply. "I'm leaving again right now."

Bay followed Jon as he walked away from Charyssa's door. Kanoa
glanced once at the closed door, wavering, then quickened his steps to
catch up with them. "Can you please tell us what's going on?" he
begged.

Jon's eyebrows drew together, more puzzled than irritated. "Charyssa
will tell you what you need to know. There's no time. I have to go."

They had reached the foyer. The main door, brightly sunlit through its panels of glass, silhouetted three figures: a woman dressed simply in a long green tunic, a slender person in a plain brown suit, and an older man in a gray jumpsuit whose shine matched his long, graying hair.

Kanoa's eyes widened. "Naraldi?"

Bay stopped arguing with Jon long enough to blink through the blaze of the sun, and she gave a sharp exhalation.

The man in gray narrowed his eyes and looked closely at Kanoa. "We haven't met," he declared confidently. "But I think I know you. Who are you, young man?"

Kanoa instinctively stepped closer to Bay. They had not spent many weeks learning their new language, but simple phrases of greetings and courtesy such as a diplomat might need to know had been covered in the very first of their lessons. To encounter the face of a VR avatar, speaking a made-up language, in the bright sun of a Havana afternoon, was completely upending his sense of the world.

"Did we step into the VR hall?" he whispered to her anxiously.

Bay gave him a look of utter exasperation that broke the spell. She squared her shoulders and stepped up to Jon. "Sir. Let me help. Why else do you have us here? For what purpose?"

"They'll find out soon enough," the person in the brown suit said in a soft, light voice. She, at least, spoke as if she were a real-world human being and not a virtual construct.

"Tareq," Jon said, his low voice a warning.

"She's right," Naraldi said, now matching his language to theirs. "Let them know what to do. But let the boy come with us."

"What? Why?" Jon protested.

"I have my reasons," Naraldi said, smiling cryptically at Kanoa.

"Fine," Jon said through gritted teeth. "Bay, go to Noriko. I'll tell her I sent you to be useful. Kanoa, you're with us."

"What? No! I have no idea what's going on—"

"Kanoa!" Bay gripped his arm, shaking him a little. "It's fine, trust me. Don't you understand? Jon is Owen."

The man Kanoa had known as Jon Newhaven raised finger and thumb to his ear and swiftly stripped the mask from his face. "Yes, I am. And we don't have much time. Let's go."

Bay pushed Kanoa's frozen body forward. "*Go.*"

Kanoa numbly passed through the glass doors of Havana Headquarters behind Jon—*no, Owen*—and his strange little band. Bay spoke reassuring words through their private channel, but a static hiss started up from his communicator bug and grew in intensity until it drowned out the sound of her voice.

When the static stopped and the message began, he knew the sense of it almost by heart, but the voice was like nothing he had ever heard on Earth.

"Hello to everyone on Earth. I am the Patrona of House Haneki, Queen of Alpha Piscis Austrini and Empress of the Galactic Council. I have bad news and good news. Your political and corporate bodies have been overrun by vermin from Alpha Lyrae. The Galactic Council has started to bring them in for prosecution. Don't stress. Don't get in the way of the Galactic Gendarmerie as they do their job. After the rats have been exterminated, you are welcome to come chat with us."

He had no time to ponder. Already Owen was leading them away from the building—not down the long driveway to the gate and the main road and the city, but on the footpaths through the grounds and toward the distant horizon that had so often teased Kanoa with its promise of a limitless infinity.

He closed his eyes on a blink and saw, like a vision or a hallucination, a flash of a dry desert, a stone tower, and a man who looked quite a lot like Tareq sitting beneath a blossoming, leaf-bare tree at the top of the tower.

When he opened his eyes, he was certain that he had died, or was dreaming.

He was home.

TEN

HAVANA HEADQUARTERS HAD erupted into chaos.

Thiago, Yrsa, and Dylan rushed into the foyer from the dining hall. Charyssa walked slowly in from the corridor that led to her office. She looked weary, but also determined.

"What was that?" Dylan demanded in a shaking voice. "It interrupted the official news feeds! It looked *nothing* like the woman in the VR scenario!"

"Let's go to the VR hall and discuss this," Charyssa said soothingly, but Dylan was beyond the power of an infatuation to control him.

"No! We stay here, in the real world, in the raw. No more scenarios, no more games. Only the truth."

"Are *you* an alien?" Yrsa demanded.

Charyssa turned sharply to her and opened her mouth as if to deliver a sharp denial, but suddenly she stopped, lowered her head, and laughed softly. "It's a fair question. No, I am not an alien. But I tell you all now"—and there it was; her fire and fierceness returned and her head held high as she glared at them—"if you think *that* is the most important question, if you go into this fixated on *us* and *them,* you have already lost."

Bay stood silently in the midst of them all, head down and mumbling to herself. Then she suddenly looked up and went to stand in front of Charyssa—not aggressively, but with conviction. "I have to leave the Project. I have to go to my cousin Noriko."

"I need to go home," Dylan moaned. "My family—"

"You *all* have to leave," Charyssa said coolly. "This building will soon be put to other uses. But you shouldn't leave without understanding what your future will look like."

"I think we got that bit," Thiago said shakily. "It's all real, isn't it?"

Charyssa nodded slowly. "Yes. And there's more."

"Put it in a file and send it to us," Bay snapped. "I don't have time."

"*Make* time," Charyssa snarled in return. "You want to get to your cousin in Amsterdam, don't you?"

It didn't quite sound like a threat. Bay looked confused, then pensive, and finally terrified. She stared at Charyssa. "You can't mean . . ."

Charyssa smiled wryly. "As I told you before, all will become clear in time. Let's go to the VR hall so I can give you the last briefing of your assignment."

Four seats were occupied around the boardroom table of the VR hall. Charyssa sat at the head, Bay and Thiago on her left, Yrsa on her right.

Dylan was not there. He had made it quite clear that he had no desire to learn more, or to participate in any further activities with the Diplomatic Group in particular and the Global Government Project in general. He had already packed his essentials and left for the ports, to try his luck getting a same-day flight back home to his family.

Bay didn't blame him. However, unfortunately or fortunately, her only way out to her own family was through.

"There is a transit station in Antarctica," Charyssa said. "The Galactic Gendarmerie have a base there, and the Lyran cartels decided to launch a preemptive strike."

"A transit station," Yrsa repeated hollowly. "So, the faster-than-light portals are real?" She caught Charyssa's tired glance. "They're real," she muttered to herself.

"There are two other transit stations operating on Earth. One is in Amsterdam." She paused to gently acknowledge Bay's flinch of shock. "One is in Havana, on this property."

"Show us," Thiago demanded.

Charyssa blinked at his audacity, but he refused to back down.

"All we saw and heard was an image and a recording. Yes, she looked a little . . . weird . . . but anything can look lifelike on a VR panel. I'm not trusting anything I can't see for myself, in the raw, in my sober mind. Take me to another planet. Let me feel the heat of another sun on my face; let me walk under a different gravity. VR can't duplicate that."

"It's not that simple," Charyssa began. Thiago leaned back with a disbelieving sneer. "It isn't," she insisted. "You can't leave Earth without going through a quarantine process. Remember your First Contact rules of exchange," she concluded, mildly mocking him as uncertainty once more took over his expression. "You wouldn't want to accidentally wipe out an entire civilization with your alien germs."

"But we can go from Havana to Amsterdam," Bay guessed.

"Yes. That we can do. But before I give you the proof you need to believe, one question. Thiago and Yrsa, are you going home, or will you join Bay?"

Bay shook her head. "I don't want—"

"You *should*," Charyssa interrupted her forcefully. "You need all the expertise you can assemble to face this. We are in the beginning stages, and there is so much more ahead. Noriko will understand."

Bay dropped her head and her fist hit the table, not in challenge, but in frustration and defeat.

"Why is Kanoa with Jon? Where did they go?" Thiago asked quietly, a small diversion to break the tension.

Bay looked up, a new glint in her eyes. "*I* can answer that. Assuming we have intelligent life in our oceans . . ." She paused to see the effect of her words on Charyssa, who opened her mouth as if to speak, then exhaled, drew back, and lowered her eyes. ". . . *assuming* that were true, who do we represent? All the humans on Earth, or all intelligent life?"

"For galactic recognition, it must be all intelligent life," Charyssa confirmed.

"And what does recognition mean?" Yrsa prodded.

"A seat on the Galactic Council. Autonomy."

"So, we've sent a delegation to speak to our monsters in the deep," Bay finished. "If we don't include them in our constituency, the Galactic Council will view us as nothing more than a bunch of scattered barbarian tribes."

"Essentially," Charyssa said.

"So, what's the problem?" Thiago said. "Do we have to be part of the Galaxy? We were doing fine when we had no idea they existed."

All eyes turned to stare at him, and Charyssa said soberly, "I'll be sure to include in that file all the ways in which the Lyran cartels have interfered with and exploited our food production, development and delivery of pharmaceuticals, media, and natural resources."

"Then why didn't someone step in earlier?" Bay demanded.

"They couldn't," Yrsa said quickly, soberly. "They only recently found out. Earth was supposed to be left alone, remember? They were watching to make sure nothing entered our orbit; they had no idea about the old portals . . . sorry . . . *transit stations* working."

Charyssa nodded in agreement. "And some think we need long-term protection as a result. A period of guardianship where we become a colony of an established civilization."

"What happened to autonomy?" Thiago wanted to know.

"Have you formed a planetary government yet?" Charyssa shot back.

"They're going to fight over us," Bay said with certainty.

"Some of them will, yes," Charyssa said with an equal certainty that was not at all reassuring.

She braced her hands on the table. "Let me sum up. Alpha Piscis Austrini, especially House Haneki, are your allies. 16 Cygni B and its Eridanian settlement—allies. Alpha Lyrae A, tentative allies. Anyone else from Alpha Lyrae—not our allies. Beta Geminorum—our allies when working with Austrinians, our enemies when with Lyran cartels. The Eridanian pilots—largely neutral in this situation. The Eridanians on Alpha Centauri—unknown, but be careful."

Various reactions, from soft cursing to forceful exhalations, sounded around the table.

"One last thing. We're all human, we all have masks, and their masks are better than ours. Some may look a little different in the raw. The Patrona of House Haneki is unusually tall and long-limbed, but even she is not outside of the range of what we recognize as human. Don't try to guess by looking."

"Enough talking," Bay said. "Let's go. Yrsa, Thiago, you're welcome to come with me. I'd appreciate your help."

"I'm in," Yrsa said immediately.

Thiago eyed Yrsa with less enthusiasm, and then shrugged. "I'll go pack."

"No need," Charyssa said crisply. "The way you're going, you can't take anything with you."

They all stared at her with a fresh, more personal anxiety, but she ignored their looks, stood up, and said, "Come with me."

Bay wasn't sure where she had expected alien technology might be hidden. In an underground bunker below Headquarters, perhaps. Behind a false wall in the VR hall, definitely.

In plain sight, bang in the middle of the landscaped acres around the main building—no, she had not expected that.

"But seriously . . ." Thiago muttered doubtfully.

The hanging garden feature, three meters or so of cascading foliage, marble ledges, and decorative lighting, was easy to notice and admire at first glance, and just as easy to forget and relegate to the background.

"Follow me," Charyssa ordered, and they followed like a line of obedient ducklings around the side. Instead of more views, more landscape, as they turned the corner, they found themselves in shadow, which dimmed and cooled the sun. A typical VR flicker passed over their vision, and they saw they were in an enclosed room behind the wall garden, a room filled with about ten uniformed personnel sitting at or near workstations, who looked at Charyssa with slightly nervous alertness.

"Don't stare," Bay growled at Thiago, who was indeed staring. Some of the faces, some of the body shapes, were *definitely* at the outer ranges of what would be considered human on Earth. Limbs in odd proportions, spacing of eyes, size of mouth, mottling of skin—they touched on the uncanny, but for every strange feature there was a familiar look that could have been either a cousin or a friend from another country.

"No, no, this is good, this is necessary," Thiago replied weakly. "I'm becoming convinced. Oh . . . and now she's asking them for . . . a driver? You see, if they'd just *told* me that was a real language, I would have paid much more attention in class."

"She's asking them for a vanguard," Yrsa corrected. "Someone to carry us through to Amsterdam and make sure our minds and bodies are in one piece when we arrive."

"That would be nice," Bay murmured.

Behind them, the back wall of the garden hummed ominously. The three spun as one and watched in fascinated horror as the smooth black surface opened up to reveal small recessed cubicles, spaces just large enough for a human body in repose.

Charyssa walked past them and stepped up to the wall. "Choose a place. Someone will help secure you inside. Don't fuss or struggle. You'll be told when to disembark."

Hesitantly, Thiago stepped into a space beside Charyssa and stayed carefully, if nervously, in place as two people strapped his body in, gently positioned a breathing mask over his face, and draped him completely in a mesh through which his anxiously blinking eyes could still be seen.

After a brief hesitation, Yrsa and Bay determinedly followed his example and let themselves be restrained, masked, and swaddled in turn. For what felt like a long time but could not have been more than minutes, they waited, seeing little and hearing only a few words they could understand, or the occasional phrase that made sense. Eventually, the humming started up again. Bay could not stop her heart from racing and her breath from quickening as the little light that filtered into her cubicle shrank from a rectangle to a line and then disappeared.

Some sedative must have been added to the mask's output, for soon she felt unconcerned, relaxed, and almost on the edge of sleep.

That did not stop her from recalling the moment when she felt the boundaries of herself dissolve and diffuse.

The dome had been untethered from its mid-ocean anchor and docked in the shallows of a bay, which lay cradled in the half-broken remnants of a reef-ringed atoll. The stabilizing shield, no longer required, had been detached and stowed, and the entrance fastened directly to a short wooden pier leading to a larger dock.

The five travelers lingered there for a while: Serendipity in contemplative silence; Naraldi in deep, earnest conversation with a still-shocked Kanoa; and Tareq with Owen.

"*Must* I call you Owen?" Tareq complained. "I am surprised you still keep that name. Has it not served its purpose?"

He regarded her with amusement. "You, who are known as Siha at home, pretend not to know the value of a different name in a different place? When Kirat traveled with us years ago, I called him Tareq, and he called me Owen. It'll do for now."

She looked away briefly, dismissing the point with a gesture as effective as a shrug. "By the way, your aunt wanted you to have this." She handed him a soft, small object.

Owen opened the folded rectangle of jersey fabric and examined words in a large black font across the back of a plain white shirt.

BE GLUE

He turned it over, knowing what to expect from his aunt, and read the smaller text over the right breast.

(NOT GOD)

He started laughing. Everyone looked at him strangely as, still chuckling, he took off his formal tunic and put on his aunt's gift.

"Family joke?" Kanoa asked politely.

"Something like that," Owen said. "A joke. A reminder. A warning."

Three people living knew that joke: his aunt, his uncle, and himself. Once it had been four, but the person who had spoken the words on his shirt had passed away some years ago. Tareq, who *was* family, or close enough to it, was well-enough versed in their past lore to understand that the choice of the name "Owen," though no joke, was also a reminder and a warning. She was wrong to suggest he discard it. He still needed that reminder, and the gift from his aunt proved that.

They were all looking at him as he pondered his life and choices, waiting for him to tell them the next step.

"Naraldi, why did you want Kanoa with us?"

The old pilot smiled. "Because I realized then, and have just confirmed, that Kanoa strongly resembles the face I saw during our expedition to the depths."

"How . . . why?" Serendipity demanded.

Kanoa directed the answer to Owen, his expression still a little stricken and vulnerable. "Naraldi thinks he saw my father."

"Your father . . . who is dead," Owen said gently.

"Yes. We never found his body, but . . . I was holding him. I remember what it felt like when he stopped breathing, when his spirit left him."

"And his last words?" Naraldi prompted.

Kanoa swallowed, unshed tears shining in his eyes. "'Don't stress. It's a good death. Can't complain.'" He laughed a little shakily. "He always said he'd rather paddle out on his old board into the sunset than die in a hospice."

"Tell Owen what happened to you after you felt him die."

In halting phrases, Kanoa told his tale. Owen's heartbeat quickened as he recognized the description of a conscious meeting with a ship in the wild, and the resulting brief coma from the encounter.

"What do you make of that?" he asked Naraldi.

"I am not sure, but there is one way to find out," Naraldi replied. He walked to the edge of the dock and looked out to the horizon. In mere seconds, a gargantuan shape reared up beyond the broken reefs, blotting the morning sun, furling and fanning the finlike edges of its bulk as if waving cheerily. After this display, it demurely settled and sank beneath the waves once more.

"Was that what you saw?" Naraldi turned around to address Kanoa and was forced to direct his voice to a point on the floor. Kanoa was flattened with horror.

"No! I would *not* have missed *that!*"

"Hmm," Naraldi murmured, considering. "Not one of our ships, but perhaps something similar?"

"Sometimes . . . I dream."

Everyone's attention focused on Kanoa as he slowly moved to a sitting position, arms clasped around knees, eyes fixed on the swirling froth of the now-empty ocean.

"I dream about how my father died. And then I dream that he's talking to me . . . but it's not quite him. Not his personality. He liked to tease me; he used to joke around a lot. In my dreams, his face is blank. Neither happy nor sad, just . . . present. Asking me how I am, listening to trivial details of how my day was or what I'm learning. Then he says goodbye and disappears into the ocean again, and I wake up. He always says goodbye before the dream ends."

"It's good that you can remember your father like this," Serendipity said with sympathy.

Kanoa gave her a lost look. "Everything I thought was strange is ordinary, and now the ordinary is strange. I don't know what's unusual anymore, that I talk to my dead father in my dreams, or that you took me from Havana to an island in the Pacific in the twinkling of an eye. Maybe I'm keeping my father with me the only way I can, but—"

He stopped suddenly.

"Go on. Tell us," Owen urged him. "We'll decide what's strange together."

"When I wake up from those dreams, I feel just like I did that day on the beach. Drained, almost drugged. Worn out, like I've been wrestling with something much bigger than me. Sometimes, especially if it's a long dream, I'm useless for the whole morning. Can't eat, can't concentrate. Takes hours before I feel like I'm fully in this world again."

"Hmm," was all Owen said, but he caught and held Naraldi's gaze.

"Many people die at sea and their bodies are never recovered," Tareq noted, her voice a cautious intrusion. "How many inhabit the dreams of their loved ones?"

"Tareq—" Owen began to remonstrate with her.

"It was a serious question," she flashed back. "I'm not talking about grief or coping or wishful thinking. How many of the dead walk the dreams of the living in this place of many islands? It might be worthwhile to find out."

"We have stories . . ." Kanoa offered.

"Legends?" Serendipity asked.

"More like urban legends. Not stories of generations long past, though I'm sure there are those too. Recent. Within my generation, my parents' generation. And not everyone who dies at sea, but a few. More than a few. People who stood out in some way, who served their community well. Did us proud. I always thought of it as our way of making them immortal."

"Maybe they are," Naraldi murmured, his eyes distant.

Owen watched him closely. His uncle had told him that Naraldi's many travels through time and space had brought him great knowledge at a heavy price, but also the wisdom to know when not to interfere. Searching for Eridanian ships in Earth's oceans was the closest he had come to interfering in the last three decades. He wondered if Naraldi was about to make another exception.

"If you know anything—" he began cautiously.

"I do not," Naraldi said regretfully. "I have used these oceans as landing site and occasionally as hiding place. I never explored the depths or asked for their stories. If we are to learn more, it must come from this son of Earth and from the paths that he walks in his dreams—if he will permit it."

"Son of—" Kanoa began to stutter. "If I'm a son of Earth, what are you? What are all of you?"

Owen spoke slowly, keeping his eyes on Kanoa to anticipate his reaction. "I'm Cygnian, which is to say, mostly just like you. Serendipity too, but less so. She's Cygnian and has a fair amount of Eridanian ancestry. Naraldi and Tareq are entirely Eridanian.

"They're telepaths, all three of them. That's a very general, imprecise word for what they can do, but just accept it for now. They want to observe you when you sleep. See where your mind goes, or what comes to your mind, when you dream of your father. And I believe, somehow, that you will do so tonight."

Kanoa stared at him. "*You're* not a telepath." His tone made the words more of a hope than a query.

"No," Owen laughed sincerely. "Not at all."

Kanoa laughed along, though still a little nervously. "In our first week at Havana Headquarters, when I saw all the old tropes in your scenario design, I seriously doubted you. I tried so hard to find a metaphor in everything."

"Well, those tropes had to come from *somewhere*," Owen said carefully. "A thing can be both a truth and a metaphor."

"Will it hurt?"

"Of course not," Serendipity exclaimed, shocked.

"We don't have all the answers," Tareq added. "We're learning about Earth the same way Earth is learning about us. But we need to know, and soon, because it could make a difference."

Kanoa nodded slowly. "Fine. And thank you for asking first, I guess."

Serendipity made a slightly strangled sound of indignation and dismay.

"Kanoa," Owen said gently, "suggesting that anyone of the Eridani culture would violate your mind without consent is . . . uh . . . rude."

Kanoa's mouth tensed into a half-wry, half-impatient line. "I wouldn't know that, would I? It appears *some* things were left out of our dossier on Epsilon Eridani."

Naraldi cleared his throat, or maybe it was a cough to cover his amusement. "The day is yet young. Perhaps we can make up for some of the gaps in your education by showing you our memories of our encounter with the stranger in the depths?"

Kanoa stood up and smiled at him. "Was that really you in our VR, or just a physical imprint for the avatar?"

"An imprint only. I cannot be everywhere at once, although I have tried to be in the past. I do not recommend it."

Owen watched as Naraldi ushered Kanoa into the dome, feeling a deep relief as Kanoa went with willing curiosity.

"He's taking it fairly well," Tareq agreed in an aside.

"I hope he will be the norm and not the exception," Owen muttered.

"Do you need to worry about that? You've been very successful in breaking the news to your team."

"That was small-scale, and they had known me for some time. This is unprecedented, large-scale, and impersonal. I told Ixiaral not to do it this way, but she insisted that the Galactic Council could not delay."

"The Patrona was right," Tareq said in mild defense. "Look at how quickly the Lyran cartels are moving. If it weren't for the groundwork you laid, I'd say we've already been outmaneuvered."

"Kind of you," Owen replied, looking out at the horizon. "I just hope it will be enough."

Bay did not have claustrophobia. If she told herself that often enough, it would be true, and she would not feel some lucid portion of her brain screaming even as her body remained lax and her breathing measured. She was conscious, but it was an altered consciousness. From the little she knew, transits were supposed to be instantaneous, but did it matter what time you arrived when there was no way to measure the duration of the journey? When each breath could have taken a minute or a second? Or even—and she panicked even more at this—maybe her breath and her pulse were still racing but she perceived them as slowed and calmed, in a stretched-out sliver of time.

Sleep paralysis. She had never suffered from it, but she imagined it might feel like this: a trapped awareness frantically knocking on the inside walls of a flesh cocoon.

Fresh air and light hit her face like the slap of water thrown from a bucket. The restraints tugged tight briefly, the mask pressed in, and then everything released all at once, and she stumbled forward into a bright, green blur with her arms outstretched. Someone grabbed her seeking hands hastily and caught her up in a hug, speaking clashing, clanging sounds that merged with the blur of her vision.

"Hana?" Bay knew her sister; the body's physical memory could not be fooled, at least. The height of her, positioning her chin to Bay's ear; the hard, strong arms and the soft torso; the brush of hair strands against Bay's eyelashes. Even when the person stepped back a little and shook her slightly, that too was a familiar move. *Get a grip, Bay,* it said, and she silently replied, *I'm trying, Hana. I'm really trying.*

Other hands tugged her away and led her to a recliner. Feeling her way with anxious hands, she sank into it gratefully and closed her eyes. Minutes passed, and the background cacophony gradually resolved into words spoken, sensible phrases, conversations ongoing. She cautiously opened her eyes. Focus was returning, though images still looked a little fuzzy at the edges. When she turned her head, she knew in advance that Hana would be sitting there.

"That was scary," her sister huffed in annoyance, as if it were all Bay's fault.

"What . . . why . . . ?" Bay's lips did not yet feel as if they fully belonged to her.

"A bad reaction. Some people have them, in spite of all the precautions." This was a far more reasonable voice, and it belonged to the medic on the other side of the recliner. "I suggest you have Dr. Kuria redo your physiological calibration. That much offset isn't acceptable."

"Okay," Bay murmured vaguely, but Hana nodded firmly, as if she actually understood what was being said.

Bay's vision grew sharper and more capable of taking in the details before her, and the world began to make more sense. She was seated in a small, open area a few feet away from another hanging garden, this one installed under a high, arched ceiling of glass and VR paneling. Thiago and Yrsa were standing in conversation with Charyssa not far away, both occasionally giving her concerned looks as Charyssa spoke intently and at length to them on some matter.

The enclosure was a vast hall, a place she remembered well from many visits in the past. Headquarters of ParaVee, the largest and best virtual reality research and development company on Earth. Back then, in her recollection, it had always been busy with personnel at work and on the move from office to office and station to station, but now it *bustled,* finally able to show the full range of its capacity.

Another person joined the small group of refugees from Havana Headquarters. Noriko, her cousin and former manager of Owen's concerts, investments, and enterprises. She went straight to Charyssa and spoke briefly. With a quick hand grip and nod, Charyssa responded, apparently saying farewell. Her glance over to Bay, warm and apologetic, also felt like a leave-taking. Then she walked away, disappearing behind the hanging gardens.

Noriko went quickly to Bay, with Thiago and Yrsa following close behind. "Bay, how are you feeling? Can you get up?"

Bay slowly swung her body around to put her feet on the floor. "I think so. Is Charyssa . . . ?"

"Needed elsewhere. She's handed you all over to me." Noriko looked rueful for a moment, but not vexed, which for her was positively cheerful.

"Can you tell me what's going on?" Bay said plaintively, getting shakily to her feet. "Tell *us*. Thiago and Yrsa don't even know the little I know."

Noriko looked back at Bay's classmates. "Hmm, good point. Let's assign you some tech and lodgings. I'll tell you everything I know, starting from eleven years ago, in Paris. And then we'll discuss what Charyssa needs us to do."

ELEVEN

AFTER THE GALACTIC Council meeting when the captured Lyrans revealed the scale and duration of interference in Earth affairs,
after the representatives from Alpha Lyrae finally and formally issued
an apology for said interference (dodging a possible Second Galactic
War that no one wanted), after the expansion of the Antarctica base of
the Galactic Gendarmerie . . . after all that and more, the white-and-
gray palette became the standard for the Patrona's wardrobe.

The first year or two had provoked shock, the next few years brought
acceptance bordering on resignation, and now the colors were merely
ordinary fashion, their origins and meaning half-forgotten. So, too,
went the commonplace view of the ending of the Earth embargo. *Is it
really going to happen? Well, it's happening. Hey, hasn't it happened already?*

The Patrona, being at the heart of it, knew two things. One, there
was still much to do to safely end the embargo, and two, there were

other things unrelated to Earth that remained to be done. She delegated and delegated, but there was information that only she could see, and matters only she could decide. And so it was that with exquisite timing, when all her attention and energy should have been on helping to guide the Antarctica counterattack, Kelaihaneki from Intelligence came into her office and presented to her the answer to a forty-year mystery.

"We've traced her." The declaration was redundant, even distracting, as the Patrona was already scanning the report on her screen, but Kelaihaneki had been working on this case for almost eight years, and she would not blame him for feeling triumphant.

"Kelai, you're a seasoned intelligence officer, so I know you won't be offended when I say—you found her because she's ready to be found."

He smiled. At the start of his career, he had been one of the best of the bright young Hanekis, with people speculating that he might yet become the House's second Patron in history. But he was sufficiently self-aware to understand his strengths, and now he lived a quiet, ordinary life to cover his very extraordinary work. He was the closest thing the House had to an old-time spymaster.

"Of course, Patrona. She may have been protecting others before, and now . . ."

Now there were amnesties for deserters from the Eridanian military and quasi-military, and protections for women of Eridanian descent. Now there was a powerful diaspora of Eridanians who slowly but inexorably were defining a new culture and crafting a new self-image for the galaxy to see as quintessentially *them*.

". . . even now," Kelai continued, looking pensive, "there are still some dangers. But we are professionals. We can ask her if she wishes to be contacted, and how. We can ensure her safety."

The Patrona considered this for a while. The mystery of this woman's disappearance had been a burden on her brother's conscience for several years, and there were other friends and relatives who would be ecstatic to learn she was alive and well. But she could think of only one person who deserved to be the first to hear this news.

"Kelai, send your report via secure channel to this contact. If he needs help, assign an agent to him, one with trauma training. It *will* come as a shock. He's been searching for his wife for decades."

With a tap of a stylus, she sent across the information. He looked at his screen, nodded to acknowledge receipt, and walked briskly away. The Patrona had already refilled her screens with military dispatches by the time her latter-day spymaster departed to carry out her orders, but she could feel resentment tainting her satisfaction. This should have been a moment of pure celebration for so many people. Why did it have to happen when everyone was distracted by crisis?

She was so, so tired of this era of petty apocalypses.

NIGHT CAME AT last to the small island—cool, dark, sparkling with stars undimmed by any city's competing glare, and murmuring with the conversation of fauna and the movement of wind and wave.

Sleep also came, but not to all. Tareq had disappeared, and Kanoa knew by now not to question this in a universe of doors as well as distances. Owen and Serendipity were in the dome. Kanoa remained on the deck, and Naraldi stationed himself a few meters away. The bedrolls that Serendipity had given them were thin yet ridiculously comfortable, and the awning that was stretched overhead kept off any sprinkling of rain or dew—but Kanoa could not sleep.

"There's quite a legend attached to your avatar," he said out loud. His own words startled him. He had not intended to speak, but his head was filled with all the day's happenings, both the trivial and the momentous, and yet somehow what came to the surface was the bizarre fact that the VR creation he had seen in the Epsilon Eridani dossier was a real person.

"My avatar?" Naraldi repeated musingly to the night sky. "Yes. I lent my name and image to the Global Government Project years ago. I trust they have portrayed me with dignity? What does the legend say?"

"That you are the only Eridanian pilot to have traveled in time as well as space. Is that true?"

Naraldi paused and shifted to face Kanoa. "Yes, that is true."

"Other pasts and futures? Alternate universes? Is all that true as well?"

"More or less," the old pilot replied cautiously. "It doesn't do any good, you know. Anything can change for the slightest reason, and of my own universe and fate I am no more knowledgeable than you."

"Yet you speak a language of Earth well enough for my translator bug to give you no accent."

"Earth was a good place to hide, or to rest, when it was properly under embargo. In some eras, that rule was more respected than in others."

"So, you don't know what's going to happen . . . but I'm sure you have some good guesses."

Naraldi exhaled sharply in mild impatience. "Along with my name and my image, I also gave all my guesses to the Project years ago. Perhaps they will be useful, perhaps not, but those who have the skill to analyze such things have taken on the responsibility."

"I only want one guess from you, Naraldi. What do you think happened to my father?"

"Hmm," Naraldi murmured to himself. "Well, that is not such a bad question. The answer is a bit long, unfortunately, but perhaps a bedtime story is exactly what you need."

Kanoa turned over and around so that he was on his stomach, head toward Naraldi and the ocean. "Tell me."

"Did your training in Havana give you any information on the origin of the Eridanian ships?"

"Very little," Kanoa lied. He wanted to hear it all again from the real Naraldi.

"All of the human-origin planets are related, and there are several hypotheses but no clear reason why this should be the case. Our oceans, lands, and skies constitute biospheres that are identical in some respects, and merely similar in others. At times, there is a marked difference, some beast or plant beyond anything seen anywhere else in the known galaxy. The ships of Epsilon Eridani were categorized as such, and there are even more hypotheses to suggest that if they had not been a part of our evolution, we would have developed to be like the Austrinians, or even the Lyrans."

A small jolt of fear jerked Kanoa alert from the spell of Naraldi's soothing voice. "Wait—like the Austrinians and the Lyrans? We were never told that the Eridanians were telepaths. What haven't they told us about the Austrinians and Lyrans?"

"Perhaps that can be told another time?" Naraldi said in very gentle rebuke.

Kanoa subsided and tried to relax again.

"Our ships were intelligent leviathans whose origins and domain were the depths of the ocean. They might never have been discovered, except for their own curiosity about the humans who dwelled on islands and coasts. They hungered for us, and they consumed us in every sense. They became the center of myth and religion: the voices in our dreams, the sacrificial meat of our rituals, the resting place of our dead, and their resurrection thereafter. In time, science gave detail and logic to the wisdom of our ancestors, and we understood what it meant to join the collective consciousness and travel across the galaxy via dimensions previously unknown. A religion became a journeying, and the paths we traveled became the routes of our empire.

"The Austrinians and Lyrans created their own forms of transit, one organic, one mechanical. In all our travels, we never found a parallel evolution to match our ships."

"And in *your* travels?" Kanoa asked quietly, hesitant to break the flow of the old pilot's narration.

"I was only one person, and that was not my focus. When I was not hiding or resting, I was trying to find a way to restore my home, to change my past. Of course, that was impossible, but it took me a very long time to accept the lesson."

"What about Tareq?"

"Tareq is . . . a special case. Not even the first case of such a skill, but definitely an unusual product of a combination of blended traditions and new discoveries. I am not in a position to say any more than that."

And he didn't, and in the silence that followed, sometime in the early hours of morning and well before dawn, sleep found Kanoa at last.

Noriko gave them time to get properly settled. "After all," she said, "the world's been ending for a decade or so by now. You won't miss a thing if you skip a day."

Bay watched the news about a fresh salvo of missiles heading toward what was now being called "the Antarctica bubble," and she doubted Noriko's calm. But then Thiago, remarkably upbeat after his twenty-four hours of world-upending discoveries, told her that they would have to focus on what they *could* do instead of imagining all the stuff that they *should* do, and she was both irritated and reassured by his pragmatism.

Noriko backed up his words. "Antarctica is not our problem. Not yet. They've stuck a finger in the hornets' nest and all we have to do is watch the fun."

Who is they, Bay thought. *And why have I been underestimating my own family for years?*

She was tired enough after her transit that she kept her protests feeble and easily overruled. They were shown into an apartment in the ParaVee compound, provided with food to eat and clothes to wear, and given a series of orders.

"Tap into your Diplomatic Group accounts—the console in your apartment has access—and put together all your files, including the new ones from today. Sleep early, get rid of the time-zone lag. Get yourselves ready by nine tomorrow morning." Noriko then gave Bay the famous Don't Shame the Family Name stare that could always bring her to her metaphorical knees. "We have a lot of ground to cover in very little time, and a long haul ahead after you've been prepared. Make sure you do whatever you need to do to function at your highest levels."

For some people, that would have meant stimulants, all-nighters, and various other stunts to push the human mind and body to their limits. But Bay understood Noriko was telling her something different. She was warning her not to burn out, to pace herself for a marathon and not a sprint. The refrigerator and larder confirmed her suspicions— they had been stocked with all the basics but also with a range of herbal and synthetic supplements for alertness, relaxation, strengthening the immune system, and pain alleviation. Noriko was mostly traditional, but also practical; she would take whatever would give her an edge.

All their clothes were tailored with an accuracy that only a 3D VR scan could provide, and if Bay needed confirmation that the Global Government Project and ParaVee were basically operating from the same database, that was definitely it. Nothing in their wardrobe was frivolous, but it was impeccably designed. Everything was both formal and comfortable, fit for standing long hours before the media or stylishly running away from an assassin . . . or an army.

Yrsa looked at Bay oddly, and she realized her dark thoughts had manifested into a dark chuckle as she fingered the sleeve of a forest-green jacket hanging in her wardrobe.

"Have you visited the ParaVee campus before?" Bay asked as a diversion.

Yrsa's eyes lit up as she took the bait. "Once, as an intern, about three years ago, when they'd just opened up the new expansion. But it was a tourist tour, just the public areas. I never got this close to the heart of it. You?"

Bay didn't know what to answer. *Yes, even the heart of it, when I was a child and didn't quite comprehend that Uncle Peter was not only the richest man in the world but also the smartest?* "I've been here once or twice," she hedged. "Didn't hold the same meaning for me as it would have for you." She gave a quick, apologetic smile. "Not my specialty, though I definitely appreciate what you do."

Yrsa gave her a wan smile in response. They were being so kind to each other, holding on to little courtesies as a way of snatching stability in a topsy-turvy world. Yrsa took her tablet out of her pocket and frowned at it. "The transit wiped it clean. Everything—files, operating systems, applications, and sub-apps." She sighed deeply in frustration and settled it into a console dock for a full write-over from her accounts. "I was adding stuff just before we left. I hope it doesn't fall between the cracks."

Thiago bounced in, still relentlessly energetic, and caught the last two sentences. "There's more than a backup on our accounts. It's a completely new system, and we've got access to information I've only ever dreamed of! I don't know whose database we're attached to now, but who cares! We've leveled up! No wonder ParaVee was always ahead of its rivals. This *must* be alien tech."

"Let's not get ahead of ourselves," Bay said dully. "Wait for tomorrow's briefing, see what the real-world situation is. We're not in a simulation anymore, so I doubt it'll be that simple." She knew she was tired, and perhaps that excused her lack of enthusiasm, but also, somewhere at the back of her mind where she didn't have to fully admit it, she hated that her own family seemed to be so involved in this entire setup. Even if they were the good guys, even if it was all to benefit people on Earth, it felt like a little bit of a betrayal to learn about it so late. And yet . . . could she blame them? She'd been a teenager who couldn't even keep her cool when a pop star walked into the room. How would she have handled meeting someone who was not of Earth?

Thiago would probably spend half the night curled up with his new and improved tablet, scanning its screen in the dark and getting even more excited about his place in Earth's future. Yrsa's tablet was taking extra long to recover—how much *did* she have on that device? Entire VR proto-games under development, complete with protective securityware? She left for her bed with a longing, uncomfortable look at her still-inert tablet, muttering something about getting up early to tweak settings.

Bay needed no encouragement to sleep. Her night was dreamless and restful, and when she rose in the morning and stretched, she felt at last as if she were once more properly situated within her own skin.

Yrsa was already at the console, as expected. Thiago was still asleep.
Only 6:30—no need to drag him out of bed yet. Bay showered, put on
one of the dressed-to-kill-or-be-killed suits provided, and opened the
fridge door with hunger and hope. Fresh fruit and herbal tea to start,
she decided, and moved herself and her meal to the breakfast bar.

"Your tablet's not ready?" she asked Yrsa, who was still stationed at
the console.

"It's . . . ready . . ." Yrsa said, speaking with the slow, halting words
of one fully immersed in some difficult task. "I'm just . . . wondering
something . . ."

Bay munched, sipped, and watched her with interest, but there
was no more forthcoming. She reached for her own tablet, fully restored from the previous day, and checked the news. There was . . . a
lot. Religious riots in various countries, with at least three different
major religions reacting in accordance with their own version of the
apocalypse. Problem was, there were more differences within than between. Aliens could be angels or demons, messengers with the word of
God or deceivers with the mandate of hell. The trick was finding out
where they were hiding. It could be a neighbor, a boss, or a friend.

"Oh shit," she said with feeling. The image of the Patrona had been
remarkable not for the style of her clothes nor the sound of her voice,
but for her unusual height. "Oh shit," she said again. "They're targeting
tall people."

"What?" Yrsa said testily, still distracted.

"Look. They had to rescue an entire basketball team from a mob in
Upper Florida."

"Seriously?" Yrsa said, glancing up and finally paying attention. She
turned back to her tablet, this time checking for the information Bay
had just told her. "Seriously. What the hell?"

It was not clear, the news report said, whether the crowd of people
had wished to beg the players for miracles or kill them.

"'Law enforcement officers appealed for calm while representatives of government gave assurances that they are working diligently to
unmask any infiltrators,'" Bay read aloud.

"Meaning to say they don't have a clue," Yrsa muttered.

"Oh, don't be so sure. In England they're dismissing it as an elaborate prank by the Celtic Union to lower morale, and they've threatened to censor any reports on it."

Yrsa scoffed. "Right now England couldn't censor my ass. They were next on my list of 'most likely to have been infiltrated by aliens.'"

Bay kept skimming the headlines and news digests. "Hysteria on one end of the scale . . . indifference on the other. Well, good luck with this global government thing we're trying, when we can't even agree on if we're being invaded or not."

Yrsa looked up again with a quick, bright smile. "Dig deeper. I've been chatting with some colleagues. It's not all flailing about out there. Some people are actually thinking."

Bay immediately joined her at the console, and they spent almost an hour with heads together, comparing messages and discussing. Thiago suddenly and noisily got up and flung himself about in a raging hurry because it was less than twenty minutes before pickup time. His excitement, once positive, was now pure nerves and entirely contagious, which was why Noriko arrived to find the three of them sitting on the sofa in a tense little row, silent and grim-faced, awaiting orders as if about to go to their deaths.

"It's not as bad as all that," she told them, mildly surprised. "Yes, we have a lot to do, but it isn't like we're not *prepared*."

They followed her docilely into an elevator capsule that carried them a few floors down before turning a corner to continue on a long sideways slide. The capsule's front VR panel, set to transparency instead of display mode, showed the top of the glittering greenhouse roof of the main hall, and beyond that another long curve of glass-paneled offices and dwellings dripping with greenery at the balconies and reflecting the sunlight in all directions.

"Are we going to see Uncle Peter?" Bay blurted out, without thinking how unprofessional it might sound.

"Yes, and Hana, and a lot of other people. I'm glad you're all looking presentable." Noriko's appraising gaze flickered a little over Thiago's haste-creased suit and misaligned fastenings, but instead of amending her words, she merely changed the panel to mirror mode and made a show of checking her own appearance. "Presentable means persuasive, and we are going to have to do a lot of persuading over the next few days."

They took the hint and adjusted their clothing to neatness and their expressions to confidence. The capsule slowed and opened, and the group of four strode out with purpose into a sizable meeting room with one long wall entirely of translucent panel, a glass-paneled table that was very likely also display-capable, ten chairs positioned around it, and four other people standing in quiet conversation.

This time, when Bay saw the familiar faces in the meeting room, she kept her composure. Greeting in order of seniority, she went first to a distinguished man dressed entirely in white who was leaning idly against the wide window opposite the elevator, ensuring that he had a good view of all who entered.

"Doctor Hendrix. An honor and a pleasure, sir."

"Little miss, why so formal with your old uncle?" he said with a light chuckle and a warm hug.

Bay smiled with sincere happiness. He looked well, and he displayed no sign of augmentation or masking. That was a sign of trust and intimacy, and she appreciated it. Peter Hendrix was not a Kaneshiro, neither by blood nor marriage, but he had become more than blood in spiritual kinship and mutual interest.

"Let me see your young friends," he continued, fixing the two with a narrow, calculating stare. "Yrsa Helgadóttir, a most promising apprentice to my former protégé Björk Jónsbur. Thiago Mendes, who has bright potential in his own right, but we should not overlook his older brother Paolo Cardoso, cofounder of CostaCardoso, my partners in the development of VR applications for governance. Glad to have you both here."

Yrsa and Thiago did the sensible thing when faced with someone who knew far too much about them and their origins—they smiled politely; spoke brief, courteous thanks in turn; and then shut up, though Bay heard Thiago mutter under his breath, "Half brother . . . much older."

"No Dylan?" Hendrix then asked in an aside to Noriko. She merely shook her head.

Bay noted quietly that he had not asked about Kanoa. That situation, at least, appeared to be known to them, and she was guessing it meant he was probably still with Owen. Perhaps she could ask Noriko to send word to him, some small encouragement and reassurance that they were still all in this together.

Hendrix gestured to the three others in the room. "Let me introduce my colleagues. Professor Emeritus Dorian MacLeod, specialist in political analysis and valued consultant to ParaVee; Professor Naomi-Joy Addo, Chair of New Economics at Oxford International University; and Hana Kaneshiro, who is a wizard of virtual currencies, a board member of Kaneshiro-Hendrix Finance, and Bay's older sister."

Bay joined her classmates in greeting the professors and gave Hana a quiet nod. She was pleased to see her sister, but apart from Uncle Peter, they weren't a huggy family when about to do business.

Led by Hana and Noriko, they took seats around the table. Hendrix took the head of the table, and his eyes leisurely swept the room, from the now-closed door, across the occupied chairs, to the view outside the long, wide window.

At last, he sighed and began. "This must be a very confusing time for you, so it seems only fair to ask you first if you have any questions."

Bay sat peacefully as a few seconds ticked by, then straightened on a jolt of adrenaline as her sister shot her a meaningful glare. "I have a question. Who is for us, and who is against us?"

"That's a good place to begin," Noriko replied. "The Cygnians, the Austrinians, and the Cygnian Eridanians and their pilots are for us. Most of the Geminorans are for us, but that can be murky. One of the Lyran planets is on our side, but cartels in the rest of the Alpha Lyrae system have been steadily undermining and exploiting Earth for about two centuries. As for the Eridanians at Alpha Centauri . . . we don't have a lot of information on them. They were here on Earth about forty or fifty years ago, but they packed up and disappeared after they were discovered."

"Just like they taught us," Thiago spoke with quiet, suppressed excitement. "Is that how ParaVee took over the VR industry? Borrowing from Lyran technology?"

Hendrix slowly turned his head to regard Thiago, and the very air in the room seemed to grow heavy and cold. "Lyran technology? You think that ParaVee's success, that *my* success, is because of alien technology? You think they offered us baubles and trinkets and worthless bits in exchange for the keys to our city gates?"

He got up, walked across the room, perched himself on the edge of the table between Yrsa and Thiago, and glared down at the young man, who had begun to sweat. "We gained knowledge! We were given nothing; we stole nothing. We observed, we learned, and we innovated! I confess it, in the first five years or so, we struggled to take it all in, but since then? ParaVee is recognized as a cutting-edge *galactic* company." The last sentence clicked and spat with fierce pride from his lips as he cocked his head to deliver another angle of glare to Thiago's shrinking, shamed countenance.

Hendrix flung out a hand to Professor Addo. "I needed to learn how a postcapitalist, interstellar economy with limited trade volume could develop from our quasi-feudal corporate empires and oligarchic systems of government!"

The imperious hand waved to Hana Kaneshiro. "Trading in data and digital art was easy. Getting *paid* in a usable currency—that was where the Kaneshiro genius was needed!"

He sighed and got to his feet again, calming his intensity as he went to Professor MacLeod and dropped an affectionate hand on the man's shoulder, a gesture that was acknowledged with a smile of warm admiration. "And, although I am an old man who will not see many more years, I wanted ParaVee . . . I wanted *Earth* to flourish and do well, not only in the present, but for many centuries to come. I am a child of the consequences of colonization, the cast-off of various manifest destinies. I know the cost of recovery, the generations and effort it takes to first survive and then overcome. I needed an analyst with foresight to show me where we might be weak and where we could be strong, so we could prepare ourselves for the coming fight."

Peter Hendrix seated himself once more at the head of the table. "We will not come to their table uncouth and ignorant, to be discounted or treated like children. A global government must be formed. You are the seed we planted. Now it is time to see the fulfillment of that promise."

Addo, who had been watching Hendrix rant with a mixture of amusement and approval, addressed the group. "Professor MacLeod and I are former instructors for the Global Government Project. We have sent out messages to five years' worth of alumni, informing them of the situation, and we have so far received replies from approximately 170 out of 247."

"Not all of them are able to join us, for various reasons, personal and professional," MacLeod continued, "but those who can will be meeting with us, either via VR or in the flesh."

"You are the first class with a Diplomatic Group," Noriko told them. "You'll carry a greater burden as a result."

"You will notice," Hendrix said loudly, "that when you arrived I made note of both your intrinsic worth to the project and your external connections. Everyone who has participated in the Global Government Project has a tie that we plan to leverage." He smiled slyly. "We have a lot of persuading to do, and sometimes the quickest way to manage that is among kindred. Elders do not mind so much if it looks as if their sons and daughters are taking their place and—"

Yrsa interrupted him boldly. "International nepotism? *That's* your plan?"

Hendrix spread his hands and widened his smile to a wicked grin. "It has worked so well in the past. Why change tactics now? We will have to spend another century or so striving for true meritocracy, but today is not that day."

He stood up. "Bay, Thiago, Yrsa, I need you to work with Professor MacLeod and develop a schedule of talks, starting with those countries and companies that remain free of infiltration and with the strongest links to Global Government alumni. I will also provide you with the names of executives and officials who are fully aware of our present reality. Some will have learned very recently; others have been working with us for years. Noriko will ensure you have everything you need."

They all rose to their feet, and Noriko moved to the doorway to usher them out, but Bay noticed that Hana and Professor Addo stayed behind. Uncle Peter gave her a wink as she glanced back over her shoulder at him, unable to hide her curiosity.

"More work," Yrsa grumbled as the elevator capsule carried them away.

"You heard what he said," Bay replied patiently. "We're the first and only Diplomatic Group. We have to represent our world to a galaxy full of civilizations that people just learned about and barely even believe in."

"That's taken care of."

"What?" Noriko and Bay said in unison, turning to stare into Yrsa's smug expression.

Coolly defiant, she replied, "This morning, or rather late last night, Dylan released my newest game. It's a free, bootleg version based on our training scenarios. I wasn't able to capture the fine detail of the avatars, but I harvested all the planetary data and repackaged it." She took out her tablet, which was seething with incoming notifications, and displayed it triumphantly to their shocked eyes. "Apparently it's already very popular. One hundred thousand connections and counting."

"What were you *thinking*!" Bay exploded. Yrsa stepped back, tucked her tablet against her jacket, and raised one hand slightly to deflect any physical attack, but her self-satisfied smile remained in place.

Noriko laughed. She laughed loudly and carelessly and for so long that Yrsa's smile froze and then slowly transformed to a resentful moue.

Finally, Noriko calmed and found her voice. "Were you expecting us to be angry? No, no punishment, but no medals either. All that information is already available in every device and information application made by ParaVee. Peter unlocked the feature yesterday. But your way works too. A little redundancy can only help us at this stage."

"I'm wondering how long it will take before people think that the broadcast from the Patrona was just an elaborate piece of ParaVee marketing," Bay grumbled.

"Oh, they think that already, but they won't think that for long," Noriko said cheerfully as the elevator doors opened into the main hall. "Am I right, Professor?"

MacLeod was the last to exit the capsule, his mien distracted. He tapped his bug in explanation as he replied, "You are right, Madame. The extractions and arrests have begun."

The main hall of ParaVee was glass where it was not green, and almost every flat surface, and a few curved ones, was display-capable. The group walked into a cacophony of a world on fire. One screen showed a baffled reporter in Paris speaking of the sudden disappearance of nine corporate jets in-flight. Another presented a news medley from the United States of Greater Texas, where a number of politicians had arrived in their offices with three months or more of amnesia and utter disbelief at the laws and decisions they had implemented during that lost time. Throughout Southern Europe and Northern Africa, key government aides had disappeared, and when their houses and offices were searched for clues, strange artifacts surfaced whose materials proclaimed them to be of exosolar origin.

Yrsa stood next to Bay, tablet aloft at eye level so she could look at her notifications and the ParaVee screens at the same time. "Five hundred thousand. Six. Damn, I should have charged people one bit for this. Half a bit. I'd be stinking rich. Seven point five hundred thousand. Nine."

"I'm not sure how to feel about this anymore," Thiago moaned. He made a neat turn to his left and, with every effort at restraint, vomited tidily into a plant pot.

TWELVE

KANOA STRETCHED, YAWNED, and pushed himself up onto his elbows. He felt the mild buzz of having slept too little combined with the restlessness of a habit of early rising. He might hope for naps later, but for now his body insisted that he get up and get fed.

"Good morning." Owen was sitting on the edge of the deck, dressed casually in his white T-shirt and a faded purple sarong. He looked surprisingly relaxed, as if all this were merely a vacation.

"I didn't dream," Kanoa confessed, disappointed.

"Not that *you* recall," Naraldi corrected.

Kanoa twisted himself around and sat up. Naraldi was a few feet behind him, kneeling on a folded bit of red cloth and with his hands placed neatly on his thighs in a meditation pose.

"The little we were able to detect from you was intriguing but not enlightening, which brings us to our next step."

"Step three would be kinder," Owen commented.

Naraldi flashed him a look of exasperation. "While *some* people have difficulties engaging their conscious minds with a ship, it's not a common occurrence." He focused on Kanoa, and his gaze radiated a gentle reassurance. "Would you like to meet my ship?"

Less than an hour later, as he gasped and flailed on the nearby sand while Serendipity sympathetically patted his back, Kanoa decided that the answer was demonstrably "no."

"Thought so," Owen said neutrally, in the manner of a scientist merely making an observation. "I suspect it's more common in people from Earth than you realized."

"Hmm. I should test that out thoroughly when I have leisure," Naraldi mused. Owen looked at him, alarmed, and he quickly amended, "Now is not the time, of course."

"Step three?" Serendipity prompted.

"Step three," Naraldi agreed. "We must sail out into open ocean and hope for an answer."

"I'm not sure of the question?" Kanoa asked timidly.

"If there is intelligent life evolving in the depths, we have a case for protecting them. Likely a new, more rigorously enforced Earth embargo. At the very least, it would buy you time to build a government and join the Galactic Council as equals," Serendipity explained.

"And if there are *civilizations* in the depths," said Owen, his voice taking on an almost reverent resonance, "they have every right to be represented in the galaxy as well."

"Of course, it might all be a wild-goose chase," Naraldi admitted. "But, if so, it's one that keeps Owen out of danger and well protected."

Kanoa saw a brief annoyance pass over Owen's face and thought he understood. It was one thing to know you were being managed by your friends and colleagues, and quite another thing to hear it so clearly and cheerfully expressed, with no pretense at preserving the illusion of choice.

"Why does Owen need to be protected?" He spoke the question idly in an attempt to divert from the slight tension Naraldi's words had created.

Instead, unexpectedly, a weightier silence descended. Owen broke it with a shrug and a joke. "Perhaps they're protecting the world from me."

Serendipity lowered her eyes. Naraldi frowned. Neither said anything.

A lower chamber of Serendipity's dome housed a lovely, light craft with three hulls and a solar sail. The moment he laid eyes on it, the last reserves of Kanoa's disbelief evaporated. He was neither a specialist nor a hobbyist in sailcraft, but the ocean and all its modes of human interaction were the warp and weft of his life, the invisible air that he had breathed since birth. No one on Earth could have made this boat, not as a prototype, nor even as a model for some VR fantasy or future world. The sleek, efficient design; the strange etchings that could have been either meaningful symbols or artistic decor; the textures and colors of unfamiliar materials—it was truly otherworldly and wonderful.

"Cygnian craft," said Owen, looking pleased at Kanoa's awe. "Old Earth's technology blended with modern galactic techniques. When all this is over, I can put you in touch with the suppliers."

"I'm not rich," Kanoa choked out, wistfully stroking the lines as he walked the boat's length. "I could never afford something like this."

Owen frowned. "Oh? Well, credit works a little differently in the galaxy. You'd be surprised at what might be considered a fair trade."

"He doesn't understand," Serendipity told Owen.

"He should," Owen replied forcefully. "Kanoa, you learned in Havana how costly and inefficient it is to move inanimate matter through interstellar distances. You already have rudimentary 3D printing on Earth. Don't you understand by now that the main galactic trade is in data, not material? Offer a bit of previously unknown Old Earth history, or a unique craft design of your own, and that should constitute

enough credit to get single-copy rights to this design. Better yet, partner with ParaVee and get rights for a limited run, and ParaVee will do
the full construction for you, personal adaptations included."

When Kanoa listened to Owen talk about the vastly expanded
boundaries of the universe, he felt the thrill of the unknown, like a
five-year-old shaking wrapped presents on a birthday morning, anticipating things wished for and things beyond imagination. A day ago he
had thought himself surrounded by beings like himself; today he was
in a boat not made on Earth, surrounded by people not born on Earth,
journeying to the middle of the ocean to call on the ghost of his father.
And then the thrill became a tingling frisson of fear, and the deep
breath of wonder he had been about to draw thickened in his chest and
choked his throat closed.

His hand clenched briefly, and then he quickly collected himself.
There was something vaguely indecent about being visibly upset in
front of people who could read your dreams and goodness knew what
else.

"Here," said Naraldi, and Kanoa had no idea what he was referring
to, but in that moment Serendipity touched controls that slowly
brought the boat to a wide turn and stop. The swells, which had not
been high to start with, disappeared completely. Kanoa was briefly
confused until he saw the grayness of the water beneath them and
understood that Naraldi's ship was stationed just below, dampening
the waves for them and protecting them from any unpleasant surprises.

"They *can* come to the shallows," Naraldi explained quietly. "They
came close to the shore to take your father. One simply has to pique
their curiosity."

Kanoa's breaths were once more even and calm. Slowly, following
an instinct that he could not explain, he moved from his seat to lie full-
length on the deck, his arms spread wide on either side and his head
turned and pressed into the warm, smooth surface beneath him. The
self-consciousness he had felt before, mid–panic attack, no longer
seemed to apply. He was trying to listen with his entire being. He was

trying to sense the layers beneath him: boat and water and living ship, and more water. *Here I am,* he spoke as clearly as he could, with every part of himself except lips, tongue, and vocal cords. His fingers flexed hard on the deck and he exhaled deeply, pushing his spirit out with that breath.

Silence.

A familiar touch drew Kanoa back to himself. He was sitting up but could not recall when he had moved. He turned in the direction of the hand on his shoulder, unsurprised to find his father sitting beside him.

"We can talk while they're talking," his father said calmly, withdrawing his hand unhurriedly.

Kanoa nodded with equal calm, as if everything made sense, as if the warmth and solidity of his father's callused hand were something mundane and not miraculous. The wood below him pulsed with the pull of the waves, like a breathing skin. They looked at each other for a while in silence, and then, finally, his father spoke first. "How are you doing?"

"Fine," Kanoa replied immediately. Ridiculous! How could anything in the last few volatile months be described as *fine?* But it was not a lie—he was managing, and at times it was even weirdly enjoyable, like a ride on an unpredictable wave that might kill you, but then again, it might not.

Perhaps his father understood all that from the single stock word, because he responded with a rare, fond smile that made Kanoa feel a sudden warmth in his chest.

"And you?" Kanoa prompted with automatic, inane courtesy.

"I like it here," his father replied simply. "There's a lot to see and do."

With those few words exchanged, they again fell silent. Just as in the past, their worlds remained somewhat opaque to each other. And yet it was better bridged; a different light illuminated their being and connected their mutual gaze.

The breathing deck shifted—or the universe did. The attentiveness in his father's eyes turned inward for a moment, then once more focused on him. "You have to go. Come see me when you have time."

Kanoa gave a murmur of assent, and then he felt a profound disorientation. The wood shifted again, tugging at his sense of reality as it moved. He was no longer sure where his body was, or what it was doing. The uncertainty gradually faded into utter oblivion, but before it all vanished, Kanoa was aware of bright points of light on the horizon, a distant sound of sweet-toned music, and a sensation like a cool, rough kiss brushing his brow.

Owen watched curiously as Kanoa got down close to the deck, almost trying to burrow through to the sea with nothing but his bare fingertips. *Would that work?* he wondered. Perhaps they should toss Kanoa directly into the water and let the scent of him pervade their environs, like any good bait.

And then Serendipity and Naraldi both cried out, the boat rocked and slapped the water as the ship beneath them shuddered, and Kanoa stiffened briefly in a seizure. Owen rushed to his side, but before he could reach him, Kanoa collapsed like a fresh corpse. No . . . not at all a corpse, because he briskly sat up and stared hard into Owen's concerned face before turning away to glare at Serendipity and Naraldi. Serendipity appeared too shocked to speak, but Naraldi stretched out a hesitant hand to Kanoa and started to say something.

Kanoa's mouth opened.

The voice hit Owen like a splash of freezing water all over his body, waking up his nerve endings in a painful itch. He tried to shake it off with a gasp, in much the same way as one blows bravely through the start of a cold shower, but he was right beside Kanoa and there was no sheltering from this.

Naraldi held himself still under the onslaught, fumbled for a reply, and ended up saying nothing. Kanoa slumped a little, fetched up against the side of a storage trunk, and began to drool. Serendipity was the first to react sensibly; she took a blanket out of that same trunk and draped it over Kanoa. The young man blinked and looked at her sleepily. "Thank you," he mumbled.

His eyes suddenly narrowed and he looked past her to focus once more on Owen. "Not God."

Invisible lightning sizzled from Kanoa and through Owen's body from skin to bone, but the vocal vibration had been tempered. Perhaps they were learning. "No, not God," Owen replied softly, answering with an uncanny thrum in his voice.

Kanoa's stern expression relaxed, but his words still crackled. "Not Gods. If you remain so, so return to us."

Owen lowered his head in a slight nod of acceptance.

On the way back, Kanoa slowly came to his senses. The light and color in his view acquired perspective and solidity and meaning until the concepts of *ocean, boat, people,* coalesced once more in his brain. He noticed the smell of the salt spray and laboriously attached it to the concept of *ocean.* The sounds in his ears settled into separate areas of attention. Water and air moving—background. The noises of the boat as it traveled—background. Voices saying words, words addressed to him—shouldn't he be understanding them? He was sitting, leaning forward in an accidentally attentive posture, and probably had been for some time. He was even nodding as he became finally, fully alert mid-conversation.

Owen was explaining what had just happened and how it had appeared to him. "You went completely limp. Then you sat up and spoke to Naraldi in ceremonial Eridanian, which, by the way, I only know because I have heard my uncle speak it a few times in preparation for meditation."

Kanoa was speechless. His head had the heavy, weary feeling of an overlong nap. He kept looking blankly at Owen, feeling a little lost, and saw Owen's expression melt from awe to sympathy. "Did you see your father?" Owen inquired gently.

What could Kanoa reply? That for a moment he had felt the blood of his ancestors in the salt water and the bones of his ancestors in the coral rock? That he had not *seen* his father because for a moment he had *been* his father?

Naraldi came to his rescue, admonishing Owen gently, "Speak with him later. For now he is a little unmoored in time."

"Say nothing of this." The words rasped from Kanoa's throat, driven out like the ghost of a banished presence.

Had his mouth moved? But the words vibrated in the air with their own life and energy, impossible to deny, request and command bound up together. Owen looked stricken.

"I will say nothing." His answer shook the air with a similar resonance, reply and surrender.

All three remained quiet for a long while as they skimmed in the gentle wake of Naraldi's ship. Serendipity broke the silence at last. "I think I understand a little better now why the pilots decided to leave Earth alone . . . and why they do not speak of it."

Kanoa felt strangely at peace. Whatever had happened, whatever part he or those who followed him might play in the future, he was neither impatient nor afraid. He had shaken the mystery for a brief moment, and learned enough to leave it wrapped in secrecy until the appointed time.

Tareq was waiting to welcome them when they sailed into the bay. They put Kanoa to bed inside the dome so he could sleep his way back to normality, and then they gathered on the deck to speak freely.

"Did you find what you were looking for?" she asked.

"Yes," said Owen. "And yet, somehow, also no."

"You understood what he said to me?" Naraldi asked Owen. "And *how* he said it?"

"A declaration of intent. 'I *do* not; I *am.*' Or, to expand for better meaning, 'I find myself not in activity, but in being.' A ritual reminder to quiet oneself before meditation."

Naraldi nodded. "Between that and the prohibition they have placed on you, I would say that our friends below decline to be involved in your plans at this time. Though I think you should be flattered that they invited you to return."

"Not flattery," Owen said bleakly. "A warning. They know the dangers I am facing, the dangers I confront every day. They are offering me a way out."

If he had hoped they would ask him to clarify, he was disappointed. Naraldi merely gazed at him, as if he were considering whether his caution was greater than his curiosity. Serendipity had barely spoken, her eyes were unseeing, and her focus was turned inward, contemplating. Tareq looked away from all of them, but Owen could tell from her stillness that she was alert and waiting for the next order, the next destination.

"They are very old—no, more than old. Timeless." Something in Serendipity's voice made Owen look at her more closely. He recognized that dreamy smile, that intimate warmth in her tone. She had seen them only a little, and already she loved them. "They move at their own pace, and for their own purposes. They remind me a little of the Eridanian ships, but so much in them is familiar! They have tasted our lives, our histories. They already know us. Already I can hear their voices more clearly, and feel their welcome.

"No, they will not interfere in our matters, but if what I sense is right, we already have a shared past, and we will have a shared future."

Owen watched her in amazement as she glowed like a saint after a visitation. Sometimes he forgot that Serendipity's heritage was both Earth and Epsilon Eridani.

"Where next?" Tareq asked him softly, ending the moment with a cold dash of reality.

Owen hesitated on what should have been an easy answer. "Back to Havana," he said at last. "Naraldi, Tareq, would you be so kind as to guide Kanoa through the transit to ParaVee? I'll join you later." He did not have to say it aloud; they all knew Serendipity was staying.

"Where are *you* going?" Tareq asked, a worried edge to her voice.

Owen gripped her shoulder reassuringly. "I need to speak to the Patrona. I won't be long, I promise."

*   *   *

Havana Headquarters had transformed overnight from institute of learning to war camp. New administrative buildings surrounded the transit wall, and temporary barracks nearby housed gendarmes and equipment pouring in from the Antarctica base. Kanoa's sense of dislocation was complete—when he looked at it he could barely imagine the vaguely boring place they had known as students.

"We can still take you home," Owen offered, looking at him with concern.

"No," Kanoa answered quickly. "Too many questions from everyone if I go home, and I have some questions of my own to answer. I'll stick with my group for now."

"Good," Owen said with satisfaction. "Your friends need you. We need you."

"Don't be long," Tareq reminded him. "Or I'll come get you."

"Save your strength," Owen chided. "I'll be at the ParaVee transit before you know it."

Mind-reading without asking first might be considered rude, but it looked like some things were so obvious that they were seen as fair game. The atmosphere was stern and significant as both Tareq and Naraldi stared at Owen. Kanoa couldn't swear to it, but he felt they were both worried that Owen wasn't coming back . . . and that made Kanoa start to worry too.

There was no time. First they saw off Owen, who was centrally placed in the transit wall for the trip to Alpha Piscis Austrini. "He's the strongest nexus they have, after all," Naraldi mused aloud, a comment that Kanoa only slightly understood and noted with great care for further investigation. Odd, and very disconcerting, that he would now need to study in depth all the material that was once the responsibility of others in the group. The gulf between a training simulation and real-life survival was vast indeed.

Then, after the wall's shield reversed and the passenger capsules reemerged open and empty, it was their turn to be pinned to the wall like specimens on a board. "Direct to ParaVee," Naraldi told their nexus firmly. "We have an unquarantined passenger who is *not* cleared for galactic travel. No mistakes, please."

I'm the alien, Kanoa thought with a sudden lurch of panic in his chest. *This is their normal. I'm the outlier.*

And then his world quietly dissolved.

The transit terminals of the Janojya Equatorial Belt were always busy, though not yet as busy as the suborbital cities, with their links to easier ways of moving large masses of matter. Where the orbital ring banked on trade in raw, physical goods, the transit terminals specialized in people and information, and kept them sectioned off carefully by place of origin and political importance.

The section dedicated to transits from Earth was small, private, and strategically close to key routes. A swift shuttle in one direction took you to Port of Janojya—surface entry to the suborbital city of Terminal 5 and, beyond that, the orbital ring. The opposite route went to Old Janojya, capital of Alpha Piscis Austrini and, some argued, of the entire galaxy, an ancient dome of climate refuge in which the Austrinian civilization had made a cozy bunker for survival in an extreme ice age.

However, if you had been vetted and cleared to a certain level of security, a series of elevator capsules located in a secret foyer would transport you by a winding, unknowable route to the fastness of the Galactic Council Hall and its administrative offices.

Owen was at such a level, and he went with confidence to his sister's offices, knowing that word of his arrival would reach her long before he did. The door opened obediently to the brush of his hand, he walked in briskly, and then his confidence stumbled slightly.

"Speak of the devil," said Charyssa. She looked very tired and a little bit annoyed, but still, underneath all that, glad to see him.

His sister, relaxed and familiar without her Council robes of state, eyed him with resignation and amusement. She got to her feet and hugged him. Owen wasn't especially tall even by Earth standards, but

Ixiaralhaneki, Patrona of House Haneki, was taller than any basketball player and always made him feel like a small child.

"Why are you here?" she asked bluntly. "Don't you have work to do?"

"He's dithering," Charyssa said drily. "I recognize the signs."

Owen thought, not for the first time, that he had a knack for discovering people with great talent, often marked by their utter inability to be in awe of him. "I appreciate you, Charyssa," he replied with similar dryness. "And yes, I have questions, although I wouldn't call that 'dithering,' precisely. You've advanced the schedule, Ixiaral, and I'm just trying to keep up."

"Our hand was forced by the attack on the Antarctica base," Ixiaral admitted, "but apart from that, the extraction process is going well. Is there a problem with your part of the process?"

Owen looked at her, tried to speak, and sealed his lips firmly shut instead. He sighed and looked apologetically at Charyssa. "May I speak privately with my sister?"

Charyssa raised her eyebrows in pure curiosity, but she nodded and quickly left the room. Ixiaral did what she would never do in public and half knelt, half sat before Owen on the floor as if indeed about to listen to a small child.

"*Officially,* no one on Earth must know about this," he began.

She nodded slowly, waiting.

"*Practically,* it is already known by a select few. I have been asked not to speak of it."

"Asked?" Her voice held a lilt of amusement.

Owen smiled in response. "Demands were made, but you know that has never worked on me. Still, I would like to honor the request with a certain amount of discretion in who I tell."

Directly and simply, he related all that he had learned about the entities living in the depths of Earth's oceans and their connection to humanity through the spirits of the dead. He reminded the Patrona of the origins of the Eridanian ships and the possibilities inherent in their parallel evolution. "They may represent a new form of dimensional travel via collective consciousness," he reasoned. "But for now, they don't wish to be disturbed, and they don't want to be involved."

Ixiaral stretched out her long legs and leaned against the wall, her face thoughtful. "That's very interesting. Who knows what they could become in the future? But . . . that *is* in the future. It's not a problem for now, and I don't see what's so urgent that you had to come all the way from Earth to tell me about it."

Speechless, Owen stared at her, not bothering to hide his dismay and frustration. She examined his appalled expression clinically. "Oh. I see. You wanted them to be your solution. To do your work for you." She kicked him lightly in the ankle. "Stay the course. I need this to be over soon. We do *not* have the resources to take responsibility for Earth. Beta Geminorum is still a divided world, and our allies in the Alpha Lyrae system need all our support. The Lyran cartels will be quiet for a while now that we've stopped them from sucking Earth dry, but the Eridanians on Alpha Centauri cannot be overlooked. What's to stop them making a strong claim to be Earth's guardians?"

"They're more concerned with the disappearance of their pilots."

"They'll adapt," Ixiaral warned. "You can't rely on an opponent's weakness or distraction for too long. No, our plan is sound. Earth needs to be our ally and equal, not our colony."

Owen looked at his feet in silence.

"You can't be afraid of this, not after all this time. Do you honestly believe you won't be able to walk away afterward?"

"I—" he began.

"You have the greatest self-control I have ever encountered in a human being. Your only problem is you get bored. You have a traveler's spirit, ever in the vanguard. Mother always had to find new challenges for you, until even being Patron wasn't enough."

"That's not—"

"And you keep punishing yourself in advance for a failure that never happens! Promise me something. When this is over, reward yourself by doing something selfish and self-indulgent. Just for yourself, no benefit to anyone else, as frivolous or serious as you please."

"I didn't come here for a pep talk," he said weakly.

She regarded him soberly for a while. "Yes, I can see that it's not helping." She got to her feet, frowned at him, and put a heavy hand on his shoulder. "I promise you this. If you deviate from what we agreed, if you show any inclination whatsoever toward becoming a dictator, I will kill you myself. Better?"

Owen inhaled sharply. Ixiaral might speak lightly, but even her jesting was meaningful. Paradoxically, he felt his back straighten, eased of an invisible burden. "Thanks. But I don't want to be any trouble. You're a very busy woman. Just send an assassin."

"You're a Haneki, and my brother. I'm not going to execute you like a common criminal. I will give you a glorious death."

They laughed together, far too much for such mild humor, exactly enough for the stress and exhaustion of their work. Ixiaral pulled herself together and tapped him lightly on the cheek with two fingers, the gesture of a senior gently chastising a junior.

"Return to your post," she said. "I *am* a very busy woman. Send Charyssa back in when you go. We were talking about diplomacy, trade, and other aspects of Earth's future. Make sure there will *be* a future."

Owen stepped out of the office to see Charyssa standing nearby, close enough to hear if she was called, far enough to be out of eavesdropping range. She looked anxious, which was unusual for her. The wrinkles at the corners of her mouth deepened and her eyes were wide and alert with tension.

"Is everything all right?" she asked him immediately.

"Yes. Yes, it will be," Owen said, trying to match his sister's certainty.

Charyssa saw through him, of course. Her entire face softened into a smile and she rested a hand on his shoulder, much like Ixiaral had done, but lightly. "You do realize this isn't all on you?"

He blinked at her, not quite in realization, but in a kind of relief that there was someone who didn't see him as the only way out. Ixiaral had assured him that he would not fail, but here was Charyssa, letting him know that even if he did, it would not be the end of the universe. "You've pulled together a great team," she continued. "We can carry this. Trust us. You do what you're good at, and we'll do what we're good at."

He covered her hand where it rested on his shoulder. "Thank you," he said in deep gratitude.

Vanguard. He might be at the front lines, but there was an entire army behind him, even if he fell.

THIRTEEN

THE TIDY APARTMENT assigned to the Diplomatic Group became quickly shambolic within a few days. Kanoa entered to mayhem — a foyer crammed with biodegradable boxes; a common area overflowing with physical files, data drives, and half-eaten meals; and the complicated fug of old food, stress sweat, and a cloying layer of floral freshener attempting to smother it all.

"Sorry," Thiago mumbled, walking by with a plate in one hand, a stylus in the other, and a secure transfer cable between his teeth. He spat it out onto the coffee table and sat down in front of his tablet and a data drive. "I opened a box of your clothes by accident. I put it in your room."

"My clothes?" Kanoa asked, confused.

"They cleared out our rooms in Havana Headquarters and shipped everything in," Yrsa said. "Excuse me, I have a call coming in." She engaged the audio midstride, speaking with a cheerful, professional briskness. "Armande St.-Pierre? Thank you *so* much for getting back to me. First year of Global Government, right? Yes, we have quite the situation here. If I may ask, how's your great-aunt handling it?"

"We're working the unofficial channels," Bay said quietly, guiding Kanoa by the elbow to a still-closed door and ushering him in. "Your room," she explained succinctly, flopping down in an armchair near the window.

He gazed around at the neatly stacked boxes, the standard minimalism of decor and furniture, and the attempt at a neatly folded pile of clothes in a tumble on the bed. He was tired and had no idea where to begin. "You're calling all the old students," he guessed.

"Yes, especially those with connections in government and boardrooms. The official channels are making contact in the usual way, of course, but we're leaving nothing to chance. Bureaucracy is a bastard, especially in a crisis. Kanoa—are you all right?"

He blinked at the worry in her voice. "I'm fine. We . . . found out a few things. Nothing that will help at the moment."

She stared at him, waiting for more, but he gave a half smile and a slight shrug. Not dismissive, merely . . . uncertain. "Another time, then," she said, getting to her feet. "Shower. Sleep. Get ready to work like hell."

Owen hovered by Noriko's shoulder, desperate for answers.

Strictly speaking, General Ahn no longer worked for him, and answered only to the Galactic Council. Owen had no reason to call them and demand answers, especially not while Ahn was in the middle of orchestrating a minor war. Noriko had been the unofficial liaison between the Galactic Council and Kaneshiro-Hendrix Finance for the past decade or so, and if there was anything she did not know about the situation, it probably wasn't worth knowing.

In an echo of Ahn's work back when the highest stakes had been a smoothly run concert, Noriko was sitting at a desk with several flatscreens and holocubes alight with images, text, and communication links. "Ahn is fine," she reassured Owen. "The Antarctica base remains secure and operational."

He nodded, although he knew that. They would have told him at Havana Headquarters if things had been otherwise.

"Ahn's people in national and global law enforcement are taking over more easily than I hoped. The chain of command remains unbroken, even when the commanders change. *But . . .* there are a few areas of resistance."

Owen didn't like the sound of that. The success of the entire exercise depended on the action being so swift, so unstoppable, that compromised officers and leaders would have no time to mobilize their military to push back against them.

Noriko gave him a quick, worried glance, before returning her gaze once more to the shifting scenes before her. "Delaying tactics, mostly. Bombs in residential areas that have to be defused, mass hostage-taking of civilians. Supervillain strategy. Put the innocent in danger, make the superhero stop to save them." She paused a moment. "Of course, we can't save everyone. Ahn is making the decisions on that. We've invited journalists to ride along, to make it clear who's responsible when things turn nasty. We have a lot of familiar faces speaking for us, people who've acquired a reputation with the viewers and readers. Trust is our best currency in this war. The Lyrans never bothered to influence crowds, just petty trillionaires who wanted to be kings and queens."

Owen leaned forward and narrowed his eyes. "Blast . . . is that New York?"

Noriko nodded. "Yes. The flooding has already begun. The Lyrans tampered with the seawalls, and they're estimated to fail completely within a couple of weeks." She looked up into his face. "You *knew* this wasn't going to be tidy."

"Yes," he said faintly. "I knew."

She went back to scanning the screens. "MacLeod is on it. We'll get there, Owen. Don't panic now."

*   *   *

"Thank you for responding so promptly to our call."

Professor MacLeod was seated in the central chair of the meeting hall. He wore no insignia, no ceremonial trappings to indicate his post and his allegiance. The only message sent by his traditional formal suit of long tunic and trousers in sober, dark materials was that he was a global professional, and that the meeting over which he was presiding concerned serious matters. The other attendees were similarly dressed, giving the entire room the atmosphere of a glum convocation of judges.

In only a week, MacLeod, aided by the Diplomatic Group, had managed to physically assemble seventy percent of the present class and past alumni of the Global Government Project. Another twelve percent were virtually in attendance, and an undisclosed remainder were listening in unofficially on audio and communicating via unmarked messages. And it still wasn't enough.

The World Council, or what remained of it, had attempted to schedule an emergency meeting, but the Lyran sabotage of New York's sea barriers had dealt a final blow to the old, fading megacity. Only the small survived: houseboats, canal barges, and cable-tethered townhouses that could ride the tides on their stabilizers. The grand edifices were being slowly abandoned as the waters nudged up by millimeters, too unwieldy to adapt in time, too big to fall.

Now, in full desperation but with utterly skewed priorities, the leaders of nations that had not been disrupted by Lyran action were arguing over whether to hold the meeting in Nairobi or Brasilia.

"In fairness, they're terrified," Professor MacLeod summarized, his reasonable tone contrasting with the look of utter exasperation on his face. "They don't know what they're facing, or which side they should be on. As far as they know, anywhere could be a target for sabotage, or they might already be infiltrated."

"Of course," said Peter Hendrix, seated in pride of place at a front-row delegate's station. "But this is why we built the Nautilus Hall." His outstretched hands swept wide, proud arcs of attention. *See?* they proclaimed. *Is it not good? Are you not impressed?*

ParaVee had designed something new at The Hague. The Nautilus Hall was a chamber of VR displays and delegate stations arranged in broadly spiraling order. Strictly speaking, the Hall was more of a pan-opticon than a nautilus, but in diplomacy and government, a beautiful name often took precedence over an accurate one. The display panels accommodated variable inputs on both sides so that the visuals of key speakers could be temporarily brought forward to the view of the cen-trally sited Chair, while multiple views continued to be shown on the other side. The desks behind the panels were functional, ready to be occupied by a delegate in the raw, and able to transmit that delegate's audiovisual inputs.

When VR displays first became common tools in government, the argument remained that it could not replace in-the-flesh meetings. What of those quick, quiet conversations in a corner, or at the mirrors over the restroom sinks? What about sharing a meal with a potential ally or a cautious drink with a known enemy? The nuance, the en-chantment of all the unrecorded micro interactions would be stripped away, and negotiation by VR alone must thereby lose some ineffable and essential quality.

The ParaVee design teams had tried their best. It was possible, dur-ing breaks between sessions, to visit the lounges and select a scenario that paired one station with another. A delegate would sit, real and raw, on one side of the mirror, and in the mirror see not their own image but a virtual projection of a colleague's reality. They could eat together and pretend it was at the same table, drink together and imagine the bar had extended, chat side by side on a bench that began in one country and ended in another. ParaVee provided the standard designs of the scenario for 3D printing, so every Governor's House and People's Sen-ate could install the same raw furnishings that would seamlessly blend with the VR backgrounds, and also with similar furnishings a hemi-sphere away.

Still they argued: it was too planned, there was no spontaneity, the charm of the unexpected and random alliance could not be captured.

Peter Hendrix was both amused and disgusted. "Six years ago, when all this was new, you would think I had orchestrated the second coming of the Messiah. Now everyone tells me what I did wrong in the original design, and what the new version should look like, and why a new version should have been launched five years ago."

"What if we could? Bring everyone into the same space, I mean, right to the Hall within minutes, and take them back at the end of the meeting?" Kanoa waved a hand at Tareq excitedly. "What you do is amazing. How many times a day can you travel? Do you have to have seen a place before you can go to it? What's the largest number of people you can take at once?"

As he babbled on, Tareq's eyes grew wider and wider with fear, and something else—the thrill of a new risk, a new boundary that had never been tested. She quietly spoke to her colleagues. "I could try—"

Naraldi shook his head firmly. "You may not. Your form of travel is still in its fledgling stages. I tell you now, if you and your sibling, alone and unsupported, exert yourselves to bring so many people to one location in such a short time, it could cause you injury at the least, and permanent displacement at the worst."

Owen leaned forward and tapped his comm to override Kanoa. MacLeod allowed the interruption.

"No," Owen said, firmly and succinctly, and sat back.

Kanoa looked crushed. Bay touched his arm sympathetically. The delegates in the hall murmured in the background, and many eyes turned to Owen with expressions of interest, awe, fascination. His sudden and mysterious retirement had only increased the Owen mythos, and his presence now, in this place, during this crisis, was a distraction.

Owen noticed it and frowned. Masks were not tolerated in ParaVee and Global Justice buildings. Filters in the mirrors and windows stripped away all attempts at VR illusion. Diplomatic meetings were traditionally conducted in the raw as a matter of courtesy, just as he and the faculty had taught their Global Government students. He was the only one who had flouted that rule to present himself as ordinary

Professor Jon Newhaven, but now, when the only currency was trust, he could do so no longer. And yet, though he had known it would be dangerous to attend in person, he had genuinely underestimated just how dangerous it could be. He could sense the hero-shaped hole in their narrative and their desire to draw him, or anyone, into the maelstrom of its center.

He sat far back in his chair, trying to erase himself from the scene, while MacLeod called for order and the discussion moved into other areas. Slowly, as the attention moved from him, he relaxed, and then he leaned in to whisper to Naraldi, "There may be another way."

During the next break in the meeting, Owen slipped out of the Nautilus Hall with Naraldi and Tareq in tow, and told them all about Dr. Kuria.

Dr. Isala Kuria had her own office within the ParaVee compound, a perk she had demanded and quickly received five years after her first meeting with Noriko. To the outside world, the partnership with Para-Vee coincided with her fourth consecutive year as top coach in the European Leagues. In reality, it had marked the start of her full inclusion into their "inner circle" of specialists. Nor was she merely a partner in VR tech. By then, ParaVee had a functioning transit wall, and Kuria quickly became known to visiting Cygnian academics, the acknowledged experts of the galaxy in matters concerning Earth. Less than a year later, she requested and received the quarantine procedure and began her own visits off-planet to the Academes of 16 Cygni B.

In Owen's opinion, Kuria almost rivaled Peter Hendrix as one of the most unflappable, pragmatic, and underawed people on Earth when it came to the discovery of exosolar civilizations with advanced science and new technologies. He liked her a lot, and trusted her even more.

With Naraldi and Tareq, neutral but supportive, standing on either side of him, Owen excitedly explained his plan to Kuria. To his dismay and disappointment, she was appalled.

"The technology is nowhere near ready. I don't want to cause an international incident by scrambling a president's brain cells with a prime minister's. It's all theory, and yes, we've managed a few successful simulations, but no trials have been attempted."

Owen nodded. "I understand, but can you do this for me, at least? Can you bring together the biometric signatures of all the attendees, not just the heads of government but also the corporate representatives, the alumni of the Global Government Project, and me?"

Kuria nodded a yes, but her expression remained doubtful. "If it will be useful, certainly. That bit's easy. Slotting the signatures into a program to get a working connection is where it all goes awry."

"If I'm right, you may not have to rely on a program," Owen said. Naraldi turned and gave him a very hard look, which Owen barely acknowledged with a quick, careless smile.

After the three left Kuria's office, they retreated to a lounge in Noriko's department, the safest place for Owen to show his face without being disturbed. Tareq took the middle seat of a large couch and busied herself with a ParaVee tablet. The room also contained a console with several screens and cubes, similar to Noriko's communications desk, which flickered with several news and link options, but Owen chose nothing. He merely sat in front of it and watched the changing menus with an expression of deep discontent.

Naraldi positioned himself near to, but not quite within, Owen's field of view, as if trying not to impose his presence and authority. "Do I need to warn you as I warned Tareq earlier?"

"Risky, experimental, I know, I know." Owen spun his chair around and faced Naraldi fully, trying to convey his passion. "But if I am to keep my promise not to speak of those who live in the oceans, I must find a way for Earth to be independent. Can you imagine what the dictatorship of Alpha Centauri would do with full access to Earth's oceans?"

"I don't have to imagine it," Naraldi said abruptly. "I've seen pasts and presents with a similar theme. Sometimes it went well. Often it went very badly. I agree with you that Earth must stand for itself, with no guardianship or oversight from elsewhere. But these things take time. You are trying to impose the kind of order and cooperation that comes with generations of mutual interest and work."

"I have to," Owen snapped. "I can't stay and shepherd this. The longer I do it, the more I'll convince myself that I'm the only one who can. And we both know that isn't true, Naraldi."

"So . . . you set up the Wall, then remove yourself as nexus and hope the transit proceeds as planned to the correct destination." Naraldi's tone was hard to judge. Flat yet not quite neutral, it sounded like a clear statement of an unlikely scenario.

Owen pushed back rebelliously. "Yes. Precisely like that."

"He's right," Tareq interjected, with support as unexpected as it was welcome. "Ahn tells me they're worried about the power vacuums we've created here by kicking out the Lyran cartels. Some of the cartels' rivals are as bad as they are, or worse. If we leave behind weak governments, or no government, we will have destabilized Earth for nothing. Either way, it'll take years in cooperation with Earth law enforcement before the Galactic Gendarmerie can call this a success."

"The Patrona should have given us more time," Naraldi complained.

"They attacked the Antarctica base. Ixiaral did the right thing," Owen said, firmly defending his sister. "I just have to make it work in a slightly tighter time frame."

"Much tighter," Tareq said, slinging the tablet aside. "And I have my own business to attend to. I can't stay here much longer."

"Nor I," said Naraldi. "Serendipity's watch is over, but I still have pilots and ships to find."

"I'm surprised you're still here at all," Owen admitted. "Grateful, but surprised."

Naraldi smiled. "You know how susceptible I am to the lure of a historic moment."

A companionable peace descended on the room. Owen could feel his heart rate slowing and his muscles relaxing. Naraldi still smiled, his eyelids half-closed. Tareq held out her hand to Owen.

"Come," she said.

He shut off the console's distracting displays, meekly took her hand, and let her draw him to sit down beside her.

"You too, Naraldi," she said with a beckoning gesture to the old pilot.

The old man opened his eyes, regarded them for a while with a considering expression, and then joined them, sitting on the other side of Tareq.

Temporarily united in purpose, and also in mind, the three meditated.

Two days later, with the World Council still squabbling and delaying action, a second, larger meeting was convened in the Nautilus Hall. Each of the present and former students of the Global Government Project had managed to convince one or two more delegates to attend virtually or in the flesh. Family, colleagues, mentors, and teachers were included, and within their number were leaders, policymakers, and the quiet ones who work in shadow to keep several systems of governance running smoothly. It was the nearest thing to full representation of all Earth that could be accomplished at the time, and under the circumstances.

Before the meeting, a select group of people arrived at the Nautilus Hall early, like generals come to discuss strategy before battle.

Owen knew the theory, broadly speaking, and knew his part of the process instinctually. However, in an excess of caution, Isala Kuria and Peter Hendrix were now trying to explain the process to him in painfully painstaking detail. How his VR interface was a design inspired by the Lyran hardware that transformed human pilots into living brains within cyborg ships. How every delegate, every attendee had been thoroughly mapped and transcribed so that their unique physical signatures, the very same signatures needed for any transit wall, formed part of the vast data array connected to the interface. How the first traveler-pair of siblings had been thoroughly studied by Cygnian academics, and according to that research, as long as Tareq kept hold of him like a Eridanian pilot attaching to a ship, she could transit them both wherever he desired.

"Will it hurt Tareq, to carry out so many transits in such a short time?"

Kuria and Hendrix looked to Tareq. She nodded reassuringly. "It may be challenging, but it's within my range."

They began to tell Owen that the central chair of the Nautilus Hall had been reconstructed with a new level of VR interface design, and at that point everything began to blur. He could hear their words, but his mind was wandering elsewhere, utterly preoccupied.

"Will this . . . uh . . . challenge me?"

"We don't know," Kuria replied angrily. "As much as we've studied you, we've never known your limits."

Hendrix gently placed his hand over her wrist. "Dushi, stop. We're not helping him. He zoned out five minutes ago. Let him take his own time to prepare." He gave Owen a fond tap on the cheek with his fingers. "We'll be here if you need us, and out of your way if you don't."

Owen blinked and gave them his full attention. "Thank you. You've both been outstanding from the very beginning. You've adapted to incredible change, learned so much, and given us so much more in return. None of this would be possible without you. None of it."

Kuria turned red-faced and mumbling in pleased embarrassment. Hendrix bit his lip and nodded once, firmly, but a suspicion of moisture gleamed in his eyes.

"You are a child of our ultimate diaspora," he said. "My child, my kin, returned from the stars. It is for *me* to be proud of *you*."

Owen might have lost it right there and then, but Tareq gave him a light mental push, nothing intrusive, just enough to return his focus. "Time to take up our positions," she said.

As they moved to sit at an unmarked station slightly behind the start of the curl of the first row and ahead of the first overlap that began the second row, Owen's thoughts, though quietened, kept spinning.

Peter had become yet another father to him at a stage in his life when he no longer looked for surrogate parents. His Eridanian uncle had given him stability and taught him control; and his Austrinian mentor and matriarch had set him to work and guided him in the effective and ethical use of his skills. But Peter had cleansed and reforged his bond to Earth, a bond that his biological father had tainted with his abuse of the power of illusion.

Peter Hendrix was all illusion with no lies, all make-believe with no harm, all shared fantasy with no imposed fantasy. He crafted tools to make imaginary worlds, and now Owen was about to use those same tools to change a real world.

Professor MacLeod acknowledged the final delegate of the roll call. That was Owen's cue. He got to his feet, faced the front row of display panels, and then closed his eyes and breathed deeply.

"Tareq," he said, "tell me when you need to stop."

She knew he had no capacity for a verbal reply; she merely came to stand behind him, placed a warm hand on his shoulder with an encouraging grip, and said, "Ready."

Owen walked forward. Kuria's interface worked as intended, expanding his perception of the world from flat planes of display panels suspended in a real-world hall to a maze of doorways into places. A slight warping of the view was due to Tareq's mind linked to his, sharing her unique manner of seeing the universe—all creases and folds, a step here and a handspan there. She traveled with ease to any place known, and Kuria's interface operated like a Lyran pilot interface, changing navigational data to human instinct and broadening proprioception beyond the boundaries of skin.

They approached the small, elderly prime minister of Bangladesh, Sunita Chowdhury, whose eyes widened in amazement as they walked into—and through—her display panel. Soldiers in ceremonial uniform standing guard at her room's entrance were shocked out of formal stance, but quickly recalled themselves after their prime minister waved a hand impatiently.

"We did not really think this could happen," she admitted, getting to her feet and running her hands over Owen's face and shoulders with fearless curiosity.

Hand firmly in place on Owen's shoulder, Tareq kept Owen like a shield between her and Prime Minister Chowdhury's overfamiliar hands. Owen did not have to turn around to see the amusement on his friend's face. Moving quickly, he captured the prime minister's hands and held them to his heart, to both restrain and charm her.

"We cannot stay long," he said truthfully. "Remember this moment."

Then he turned back to the full wall display panel, Tareq as always within an arm's length. The display no longer showed the Nautilus Hall that they had just exited, but their next destination—the office of Simon Accola, the president of the Swiss Confederation. The man quickly stood, bracing his hands on his desk, and swore fluidly in shocked delight when Owen and Tareq glided through his display wall and stopped beside him.

"Don't worry," Owen reassured him with a light touch on the arm. President Accola flinched, looked ashamed at his unconscious reaction, and grasped Owen's forearm in a deliberate reciprocal action. "Remember this," Owen said again as he slowly disengaged. A fresh scene and a new destination were already on Accola's display. Owen moved swiftly on, helped by Tareq's sure hand.

No rule of geography or alphabet determined their journey. Tareq went from delegate to delegate, and country to country, guided by her own sense of some unmappable topology. At each brief encounter, Owen spoke, touched, and gave a single command—*remember*. The speech was to communicate, the touch to prove his presence in their shared raw reality, and the command was where he used his skill, gathering each moment of connection and strengthening it with their intent, using their willing effort to be a part of the thread he was spinning from each to each.

As Owen passed through them, the leaders' eyes followed him for a while, and then they looked at each other as if freshly awakened—

which they were—and as if something had changed—which was true. He missed who discovered it first, but all around, the story repeated, beginning with a tentative finger outstretched to touch another's image on their display. Fingertips touched and found not the cool barrier of a VR panel but warm, responsive skin. Hands plunged through to clasp and grip, and then the bolder ones took it a step further—and walked right through, following in Owen's footsteps to another place.

While the disruption increased, Owen continued, until without warning he found himself back in the Hall at their station, with Tareq's grip on his shoulder no longer firm with purpose, but heavy with exhaustion.

"Tareq," he began, alarmed and contrite.

"No, wait." The words were breathed out laboriously, dark with determination. "I can do this. We can do this. Wait."

The weight on his shoulder vanished, but before Owen could turn around, it returned with a different hand, a lighter fall, and that richer shading of timbre that was Kirat's voice. "I'm here."

"Is Siha—"

"We're fine," Tareq interrupted with the rude-seeming haste of one who dare not be distracted. "Ready? Let's go."

The journey went on, and at some latter stage, near the end, Owen felt the hand-shift once more as Kirat left him and Siha returned. He did not falter, giving them full trust as Tareq decided for themselves who should anchor and who should journey. For his own part, he kept focus on his task, touching every delegate within and without the Hall and drawing them into one space in the only way that mattered.

The Hall buzzed, then roared with unrestrained chatter. From his vantage point in the very center, Professor MacLeod could see the displays vibrantly flickering and changing. No longer were they staid portraits of world leaders and representatives speaking in orderly fashion to the meeting's agenda. One panel showed a trio of laughing men—one of them had scooped up snow from his windowsill and brought it through to a far higher temperature, where it melted at speed and dripped between his fingers; another, thinking more clearly, had as his guest-gift a bottle of rare gin, snatched up from a shelf as he attempted the portal. Two women embraced in another panel, colleagues or old classmates in a long-delayed reunion. Some panels were silent, empty, their occupants gone on a round of greetings. Many stayed where they were, still shocked and uncertain after Owen's initial appearance, and let the world come to them.

Primed with his background knowledge of all the delegates present, MacLeod observed and learned . . . and also acted as ParaVee, Kuria, and Owen had trained him, drawing to himself the threads Owen was creating and gathering them in a semipermanent binding knot.

Like the greeting of peace among a tight-knit congregation, the moment lengthened and lingered but could not last. MacLeod was interrupted in his blissful, busy musing by a tap on the shoulder. He tilted his head toward Dr. Kuria to better catch her frantic whisper. What he heard made his eyes widen a little, and he hastily activated his communication bug.

"Please return to your desks. The dimensional effect will soon fade and you may be stranded in another country. I say again, *please* return to your desks. Thank you." His voice was far too calm, but the controlled intensity made everyone pay attention. Gradually, like misbehaving pupils slowly settling down after a teacher's return to the classroom, the Hall became quieter, people found their places once more, and their newly sparkling eyes focused on MacLeod in his central chair.

He stood and gathered them in with a wide sweep of his arms, a gesture that was more than metaphor. "Let us take a five-minute break to compose ourselves, and then we will begin to vote on the tabled motions."

At the moment when the final vote was taken and the first Global Council of Earth approved, Owen was nowhere to be seen. After the last crossing, Tareq had taken him directly to where Naraldi stood waiting outside the Hall. They did not bother with the formality of a transit wall, nor did Naraldi consider a return to his ship. They held their nexus between them, drained and half-conscious, and immediately brought him home.

FOURTEEN

WHEN OWEN OPENED his eyes and saw the rough stones of the walls, the shafts of dusty sunlight through the narrow windows, and the bright colors of tumbled draperies softening the hard edges of his room, he smiled. He stretched languidly and kicked off the covers, superfluous for the rapidly warming morning. Enjoying the utter lack of need or desire to think, he lay for as long as he could, drifting from half slumber to alertness. When he was alert, he spent his time on small things—the feel of the smooth sheets beneath his fingertips, the occasional breeze that puffed through the windows or around the open doorway, a familiar voice sounding distantly down a nearby stairwell.

When he drowsed, he did not dream, or wish, or wonder.

His aunt and uncle folded him easily into their daily routine without question, and he gratefully surrendered his life to them. His aunt spoke little, and his uncle less, but something about the relaxed warmth of their care told him that whatever he had accomplished, it had not been in vain. The details he left for another time.

Much later, after good food and regular meditation had restored his body and mind, Owen allowed himself to briefly wonder where Naraldi and Tareq had gone. Not so much Naraldi . . . Tareq must have returned him immediately to Earth and to his ship after they had delivered Owen to his family. But Tareq—Kirat and Siha both—were not there.

Before he could summon up the will and energy to ask, a visitor arrived at the watchtower. When Owen slowly descended to the ground floor and saw the stranger in the atrium, for a moment he thought he recognized Kirat's stance and heard Siha's cadences. But then he saw the additional breadth and height, heard the deeper tenor, and was startled into paying attention for the first time in days. He moved quickly down the remaining stairs and stared in amazement and joy at Kirat and Siha's father.

"Tarik," he said. "It's been so long."

Tarik did not quite smile, but his face brightened. He started to speak, then glanced at Owen's aunt nervously, as if asking permission. His aunt looked doubtful, but his uncle gently touched her waist and she blinked and relaxed. An entire conversation in a moment. She smiled bravely at Owen and Tarik. "Why don't you two sit here and catch up for a while?"

"I'd prefer the roof, if it's no trouble?" Tarik asked.

"Of course," Owen said. "Go up the stairs. I'll bring us tea."

Minutes later, he came to the rooftop, tray in hand, to find his uncle, his aunt, and Tarik seated comfortably under the tree, which was now bare of blossoms but showing some small, spiky leaves in patches of new, green growth. Owen poured out the sweet, spicy mix over three cups of crushed ice and served his family and guest before sitting down beside Tarik with his own cup.

"I've been . . . a bit out of touch. Are Kirat and Siha with you?" he asked.

"They're in Grand Bay at the moment, arranging some business for me. Will you be returning to Earth soon?"

Owen drank deeply to delay his answer. "Yes, soon. There's a saying on Earth. It ain't over till—"

"—it's over," Tarik guessed.

"—the paperwork's filed," Owen continued, overlapping him.

They looked at each other, and both Owen and his aunt burst out laughing. His uncle and Tarik managed a blink and a slow smile, pure Eridanian hilarity.

"Where have *you* been?" Owen asked Tarik.

"Here and there. Passed through Janojya several times en route, but of course you'd moved on by then. Earth, most recently."

Owen froze, startled.

"Didn't stay long," Tarik said, waving a hand dismissively. "Got the information I needed, thanks to Naraldi."

Owen gazed at him but couldn't bring himself to speak. Tarik nodded in reassurance.

"She is alive. My Nasiha is still alive."

The unfinished business that Kirat and Siha spoke of was all this . . . the search for their mother, vanished decades ago. Owen had been the last person to see her, and he still felt vaguely guilty about that.

"Kirat and Siha want to join me on my next journey, but I think they feel . . . concerned about leaving you," Tarik continued.

Owen started to speak, about to assure Tarik that he had no further need of Kirat and Siha, and of course they were free to travel with him, but his aunt's voice cut in before he could do more than part his lips.

"I was saying *just* this week that it's time we moved back home," she said cheerfully. Her husband gave her a look of fond exasperation, which bothered her not one bit. "You know I'm right," she told him. "You've had more than a decade's worth of retreat, and they will have learned to do without you by now. Go find your wife, Tarik, and bring her home."

Owen closed his mouth and lowered his head humbly. Once more, he had caught himself assuming he was the center of the universe. Kirat and Siha had been taking care of his uncle and aunt; they were merely occasionally on loan to him. And there had been a hint of a tremor in his aunt's last words. Before her disappearance, Nasiha had been one of her closest friends, and she and her husband had unstintingly funded Tarik's long search and many travels out of their own accounts.

Later, his aunt joined him in the kitchen to make more tea, and it was then, while they waited for the kettle to boil, that he spoke on impulse.

"Ixiaral told me, when I finished my work on Earth, I should do something selfish, just for myself. Can I come back home with you?"

His aunt gave him a searching look. "That's your idea of selfish? Don't say that just because you think we need someone to wait on us hand and foot. The homestead's expanded to nearly eighty people now. We'll be fine."

"Yes, you will, but I said I was being selfish, remember? Maybe it's my turn to have a retreat."

She paused to take the boiling water from the stove and fill the teapot, smiling knowingly all the while. "And what happens when you get bored? Because you will."

The echo of Ixiaral's words hit him hard. "Can I try for a while?" he asked in a small voice.

She gave him her full attention. "Do you know the real reason we moved here, so far from home, with only basic communication? People could not forget what your uncle had been. He was no longer a teacher, no longer a councilor, no longer the head of a planetary government. But they kept knocking on his door and asking him to be those things again for a minute, an hour, a day. So he left. He left the new teachers and leaders to become legends in their own right. That was the correct decision, and an easy one for a man who has always loved meditation and quiet.

"But *you*, you need people. You've always been a beast with a pack. Sure, you take a little time off here and there, but you need the team, the crowd, the many minds and hearts all tangled up in your web of care.

"You'll always be welcome at home, but don't promise you'll stay and settle. We'll love you anyway, as you are, wherever you are."

Owen returned the long way around—by train and hydrofoil to Grand Bay, by Eridanian ship to Port of Janojya, by transit wall to Amsterdam, and by hopper to The Hague. Each leg of the journey required a brief stop: Grand Bay to find and thank Kirat and Siha, and to visit the old homestead that would soon be home again; Janojya to meet his sister, to hear her words of approval and be reassured that she was not going to assassinate him . . . yet; and Amsterdam to overnight with Peter, and spend a day shaking off the exhaustion of accumulated dimensional lag with the help of strong tea and light conversation.

When he reached the Global Justice compound in The Hague, he was braced for the worst, but when he disembarked, Professor MacLeod was there to greet him with an actual smile. Slightly strained, definitely sleep-deprived, but optimistic nevertheless.

"It's still a mess," he explained, "but it's *our* mess. The World Council is re-forming and will meet in the Nautilus Hall to coordinate domestic response to the post-Lyran cleanup. *Your* team, the delegates you connected, are still insisting on calling themselves the Global Council. Odd but interesting mix of Global Government alumni, diplomats, and quite a few heads of state. Significant overlap with the World Council at the moment. For now, that's in our favor, but I doubt it'll continue."

He walked as he talked, leading Owen from the hopper pad into the Global Justice complex and directly to an elevator capsule. Owen followed, listening intently.

"The Global Council's mandate is to elect and support one of the members to represent Earth at Galactic Council meetings. Sounds precipitous, I know, but your Patrona insisted. Said something along the lines of Terran-types thriving when they're thrown in at the deep end, and stagnating when they're coddled."

Owen coughed discreetly into his sleeve to hide a smile.

"We have about one hundred delegates and support personnel now undergoing the quarantine process. Two stages: one week at Amsterdam ParaVee, the remaining time at Terminal 5 in Alpha Piscis Austrini. That's just the first wave of essential staff. There's a very long waiting list."

The capsule opened to reveal the lounge of a large suite with two doors, both closed, leading to other rooms. The lounge was designed for leisure and work, with comfortable furniture around a low table, a public tablet console at the side, and a long wall with a series of VR screens showing a soothing forest view. MacLeod waved a friendly hand forward, inviting him to proceed. "So much to do," he said. "And here is your office. We need some documentation from you, and I believe your Patrona is also requesting some reports on behalf of House Haneki?"

He paused in the middle of the lounge, gave Owen a close, concerned look, and said sincerely. "How *are* you? What you did was . . . not easy."

Owen gave him a firm nod, gratified that he had asked. "Better. Much better. There's no need to worry about me."

MacLeod visibly relaxed. "Well, just in case, we've given you an assistant." He went to one of the closed doors, knocked perfunctorily, and opened it.

Noise immediately spilled from the entrance. Bay paced the length of the room, talking animatedly and persuasively into her communicator bug. A series of screens clustered around the desk behind her, bright, blinking, and busy. She saw them and quickly concluded the call.

"Oh, Professor Owen, thank God you're here at last," she said.

"So much to do," MacLeod murmured, clapping Owen bracingly on the shoulder. "Good luck. I'll be on the floor above if you need me."

*   *   *

A week later, Bay sat in Owen's office, wearily delivering the daily summary of correspondence.

"This final item . . . it's the Swiss. They're asking you if you could . . . if you would consider visiting their next Federal Council meeting." Bay paused to clear her throat apologetically. "To . . . lay hands on everyone. Stop the contentiousness and improve cooperation."

Owen leaned back in his chair and blew out a noisy, exasperated breath. "One of my first mentors had a saying: *Not God, but glue.* I think I should have it embroidered on all my clothing, just over my heart. Or perhaps a little higher, so it stays within people's line of sight."

He made eye contact at last. Bay had noticed that even when he played the part of their instructor Jon Newhaven, bland in name and form and manner, he had been careful never to look too long at any student. He would stare at the tablet in their hands or address the ceiling above them, but eye-to-eye had been a rare, fleeting experience.

"Did you know, I was once the Patron of House Haneki?"

Bay did not know. Perhaps Yrsa, with her greater knowledge of the Austrinians, had picked up that tidbit; or perhaps Owen had accomplished it with another name and another look as part of his chameleon career. He was waiting for her to reply, so she shook her head.

"I lasted five years. Long enough to prove myself competent, which was a relief to me and to the former Patrona, who had appointed me her successor over her own daughter. But also long enough to show that I did things a little too differently. The Austrinians and Geminorans have a tradition of long, empathic speeches from their leaders. Yes, it is a way to convey information, but it is also a means of connecting emotionally to the people. The mental and physical stamina required for such a task is considerable. It remains a common practice because it's worked so well to weed out those who lack the strength, intellect, and empathy to govern well. Until I came along.

"At first I did precisely what they expected of a Patron, but eventually I found I didn't really need to speak for that long. I acted in the same way I did when playing the nexus position for Wallrunning teams. I made connections, yes, but with few words, brief physical contact. I encouraged people to communicate with each other, work with each other, and not just with me. My approach upended generations of tradition. It worked, but people didn't understand it, and some didn't like it.

"Haneki is one of the oldest Houses, and their reputation is such that they have never had to cling to illusions of bloodline purity or psionic strength. But not all Houses feel the same way, and newer, less influential groups such as the Lyran-influenced Geminoran Houses are particularly intransigent. Unfortunately, my presence and my style began to interfere with our work. At the same time, the situation on Earth was calling to me. I felt I could be more useful to my House elsewhere.

"So I stepped down and our old Patrona's daughter took the mantle. By then, she had found such success in her own endeavors that House Haneki eventually gained not only a new Patrona, but also the Chair of the Galactic Council. Quite a coup, and utterly unexpected by those who foolishly assumed that my elevation was a sign of bad blood between mother and daughter."

Owen stood up and turned away from Bay to gaze out the window. "My point is this: there is no place in the galaxy that has developed a safe political framework for what I can do. Frankly, the only place that might be able to do that in time . . . is Earth."

He turned slightly and smiled over his shoulder at Bay, a brief, unguarded moment in which he allowed himself to show a little of his natural, wicked charm.

"You weren't thinking that I'm the only one on Earth who can do this, were you?"

He seated himself once more and addressed his next words to the tablet Bay held in her hands. "My answer to that request, and any more like it, is that a team of consultants from the Kuria Institute and Para-Vee will visit them at a mutually convenient time to assist them in their work of strengthening communication and cooperation in governance."

"Yes, Professor," Bay said, the old title slipping from her without thought, and she began to walk away, her fingers flying over the tablet as she composed the response.

She had almost reached the door when he spoke to her again. "Bay, you know I'm not going to be in this office much longer? You should think about what you want to do next. Whatever you choose to do, I'd be happy to give you a recommendation."

She didn't turn around. "Yes, Professor. I know. I'll think about it."

In time, the new routine of work established itself. The inaugural group returned from quarantine, a smaller group took their place, and suddenly there were more people who knew what to do and whom to speak to, and could travel widely to build and strengthen their networks. MacLeod began to look less haggard. Owen gladly completed the last of his duties and handed over to Bay what trailing matters remained for wrap-up. After a quick, quiet, unsentimental gathering to say au revoir to his inner circle, he was more than ready for a break.

With no urgency of task or privilege of identity, he once more traveled the long way around on the routes that permitted less scrutiny. Havana Headquarters remained in near–battle mode, so Owen took a passenger berth on a high-speed, transatlantic cargo ship to Panama. A private charter jet to Samoa gave him time for a discreet courtesy call on Governor Crawford, and then he was on a ferry to visit Serendipity in her dome, still anchored in the bay.

She accepted him without questions, for which he was deeply grateful, and whatever her means of staying in touch with the galaxy, her dome itself offered no visible temptations, no screens or bugs or other links to the several bubbling pots of trouble on Earth and beyond. He slept within when he wanted a cocoon of peace and seclusion, and lay on the deck onshore when he wanted fresh air in his lungs and dew in his hair. And then, eventually, he spent one or two hours at a time floating in the shallow waters of the bay, quietly hinting, hoping, and waiting.

His patience paid off. One day, he felt a presence beside him, and when he carefully turned his head he saw an older man with a wide cloud of gray hair and dark brown skin, who was very much in appearance like Kanoa. The ghost floated beside him, squinting into the sun, and for a while it appeared to ignore him.

"Why didn't you bring my son back with you?" the apparition said at last.

"He is busy working in The Hague. He'll be back home when he can," Owen said truthfully.

The specter accepted his words with a grudging nod and then vanished. Owen blinked, not sure whether to feel pleased or worried at the commonplace discussion.

Early the following morning, with the sun still low on the horizon and the breezes cool and moist, he swam steadily out. He paused at the deepest part of the bay, calm and sheltered by the encircling reef. The water was a rich, crystal aqua, the sky overhead cloudless and intensely blue, and when he tipped back and floated in place, he thought dreamily to himself that there were other ways, far more pleasant ways, to drown. Here, too, was a cocoon of peace and isolation, blue and bright, wide as the world and separate as his soul.

Ixiaral had hypothesized that, with his talent, he must have just enough empathic skill to be subconsciously aware of those around him. If that were indeed so, how blissful must be the lonely quietness of the Pacific, with Serendipity the only other mind in range, kindly and carefully shielded against his thoughts! But he could not tell for certain, he could only feel the brush of a fall of fabric rather than the trace of a single thread.

It took him a while to feel and comprehend the prickling sensation from the water surrounding him.

This time, the presence beside him looked a little changed: gray hair turned full white, brown skin bronzed to a near-metallic shine. The face, when it turned toward him, was smooth, not wrinkled with age or cheer or sorrow. No words were exchanged, but in the stranger's lazy blink, Owen perceived a multitude of souls looking out through one pair of eyes, brushing against him with the rough caress of a densely woven tapestry.

And that too was bliss, a bliss he could be certain of, a bliss he could feel and comprehend.

Once upon a time, on another world, Serendipity had looked down into the shallows of Grand Bay and seen a wounded pilot floating and framed in the restorative filaments of her ship. Years later, both ship and woman vanished from the waters of Grand Bay and reappeared in the heavens as a creature of legend: a wild ship that journeyed on a whim, tightly bound to a pilot who had forgotten how to vocalize, but not how to communicate. No one could capture them for testing, but many had encountered them for conversation.

What was it like?

Did the universe look the same?

When would they die?

Would they die?

Ships did not die. When they lost their pilots, they fell into dormancy and drifted in space, occasionally fragmenting into smaller entities that might, in time, gather enough mass and purpose to become a new ship seeking a new pilot. No one knew what might happen when a ship and a pilot fused not only mentally and temporarily, but physically and permanently.

The question remained unanswered, and yet Serendipity had enough faith in those unknowns to be present as witness at a moment of unusual sacrifice.

"I must ask you again," she said, "are you sure?"

Owen floated lightly against her arms as she stood chest deep in the pale blue sea, holding him up like an offering against the insistent tug of the tiny swells from over the reef.

"I will tell you again," he replied, "I *am* sure."

That strange resonance in his voice, which she had first heard when he answered not-Kanoa's silencing command, came more frequently now, especially when he was relaxed. He turned slightly to face her, as if reading her mind—a thing she was quite sure he had never been able to do.

"I know you hear them whispering to you in the daylight. They speak to me too, not in words, or whispers, but in a kind of yearning curiosity. I could wait, live my life, and return to join them when I'm dying, like so many of Kanoa's people have done. But they want something more from me, and I am willing to give it to them."

"You understand the risk. If this is a mistake, if it means your death and nothing more, how will I be able to face your family?"

"Trust them to know me a little better than that. They will not blame you. They will blame me, which is as it should be."

More comfort than that could not be expected. Owen fell silent and relaxed into the water, floating freely so that her hands touched only lightly under his back. There was no magic to this, no supplication. Sacrifice and witness were all that were required.

When the waters turned dark and the horizon bent over them, she saw, with eyes more experienced than Kanoa's had been, that there was a dimensional warp, a temporal shift, and the change of color and shape were all due to the bending of light and the confusion of the human, time-bound perception. She sensed the slowing of Owen's pulse but could not be sure. She was sure when his face grayed to match the waters and his body yielded to the light pressure of her palm's push with a scattering, a pulverization, like dust if dust could trickle through the skin and between the cells of the body. She grasped nothing but salt water, and yet Owen's consciousness was still present and active to her sensitive mind.

"Ahh," she exhaled softly as her knees weakened and she dipped lower into the sea. No words existed for this. And it was without words, in the primal communication of her earliest days growing up in a telepathic community, that Owen spoke to her of happiness, freedom, and certainty.

She came to her senses washed up on the beach like a log of driftwood, with the tide drawing out and the occasional wave splashing at her toes. Disoriented and weak, she staggered upright and slowly made her way to the dock and into the moored dome. There she stripped off her clothes and sat curled on a wooden bench under a lukewarm shower. When her skin was clean of salt, she turned off the water, wrapped herself in a large cotton wrap, and collapsed into her bed.

She did not dream. She would always be sure of that; she did *not* dream. She woke and there was Owen, sitting on the edge of her bed, looking at her with such complete attention that it was almost a kind of fascination. When she sat up to speak to him, he put his fingers gently over her parting lips and told her, clearly, mind to mind, "*Safe.*"

What could one word convey? By voice alone she would have missed at least four different meanings: he was safe, not dead; it was safe for him to be with her; safe for her to speak to him like this; safe for him to look at her directly in the full knowledge of years of boyish yearning and fearsome power. They would keep him safe; they would keep Earth safe from him. He could now safely walk with his strong step and his big boots and never again fear for the safety of the ants, a fear that had kept him tiptoeing all his life. He was safe from becoming the monster his father had been; he had become a different kind of monster—safe, benign, beyond, unleashed, but above all . . . safe.

He was so happy. He felt more real to her in this earthly incarnation. He allowed himself to be touched, to be looked at. His mind was now alert and awake, not hidden in shadow and unwilling to engage. She kissed him, and then she let him kiss her. And then they laughed.

"*Who* are *you?*" she said—not a question for an answer, but a teasing challenge.

He held her hand tightly so she could feel the pressure slowly ease as he faded away. "*Finding out will be . . . an adventure.*"

FIFTEEN

NARALDI SAT ON the dock alone, gazed out at the untenanted bay, and thought about those who had once shared that view with him.

Kanoa was once more at home with his family. He now possessed a state-of-the-art VR system, which was completely appropriate considering the very important work he had done and was continuing to do for the Global Council. That work allowed him to stay physically within the Federated States of Polynesia with virtual appearances in The Hague. No more was possible, not yet. ParaVee scientists claimed that the multi-portal, dimensional phenomenon created by Owen and Tareq could, theoretically, be replicated, but after the initial euphoria had worn off and caution set back in, everyone seemed to be happy to hasten slowly along that path. Perhaps that kind of immediacy or presence always required a balancing intimacy, to ensure that no harm could be done.

Kanoa would not miss it. Unlike Thiago, unlike Bay, he had declined the offer of a full quarantine procedure, a necessary step to travel to another planet. The Pacific, with its mysteries deeply bound to his soul, was sufficient universe for him to explore.

Serendipity remained in her sea home, sometimes docked near an island, sometimes anchored in deep waters. She no longer had a mission, nothing to search for in the world or within herself, and she was more than at peace with that. Peter Hendrix had bought her a new identity, confirming her permanently as a citizen of Earth. ParaVee kept her secure and supplied her needs, and she repaid them with the occasional bit of consultancy work.

They called her a hermit—was that the right term for one whose life had been spent in pursuit of perfect communication? She was learning the language and ways of Earth's undersea, and that, too, was an exploration of a universe.

And—on the topic of purchased identities—the artist formerly known as Owen had retired that identity and disappeared from all Earth's databases. His colleagues on Earth mourned his disappearance as they would have mourned his death, though at least they'd had warning of the former. His family and close friends elsewhere had no need to mourn; he still visited them often, unannounced and unburdened, sometimes in the company of Tareq—no, not Tareq. That name, which had been chosen for Earth, for a certain time, and for a set purpose, had also been retired. The twins Kirat and Siha anchored and journeyed their way through the galaxy under the name Narua once more, pursuing their own personal quest with greater vigor and hope.

About that, about many of these things, Naraldi had thoughts, and it was pleasant to think in such beautiful surroundings.

A vibration of the deck alerted him to the fact that he was no longer alone. "I knew you would come. What took you so long?" he said without bothering to turn around.

"Dear Naraldi, how many times must we go through this? I am never late. I am never early. I arrive where and when I am meant to be."

The voice of his old traveling companion and mentor through space and time rang lightly in concert with the breeze amid the palm fronds and the waves gently breaking on the sand. At last Naraldi turned, taking in that otherworldly face, bright bronze illuminated from within, haloed in a cloud's glory of white hair, angel to some humans, alien to all. "Sayr. I have missed you, although I am sure you will tell me how foolish that is as well."

Sayr did not reply with the expected quip but merely came to sit beside Naraldi, their expression unusually pensive. Companionable silence followed for a while, and then Sayr said, "Do you understand what has happened?"

"Of course not," Naraldi scoffed. "Do *you*? You never warned me about the dwellers in the deep. Did you even know they were there?"

Sayr gave him a withering look. "There simply isn't enough time in the universe to teach you everything I know."

In momentary truce, they fell silent again, and again Naraldi was the first to speak.

"So this is why you, who taught me to never interfere, allowed yourself to interfere a little in the lives of an obscure group of humans. You knew they were linked to *him*."

Sayr tilted his head in a quick, dismissing gesture. "He is not the first of his kind, and he will not be the last. It is, however, a most significant step."

Naraldi stiffened. "A road that leads to you, or something like you?"

Sayr roared with laughter. Naraldi waited, not sure if the laughter was at him or at some cosmic joke in general.

"Let me tell you a story, more of a history, in fact. Did you know that on Earth, before virtual reality technologies became so sophisticated, human scientists studying animals would try to imitate them? They would mimic their calls, and even their appearance or their scent, depending on what senses were dominant.

"Of course, this was only a continuation of a long history of interspecies interactions. Consumption, domestication. A range of attachment and identification, from the useless pet to the religious symbol. But often from a position of strength. Humans in control, or striving to be, always."

Sayr's voice grew stern and deep as they left behind their usual playfulness. "Control and attachment go hand in hand. Your young man knew that intimately—that love, or what passes for love, does not turn from using leashes and shackles. It will not shrink from mercy killings and culls. If there were a species as far from humanity as humans are from ants, *if* there were, can you imagine them keeping watch, occasionally calling out with human words, sending themselves out camouflaged in human appearance? Even setting up their own colony of humans a safe distance away in case it became necessary to exterminate the original nest?"

Naraldi felt a cold prickling walk over his skin. He held himself very still. Sayr sensed his distress and gentled their tone. "But we evolve, we find better ways, we discover new approaches. Symbiosis, mutual beneficial coexistence. You're a pilot. You know all this in the very marrow of your bones. All roads that do not lead to destruction lead to us. In communion. One flesh, one spirit. One heart, one mind. A transformation like that . . . it makes a vast, unfriendly universe as small and close as home. Wouldn't you agree?"

Sayr's smile was small, apologetic. Perhaps it was the contrite, absentminded pat you gave to a dog that had cringed at your raised voice. Perhaps it was the genuine concern of a friend for a friend. For a fraction of a second, Naraldi was entirely unsure which it might be, but he nodded and allowed himself to relax and breathe normally once more.

"That's quite a message," he said neutrally as he got to his feet. "An appropriate message for me to convey to the pilots of Alpha Centauri."

Sayr stood up as well, accepting his segue as the precursor of a leave-taking. "Ah, so you have discovered their hiding place."

"After eliminating Earth as an option, I merely guessed, but other pilots have confirmed it. Epsilon Tauri, our enemies, our brothers, have offered them sanctuary. I should be accustomed to life's ironies by now, but this . . . in all my voyages and dreams, I did not see *this* as a possibility."

"And will you go there, now that your work on Earth is done?" Sayr asked.

"I will, and also to Alpha Centauri, to do what I can to stop the cycle of trauma among our people. But before that . . . I plan to spend some time with an old friend who is nearing the end of his days, to celebrate his legacy and his life's work."

Sayr's parting words were almost wistful. "Sometimes a hero, or an angel, isn't much more than a person trying their best to do the job they've been set to do."

Bay walked with a confident but controlled bounce in the lighter gravity of an alien land. Before they had parted, Noriko had warned her that Saro City on Beta Geminorum would feel like a high-altitude city, and she should pace herself accordingly. So she did, absorbing the buzz of excitement that made her want to run and yell to test the gravity and air. She glided along the pathways of the courtyard, enjoyed the color and fragrance of their various flowers and herbs, and observed the walls of the City Tower with cool interest while the young man who had been assigned as her guide pointed out the features of the building. This tower, which was modeled on the original spires of the Academes in the war-torn Metropolis on the other side of the planet, housed the Austrinian-Geminoran and Cygnian-Geminoran transits. The Cygnian Center of Culture and Commerce was there; a deep, underground lake for Eridanian ships to dock was there; an orbital spire, soaring up and into the clouds, was there. All manner of crossroads, visible and subtle, converged on this oasis.

And soon the Geminoran headquarters of House Hendrix, a.k.a. ParaVee, would be there.

A new planet, and not even her first new planet! Alpha Piscis Austrini had been her first post-quarantine experience, but she barely counted that world of interiors, domed and tunneled and swaddled against the trailing edge of a severe ice age. She had certainly been awed, but she had already worked for so long in the VR versions of similar interiors that there had been no shock, no sense of the alien. Which, now that she was able to truly ponder the scope of Peter Hendrix's genius, had been entirely the point of ParaVee's acquisition of

Yrsa's popular yet deceptively simple Galaxy Game. With Yrsa's expertise and the added resources of ParaVee, the game evolved into something that was positively addictive. People were now playing the Diplomatic Group's old simulation like it was their job . . . and in a way, it was. "We will come to the table as a peer, not a pawn," Uncle Peter insisted. "We must not expect doors to be opened to us. We will go to them, and we will not wait to knock."

That was her mission now. The crush of her teen years, the pop star she had thought was out to rule the world—back when she only knew of one world to rule—had given her a recommendation to beat all recommendations. If your sponsor is a former ruler of a planet, the adopted brother of the elected head of the galaxy, and a living legend who might be partly immortal and is definitely nearly omnipresent, it *means* something to people. At least, it *should*.

House Hendrix, the newest player in the Austrini-Cygnian bloc, was unique for being the first economically viable galactic entity out of Earth. That made them an object of curiosity, but not respect, not yet. Bay didn't need psionic abilities to detect the whiff of condescension from her guide, a slightly patronizing aura that went well with the extra meter of height from which he regarded her. *First Contact, and we are the savages,* she thought resentfully behind her smile. The Patrona had been gracious and sincere during her brief meeting with Bay and Noriko, but this boy, the offspring of a lesser Haneki, was perhaps a more accurate example of the attitudes they would face.

And then Owen materialized on the path right in front of them, causing the youth to jump and yelp in a satisfyingly undignified fashion. Bay stood calmly, waiting for Owen to come to her and clasp her hands with welcoming familiarity. It was even more satisfying when he politely but firmly dismissed the trembling guide, who now exuded no sense of superiority whatsoever.

Bay paid the boy no further attention. She returned the warm smile of her mentor. "I can't thank you enough, Professor," she began.

He started laughing. "I blame Thiago for that 'Professor' thing. I'm not an academic, Bay. Never have been. Don't call me that."

"Very well . . . Owen," she said almost proudly.

"Don't call me that either," he said sharply, all laughter gone. His sudden seriousness shocked her into a deep embarrassment. What had she done wrong?

He saw her confusion and quickly began to explain in a low, intense voice, "My father had everything that I have, and he made himself into the petty, evil dictator of a small domain. His name was Ioan, and I hated him more than I've hated anything in my life. When I came to Earth, I took my father's name to remind myself to despise what I was doing, so I wouldn't get used to playing god. I'm very glad the time for that name is over." He paused, took a deep breath, and spoke more lightly. "Call me Rafi."

"Rafi," Bay agreed quietly.

He smiled sheepishly, apologetically. "I'm proof in more ways than one that blood means nothing to House Haneki. Promise me that House Hendrix will be more than just a family business."

"Shouldn't you ask that of Uncle Peter?"

Rafi tilted his head and looked at her quizzically. "But you're his successor. Hasn't he made that clear to you by now?"

Bay froze, pondering, and then shook her head. Tears gathered and stood in her eyes. "If that's the way it is, then I can confidently say that blood will mean nothing to House Hendrix, but family will mean everything."

Rafi gazed at her in perfect understanding and complete approval, and then the moment was shattered by the arrival of an older man, a slightly greater Haneki than the prior representative. Bowing with profuse apologies and fulsome greetings, he offered a tray with cool liquid, cups, and damp hand towels. Bay took the tray from him, rested it on a nearby bench, and sat beside it to wipe her hands and fill the cups. She listened as Rafi asked the man about the welfare of his family and career with all the sincerity and politeness of a Patron, and then guided him inexorably toward a farewell of his own uttering. When she looked up again, the man had gone and Rafi was looking down at the tray with a slightly exasperated, slightly bemused expression. Bay was reminded of a similar look, that day when she had made such a fangirling fool of herself, and felt a pang of sympathy. He'd suffered the strain of being the center of attention long before coming to Earth.

Rafi sat with a thump, hovered his fingers hesitantly over the towels, and then snatched one up and cleaned his hands with studied diligence. "Before I forget, Kanoa sends greetings." He tossed the towel back onto the tray and picked up a cup.

"How is he?" Bay asked before taking a sip from hers. Not only water . . . there were hints of fruity sweetness and herbal tang.

"Better. More comfortable with the possibility of exploring and experimenting. His father had to get very stern with him. He had quite a few nightmares while they argued it out in his dreams."

Bay looked at him with wide eyes and sipped while he spoke. Here was a thing that still had the power to shock her, and it was home-grown, of Earth, yet beyond anything for which she had a frame of reference. Kanoa's explanations had been as incomprehensible as a religion to the uninitiated. But then again, if she had not been present in the Nautilus Hall at that transformative meeting, if she had only heard the tale from another witness, wouldn't that also have sounded like an overwrought delusion?

Rafi drank deeply and brushed a thumb meditatively through the condensation on his cup before continuing, "The ghosts who live in the deep will make themselves known on their own terms. They do intend to move from myth to accepted fact. But they choose who they want, and their time is not ours. They don't want to rule, or be ruled. They seek mutual communion, not dominion. Kanoa could go to them now, but he is still enjoying his human body. In two or three decades, he might change his mind. I don't think they should rush him. That's a big step, even though I know some scientists who are dying to observe the transformation firsthand—if it's allowed."

Bay nodded, but the gesture was a lie. She had no idea what he was talking about.

"I don't think he'll be able to do what I do. Interdimensional traveling . . . you need a level of skill plus training for that. Nexus, or pilot, or anchor. But none of those things are of Earth. Maybe you'll find your own way in time, if we don't interfere too much."

She gave up. She was watching him speak and not understanding a damn thing. "Maybe," she said. That was a safely ambiguous word.

Rafi sighed and stood up. "I have to go. I've enjoyed our chat, but I promised to take my aunt out for lunch."

Bay set down her cup and grinned at him. What a delightfully human thing to say. "When I was little I wanted to marry you," she said impulsively, more teasing than confessional. "I'm sorry."

Rafi laughed loudly, sincerely and not at all politely. "You had a merciful escape. And now I'm spoken for, and you're safe. Everyone is safe."

He faded from her view, the laughter still bright in his eyes.

Bay smiled and shook her head. She leaned to pick up the tray . . . and stopped.

There was her cup, holding the dregs of clear liquid and leaf-petal debris. There was the half-full pitcher with her hand towel scrunched beside it. And there, on the far side, was a neatly rolled, unused towel and a full, untouched cup, glistening all over with beads and trails of undisturbed condensation.

Bay still did not understand, but she hoped that wherever in the galaxy they were going, Rafi and his aunt would have a good lunch. She was sure at least one of them would.

She sat a while longer on the bench, pondering the taste of alien herbs on her tongue and the scent of alien blossoms in the breeze, and imagining her new life beyond Earth.

Six months later

THE DEEP BLUES of the Pacific soothed the Patrona's spirit, even in simulation. She was standing on a beach created within a newly installed VR chamber, courtesy of ParaVee. She marveled at the quality and skill demonstrated in Earth's gift to the Galactic Council. A gift, and a warning. *Don't underestimate us.*

Earlier that day, Rafi had visited her. For the first time in their many years of kinship, they had looked at each other eye to eye, physically equal in apparent height. A trick of material manipulation, he had explained, without pride but with the innocent enthusiasm of one still exploring the possibilities of his transformed being.

She had examined him intently, not knowing what she might find, but there was no malice in his expression or bearing. He showed only the fond teasing of a younger sibling finally grown past the height of his senior. She had smiled at him and let it go, still strong enough in her own abilities to maintain a calm exterior in front of him.

(Or did he not probe beneath the surface because of the long habit of trust and courtesy between them? Too early to tell.)

The Patrona was old enough and wise enough to be brutally honest with herself. Little Brother Rafihaneki had always been her lesser in age and size and power, and this new, grander version of him disconcerted her profoundly. Moreover, his ever-shifting allegiances had shifted once again . . . No, that was incorrect. His allegiances had expanded. That curiosity of mind that had taken him from Cygnus Beta to Punartam to Ntshune, that generosity of spirit that caused him to embrace new friends, family, and colleagues in every place—was it really any wonder that such a deep-hearted man would eventually go beyond humanity to the realm of the *not-gods* and surpass her, surpass them all, in completely unexpected ways?

No wonder . . . and yet she felt a chill . . . a chill that even the warmth of a tropical simulation could not dispel.

ACKNOWLEDGMENTS

The title *The Blue, Beautiful World* is a line from the poem "The Question" by Theo Dorgan, which I found in the June 1, 2015, edition of *The Guardian*, a UK news publication.

I can think of no better phrase to describe our planet. I love the emphasis on "blue," which reminds us that this is primarily a world of deep waters. I love the fondness of the words, the blown kisses of the alliterative B. It's a way to describe home, a place that we find both intimately familiar and shockingly unfamiliar.

That tension between the familiar and the unfamiliar is what inspires my fiction. More sociological than speculative, it is a fiction that grapples with all that is mundane and holy in this world, and breaks the reality to pieces to create a fresh mosaic. Of course, I'm not the only writer who does this, but I want to single out two authors in particular who have enriched my understanding of the craft and of my own work.

Zen Cho is, like me, a Commonwealth writer. She knows what it means to have the influence of the British Empire in your history, your literature, and your use of language. She has experienced the joys and challenges of writing for a global audience without flattening and fading the unique textures and hues of your culture. She writes people with complexity far beyond the hero-villain binary. The humor in her stories is warm and clever without ever being trivial, a sweet contrast to the bitter realities her characters may face.

Tessa Gratton is a writer who, like me, is always prodding that boundary between divinity and humanity. She understands monsters, power, transformation, the importance of names, and the satisfaction of a journey that ends with home. Her characters challenge the powerful and triumph in unanticipated ways and by unexpected means. She embraces drama and pathos, and will rip a reader's heart out without apology.

I've spent several years immersed in the Cygnus Beta universe, growing the story and growing with the story: a Commonwealth of nations and a Commonwealth of worlds, a monster who finds a name and a home, humor and heartbreak wrapped up together, the stage-worthy drama of rulers and gods, the quiet intimacy of two friends drinking together. Tessa and Zen and I have different styles and stories, but we pull the pieces for our mosaics from the same pile of glorious rubble. The world is always being smashed to bits; we're always building new ones.

They say writing is a solitary endeavor, and it is, in some ways, but in all the important ways it is also a journey with colleagues and friends. Tessa and Zen, thank you, and stay awesome.

Finally, I must mention my agent, Sally Harding. More than a decade ago, she read the manuscript of *The Best of All Possible Worlds* and decided to add me to her client list. It's not easy representing an author who is constantly evolving, often shifting genres, and never writing the same story twice! Sally, many thanks for taking on the challenge, and may it pay off handsomely someday.

THE PEOPLE AND PLACES
OF THE CYGNUS BETA SERIES

THE BEST OF ALL POSSIBLE WORLDS

Cygnus Beta (16 Cygni B)
Sadira (Epsilon Eridani)
Ain (Epsilon Tauri)
New Sadira/Tolimán (Alpha Centauri)
Ntshune (Fomalhaut/Alpha Piscis Austrini)
Punartam (Pollux/Beta Geminorum)
Zhinu (Vega of the Lyre/Alpha Lyrae)
Terra, Sol (Earth, Solar System)

The Visiting Mission of the Central Government of Cygnus Beta

Qeturah Daniyel Doctor and commissioner.
Grace Shadi Delarua Biotechnician and civil servant in the Central Government of Cygnus Beta. Hobbyist specialist in languages and dialects. Aunt of Rafi Delarua.
Dan Fergus Sergeant and specialist in security and survival.
Lian Corporal and specialist in security. Dr. Daniyel's assistant and bodyguard.

Dllenahkh Former civil servant of the government of Sadira. Councilor in the government of Sadira-on-Cygnus.

Nasiha Scientist and commander of the Interplanetary Science Council. Wife of Tarik.

Tarik Scientist and lieutenant of the Interplanetary Science Council. Husband of Nasiha.

Joral Secretary/assistant to Councilor Dllenahkh.

Other Characters of Note

Naraldi Pilot and time traveler. Later the consul for New Sadira in Tlaxce, Cygnus Beta.

Freyda Mar Academic. Acting as senior biotechnician in the Central Government of Cygnus Beta while on sabbatical.

Lanuri Elder and scientist of Sadira-on-Cygnus.

Rafi Abowen Delarua Nephew of Grace Delarua, son of Ioan Adafydd.

Sayr Traveler through many dimensions of time and space. Possibly not human. Mentor of Naraldi.

Zhera Sadiri elder and spiritual leader. Former mentor of Dllenahkh.

THE GALAXY GAME

Cygnus Beta (16 Cygni B)
Sadira (Epsilon Eridani)
Ain (Epsilon Tauri)
New Sadira/Tolimán (Alpha Centauri)
Ntshune (Fomalhaut/Alpha Piscis Austrini)
Punartam (Pollux/Beta Geminorum)
Zhinu (Vega of the Lyre/Alpha Lyrae)
Terra, Sol (Earth, Solar System)

Prologue

NTSHUNE

Rafi Abowen Delarua Nephew of Grace Delarua, son of Ioan Adafydd. Student of the Lyceum. Known as Rafidelarua during his training as nexus at Academe Maenevastraya. Officially named Rafihaneki after his kin-contract to House Haneki. Patron of House Haneki.

Narua The name and identity used by the twins Kirat and Siha when traveling in Ntshune and Punartam.

SADIRA-ON-CYGNUS

Nasiha Mother of Kirat and Siha, wife of Tarik. Cultural consultant of Sadira-on-Cygnus. Former officer of the Interplanetary Science Council. On leave from the New Sadira Science Council.

Tarik Father of Kirat and Siha, husband of Nasiha. Former officer of the Interplanetary Science Council.

Grace Delarua Aunt of Rafi, wife of Dllenahkh, godmother of Kirat and Siha. Cultural consultant of Sadira-on-Cygnus.

Dllenahkh Husband of Grace Delarua. Former councilor and governor of Sadira-on-Cygnus.

Part One: Cygnus Beta

THE LYCEUM

Silyan Teacher. Galia's brother and cotraveler. Tutor and guardian of Kirat and Siha.

Galia Teacher. Silyan's sister and cotraveler.

Ntenman Student. Junior entrepreneur and heir to his father's business networks on Cygnus Beta and Punartam. Fan and amateur player of the sport of Wallrunning.

Serendipity Exchange student and telepath from Tirtha. Affiliate member of the Union of Pilots.

BRIEFLY IN, BUT NOT OF, THE LYCEUM

Ixiaralhaneki Wallrunning talent scout. Daughter of the Patrona of House Haneki. Rafi's nexus in Punartam.

SADIRA-ON-CYGNUS

Freyda Mar Academic and biotech specialist. Wife of Lanuri.
Lanuri Scientist. Husband of Freyda Mar.
Naraldi Semiretired pilot. Time traveler.
Zhera Elder and spiritual leader of Sadira-on-Cygnus.

Part Two: Punartam

Lian Second lieutenant in the Galactic Gendarmerie. Assistant to Dr. Qeturah Daniyel at Academe Bhumniastraya.
Baranngaithe Wallrunning coach and nexus at Academe Surinastraya. Retired historian of Wallrunning. Former manager in the Wallrunning Galactic League.
Syanrimwenil Research consultant in transport at Academe Maenevastraya. Retired corporate nexus of the Wallrunning Galactic League, Logistics Division. Rafi's teacher and mentor.
The Patrona Head of House Haneki. Mother of Ixiaralhaneki. Also named Ixiaral, though few can address her in that manner.

Part Three: Ntshune

Dr. Qeturah Daniyel Scientist and leader of the Academe Bhumniastraya Research Mission to Terra.
Dan Fergus Captain and security specialist of the Academe Bhumniastraya Research Mission to Terra.

THE BLUE, BEAUTIFUL WORLD

Earth, Solar System (Terra, Sol)
16 Cygni B (Cygnus Beta)

Alpha Piscis Austrini (Fomalhaut/Ntshune)

Beta Geminorum (Pollux/Punartam)

Alpha Lyrae (Vega of the Lyre/Zhinu)

Epsilon Eridani (Sadira)

Epsilon Tauri (Ain)

Alpha Centauri (Tolimán/New Sadira)

Chapters 1–5

ALPHA PISCIS AUSTRINI

The Patrona Head of House Haneki. Chair of the Galactic Council. Adoptive sister of Owen and daughter of a former Patrona of House Haneki. Former Wallrunning talent scout. Ixiaral to her close friends and family.

EARTH: THE TOUR

Owen Pop star. Official name Rafihaneki. Adoptive brother of Ixiaral, the Patrona of House Haneki. Former Patron of House Haneki. Also known as Jon Newhaven, instructor in the Global Government Project. Nephew of Grace Delarua and Dllenahkh. Formerly known as Rafi Abowen Delarua.

Noriko Kaneshiro Fournier Owen's manager. Related to the Kaneshiros of Kaneshiro Finance (later Kaneshiro-Hendrix Finance).

Lee Ahn Owen's security chief. General of the Galactic Gendarmerie. Captain Lian, the Diplomatic Group VR avatar instructor for Cygnian law and order, is based on a younger version of General Ahn.

Bernice Jones Driver and pilot on Ahn's security team. Captain of the Galactic Gendarmerie.

Tareq The name and identity used by the twins Kirat and Siha when traveling on Earth. Owen's aunt Grace is their godmother.

EARTH: THE SPECIALISTS

Isala Kuria Academic and specialist in teamwork research. Later head of the Kuria Institute.

Peter Hendrix Founder and CEO of ParaVee, and Patron of House Hendrix.

Dorian MacLeod Professor affiliated with Global Law, and later Global Justice. Instructor in the Global Government Project. Consultant and specialist in political analysis.

Charyssa Former beauty queen. Actress and icon. World Council Ambassador. Instructor in the Global Government Project.

16 CYGNI B

Dllenahkh Uncle of Owen, husband of Grace Delarua.

Grace Delarua Aunt of Owen, wife of Dllenahkh, godmother of Kirat and Siha.

Chapters 6–11

EARTH: THE STUDENTS OF THE DIPLOMATIC GROUP OF THE GLOBAL GOVERNMENT PROJECT

Kanoa Havili Representing the Federated States of Polynesia.

Bay Kaneshiro Representing Upper Pacifica.

Yrsa Helgadóttir Representing Iceland.

Thiago Mendes Representing Brazil.

Dylan Cardinal Representing Quebec.

EARTH: THE OBSERVERS IN THE PACIFIC

Serendipity Telepath and hermit. Owen's former schoolmate. Foremost nonpilot specialist in Eridanian ships.

Naraldi Semiretired pilot, former time traveler. The Diplomatic Group VR avatar instructor for Eridanian history and culture is based on an older version of Naraldi.

Chapters 11–15

OTHER NAMES OF NOTE

Tarik Father of Kirat and Siha. Husband of Nasiha.

Nasiha Mother of Kirat and Siha. Wife of Tarik.

Narua The name and identity used by the twins Kirat and Siha when traveling in Alpha Piscis Austrini and Beta Geminorum.

Sayr Traveler through many dimensions of time and space. Definitely not human. Mentor of Naraldi.

Read on for an excerpt from

REDEMPTION IN INDIGO

BY KAREN LORD

The enchanting tale of mischief and myth—inspired by West African folklore—that became a fantasy classic, from the award-winning author of *The Blue, Beautiful World*

INTRODUCTION

A RIVAL OF mine once complained that my stories begin awkwardly and end untidily. I am willing to admit to many faults, but I will not burden my conscience with that one. All my tales are true, drawn from life, and a life story is not a tidy thing. It is a half-tamed horse that you seize on the run and ride with knees and teeth clenched, and then you regretfully slip off as gently and safely as you can, always wondering if you could have gone a few metres more.

Thus I seize this tale, starting with a hot afternoon in the town of Erria, a dusty side street near the financial quarter. But I will make one concession to tradition . . .

Once upon a time—but whether a time that was, or a time that is, or a time that is to come, I may not tell—there was a man, a tracker by occupation, called Kwame. He had been born in a certain country in a certain year when history had reached that grey twilight in which fables of true love, the power of princes, and deeds of honour are told only to children. He regretted this oversight on the part of Fate, but he managed to curb his restless imagination and do the daily work that brought in the daily bread.

Today's work will test his self-restraint.

'How long has she been . . . absent?' he asked his clients.

In spite of his tact, they looked uncomfortable, but that was to be expected of a housekeeper and butler tasked by their master to trace his missing wife, a woman named Paama. 'Nearly two years,' replied the housekeeper. 'She said she was going to visit her family, but the entire family has moved away from Erria,' the butler explained. 'No forwarding address,' the housekeeper whispered, as if ashamed. 'Mister Ansige is distraught.'

Kwame eyed the pair, then glanced down at the papers before him. These were letters from minor chiefs and high-ranking officials politely demanding his assistance. If nothing else, Mister Ansige was well connected. It was a tawdry shadow of the power he had dreamed of—was the true love of this deserted husband similarly tarnished? And what of his own honour? He was very wary of trying to find people who did not wish to be found, but the names on those scraps of paper ensured that any refusal from him would not be quickly forgotten.

Fairy tales and nancy stories, his adult self said, trying to sneer at these scruples before he had time to question whether it was cowardice or prudence that made him cautious. *Do the work and stop your dreaming.*

'I'll see what I can do,' he sighed with a faint grimace.

He had little choice. The rent of an office, even in a town like Erria, was more than his business could support, and he needed this case to conclude his affairs honestly before he could resume his itinerant ways. He yearned for those days of walking free, with not a townman to pressure him about which case to take and which trail to leave. Leaner days, too, if truth be told, but Kwame had always found liberty more satisfying than comfort.

Poor Paama, his conscience murmured. *Do you want to go back, or do you prefer liberty, too?*

*   *   *

While Kwame is sniffing out the trail of Ansige's wife, let us run ahead of him and meet her for ourselves. She and her family have resettled in Makendha, the village of her childhood. Much is familiar there, little has changed except, of course, for those who return.

Paama's father, Semwe, had left when a youth, returned, then left again when a man. Now an elder, he will never leave again . . . at least not the mortal part of him. He had wanted this final return to be a peaceful retirement; he acknowledged with regret that it was a retreat. The townhouse in Erria had lost all peace with regular visits from messengers bearing Ansige's variously phrased demands for Paama's return. Semwe refused to argue with such a man, preferring to go to a place of quiet and safety where unwanted company could be more easily avoided. In a town, houses crowd together and everyone is a stranger, but in Makendha, a stranger was anyone who could not claim relation to four generations' worth of bones in the local churchyard.

Semwe's wife, Tasi, was coming to Makendha for the second time, no longer the timid young wife, but not yet the matriarch. She needed grandchildren for that, and how, she murmured, blaming herself, could she get those while her daughters stayed husbandless? She had no hope that Paama's marriage could be salvaged. She had chosen poorly for her first child, and she only prayed that she might choose more wisely for the other. Paama at least had strength and experience to sustain her, but her sister, Neila, ten years younger, had only a combination of beauty and self-centredness that both attracted and repelled. She took the move from Erria as a personal attack on her God-given right to a rich, handsome husband. Tasi deplored such selfishness but silently admitted that prospects in Makendha were certainly limited.

And what of Paama herself? She said little about the husband she had left almost two years ago, barely enough to fend off the village gossips and deflect her sister's sneers. She didn't need to. There was something else about Paama that distracted people's attention from any potentially juicy titbits of her past. She could cook.

An inadequate statement. Anyone can cook, but the true talent belongs to those who are capable of gently ensnaring with their delicacies, winning compliance with the mere suggestion that there might not be any goodies for a caller who persisted in prying. Such was Paama. She had always had a knack, but the promise had come to full flower through constant practice. It was also a way for her to thank her family. Life, even life without grandchildren and a pair of rich, handsome sons-in-law, could be sweet when there was a savoury stew gently bubbling on the stove, rice with a hint of jasmine steaming in the pot, and honey cakes browning in the oven. It almost cured Semwe's stoically silent worry, Tasi's guilty fretting, and Neila's bitter sighs.

Besides, it kept Paama busy enough to ignore the nagging question of how she was going to tell Ansige she was never coming back. She will have to consider that question soon, for efficient Kwame has already traced her whereabouts and, not without a qualm, reported to Ansige.

And Ansige, in his desperation, will not be sending messages or servants this time. He is coming to speak to her, face to face.

'Is that the one?'

'It is. She is.'

'I don't see it.'

There was a meaningful silence. It said a lot about what might not be seen by such minor beings as the first speaker. The quiet rebuke was absorbed with equal quietness, and then the first speaker tried again.

'Ansige is on the way. He is coming to fetch her back.'

'Delay him. She will be strong enough to deal with him by the time he arrives, and she will only grow stronger from there on. Then, when they meet, watch, and you will see. She alone can safely wield the power that I shall take from our . . . former colleague.' The last two words rode on the breath of a regretful sigh.

'Will you really? I mean, to involve a human! Are you certain?'

'I am certain that Paama can wield it, and I am equally certain that *he* must not. Isn't that enough?'

Another pause, then, 'He is going to be very angry. He will try his utmost to get it back.'

The reply held a subtle glimmer of a smile. 'That is indeed my hope.'

These two unknown figures have plans for Paama, fate like plans in which Ansige, if he is not careful, will be brushed aside like a fly. It is the pause point of the wave at its crest, the rumbling of a distant storm, the thrill in the backbone when the eyes of the predator glitter in the moonlight from the darkness of the trees and tall grass. Something is going to change, and it is for you to judge at the end of the tale who has made the best of the change and of their choices.

Read on for an excerpt from

UNRAVELING

BY KAREN LORD

The search for a notorious serial killer takes a therapist on a nightmarish quest to an alternate world to find the sinister secret behind his crimes, in this dark fantasy inspired by Caribbean urban myth, from the award-winning author of *The Blue, Beautiful World*.

SIX

HIS EMOTIONS WERE layered in this strange state. At one level there was the sulky, smoldering anger of a person forced to perform an unwanted duty; at another level there was a lighter, somewhat sorrowful acceptance born of the wisdom of hindsight. He whirled into a darkness of night and close walls and low ceilings, hovered and sat cross-legged with remembered elegance, then raised his head to see who had been so foolhardy as to summon him.

Two boys crouched before him around a low, fat candle with a sheltered flame, their poses suggesting that they had not yet decided whether to stay or flee. The smaller, younger boy, barely recognizable in the shadows, was Lukas, and Chance suspected that the other boy bore a name that would soon feature in a pathologist's report. He froze them in place with a glare.

"You bring me to this miserable hovel. You do not speak the right words or present the required offering. Explain yourselves."

The older boy pulled himself together in a show of bravado. "You have to obey this!" he protested, holding up a coin-like amulet on a leather thong. The metal circle was inscribed with a coiling symbol that showed a path with neither beginning nor end, but half of it was obscured by a dark smear. It was still smoking from being passed through the flame.

Chance's lips curled in a mockery of humor while his eyes narrowed in calculation. "Where did you get that?"

"It belonged to my grandmother. She met one of your kind, and they gave her this." The boy was bolder now. He spoke with authority.

"I see," said Chance. "And she knows that you have it? She gave it to you?"

The boy opened his mouth, faltered, and said nothing. No doubt he had been warned not to lie to whomever the amulet brought. "I stole it," he admitted. "I stole it from my father, who never gave me anything. But his mother, she was kind to me sometimes, when my father's wife couldn't see. She's old now. She hasn't remembered me for more than a year."

Chance leaned forward slightly, frowning. "Stealing another's rewards is a risky thing, as foolish as taking on another's debts. You still have time. Return the amulet."

"Please, Xandre!" Lukas squeaked, breaking his silence at last. "We should do as he says!"

Xandre turned on Lukas, his face changed in an instant from fear to contempt. "He is the one who has to do as we say! Do you *want* your father's murderer to walk free?"

"What's this about a murder?" Chance interjected. "I don't kill people. If you know anything about the amulet, you know that."

"No," Xandre breathed. "You don't get to kill him. I do. You just have to help me get close."

It was hard going through that emotion again, the mingled pity and disgust that filled him both then and now as he looked at the boy's fanatical face. "What makes you so eager to kill his father's murderer? Who appointed you his avenger?"

The boy stared at him as if trying to impress him with his steadfastness of purpose. "He's killed others—people I knew, people who helped me. And he'll kill again."

Chance pondered. He hated amulets, but occasionally there were instances when humans did some favor that deserved compensation. Of course, the idea was that they would use their reward to benefit, not harm. Where did killing a murderer fall on the scale of good to evil? Particularly a murderer who might kill again? And did this boy really have the strength of mind to do it?

"Show me the man," Chance said.

Xandre led the way to a landing at the back of a town house, then three stories up a narrow stone staircase that ended far below in the suck and slap of waves at high tide. The three looked in through a window at the small, cluttered lodgings where a man lay sleeping on a narrow bed, bare-chested in the heat. Chance stared at him—not because he looked harmless nor yet because he seemed familiar in that odd way that hinted at future rather than past acquaintance, but because of what he wore around his neck.

Chance smiled again with that humorless smile. "I'll make you a bargain," he murmured in Xandre's ear. "Don't kill him. That thing around his neck—get it for me, and I will make sure he never troubles anyone again."

The boy's eyes were wide and terrified as he finally began to grasp that he was dealing with something he did not understand. "The window grille is bolted," he whispered, his breath coming shallow and fast.

Chance laid a gentle hand on the boy's shoulder, gradually increasing the pressure to something less friendly as he moved behind him and said, "Should that stop a thief of your experience? But here—iron *does* rust, and it's a shame that the landlord won't do the proper maintenance."

There was a dull chime, the sound of metal unleashed from a point of stress, and the grille sagged very slightly.

Seizing both shoulders, he turned the boy to face him. "Breathe easy," he said softly and not at all kindly. "He'll hear you coming."

Shivering, Xandre went in through the window, too distracted to notice that somewhere amid all the touching and turning about, he had lost his spent talisman. Chance watched him go, absently crushing in his fist the amulet that had summoned him there. When his hand opened again, an insubstantial dust floated out and was quickly taken by the wind. Lukas was a weeping, trembling heap of fear in the far corner of the landing. Chance gave him a brief, direct look, wondering if he would have to prevent him from crying out at the wrong moment. Lukas eyed him and tried to crawl farther back.

A shout rang out from inside, then a muffled scream, and both of them turned. Lukas had of course reacted to the sound, but Chance had been jolted by a less human stimulus, the sudden sensation that one of his own kind had just torn open a passageway in spacetime. He rushed to pass into the room—and found himself blocked, blocked as solidly as if a wall had been placed before him, a wall that even the undying could not pierce. Silently he railed, sending static crackling into the night like stunted lightning as he fruitlessly tried with all his knowledge and skill to break through.

Then it happened, as he had somehow known it would from the moment he began this duty. Xandre came through the open window, thrown like a kitten in a sack, his arms bound in deep red tendrils that began to fade as soon as Chance perceived them. The boy cleared the narrow landing and began the long tumble down. Now his arms were free, and as his limp body spun, they flung out dark, liquid tendrils of their own that carried a rich, choking scent to rival the sea-salted air.

Chance grabbed Lukas and dived off the landing, knowing without seeing that the murderer and whatever it was that had aided him were coming out to see their work. His hand smothered Lukas's face so that even the shock of hitting cold water did not elicit more than a short gasp. Then he remembered his limitations.

"Swim, boy," he growled, releasing Lukas to the mildly surging water. "I cannot help you any further. You must choose for yourself. Swim or die."

Softly crying, Lukas did as he was told. Chance flashed to dry land in a single step and stood watching, invisible, until the small shaking figure clambered up the big rocks lining the coast road and started stumbling homeward. He gave a thought to following Lukas, then wondered if it would be any good to see if Xandre had survived. Before he could decide between the two, another tearing sensation sent a crackle through him. He whirled around and stared into the murk, already furious at whomever this intruder might be.

"Chance? Is that you?"

He tilted his head and peered more closely, considering. "Do I know you?"

An ordinary figure, very human-looking but with an otherworldly glitter about the eyes, stepped forward out of the darkness and into the amber circle cast by a streetlamp. "You might. You will."

Chance pondered that and risked stepping a little closer to examine the shadow carried by this undying one. It was unfamiliar in a way that was disconcerting, as if the undying one had actually transformed himself into some other being rather than merely crafting a facsimile. As to whether the substance below the shadow was familiar, Chance could no longer say. The entire event was beginning to ring so loudly of déjà vu that he couldn't even trust himself to know which direction he was facing.

"I was watching earlier from the edges," the stranger continued. "How did you come here? What duty did you have?"

"Amulet," Chance spat. "And not even wielded by the right person. I'm not responsible. I gave him plenty of options, and he chose the worst ones."

The stranger smiled a bitter smile and looked keenly at him. "Not a lie, but not the truth. He would not have gone for that other amulet if you hadn't put the possibility into his head."

"We shouldn't allow amulets at all," Chance hissed in anger, livid at being seen through so quickly. "That one left back there will do some damage yet. I'm not responsible. I've done what I can within my limits."

The stranger shrugged. "For now. I must get back. There's nothing more to see here."

"Wait," he began, but the stranger slipped away before Chance could ask any more questions.

Dizzied and sickened by the doubling, echoing vibration of the place, Chance ripped open an exit rift and left with more haste than skill. He stumbled into the center of the labyrinth, fell to his knees, and retched. Hands rested on his shoulders, tentatively concerned.

"Give him a minute," he heard the Trickster say.

He was grateful, not only to Miranda for the human concern she showed but to his brother as well. The Trickster held the made-world steady as Chance collected himself, a gesture as good as physical support would be to a creature of flesh and blood. Slowly he raised his head.

"Well," said the Trickster.

"Well indeed," replied Chance. "I think I know where we must go next."

He turned to look at Miranda. She was still touching him lightly with bewilderment in her eyes that he could be capable of showing such weakness. "I have to leave for a moment. Literally a moment, for you. Wait on us. You'll be safe here."

"Where could I go?" she answered, spreading her hands wide but tempering the helplessness of the gesture with a shaky smile.

The Trickster helped him to his feet. Chance thought for a moment, his resurrected memories swirling, settling, and organizing themselves. Then he looked at his brother, a look that held all the information they needed. Quietly they flashed out from the center of the labyrinth.

Barbadian writer Dr. KAREN LORD is the author of *Redemption in Indigo,* which won the William L. Crawford Award and the Mythopoeic Fantasy Award for Adult Literature and was nominated for the World Fantasy Award for Best Novel. Her other works include the science fiction novels *The Best of All Possible Worlds* and *The Galaxy Game,* and the crime fantasy novel *Unraveling.* Lord edited the anthology *New Worlds, Old Ways: Speculative Tales from the Caribbean.*

karenlord.wordpress.com

X: @drkarenlord

Instagram: @drkarenlord